THE WIVES

VALERIE KEOGH

Boldwood

First published in Great Britain in 2024 by Boldwood Books Ltd.

Copyright © Valerie Keogh, 2024

Cover Design by Head Design Ltd.

Cover Images: Shutterstock and iStock

A CIP catalogue record for this book is available from the British Library.

Paperback ISBN 978-1-80549-441-6

Large Print ISBN 978-1-80549-442-3

Hardback ISBN 978-1-80549-440-9

Ebook ISBN 978-1-80549-443-0

Kindle ISBN 978-1-80549-444-7

Audio CD ISBN 978-1-80549-435-5

MP3 CD ISBN 978-1-80549-436-2

Digital audio download ISBN 978-1-80549-439-3

This book is printed on certified sustainable paper. Boldwood Books is dedicated to putting sustainability at the heart of our business. For more information please visit https://www.boldwoodbooks.com/about-us/sustainability/

Boldwood Books Ltd, 23 Bowerdean Street, London, SW6 3TN

www.boldwoodbooks.com

For Lynda Checkley, with love

1

NATASHA

Natasha met Daniel at a gallery opening she'd gone to with a friend. It had been a crowded event, full of minor celebrities posing for cameras trying to look as if they understood, or even liked, the garishly coloured artwork that had been chosen for the opening. She'd spied him chatting to Jason, the gallery owner, and made her way through the crowd to their side. She was never one to hang about, nor was she one who bothered with being subtle, so after offering Jason glowing praise for the opening and wishing him every success, she turned to the man at his side and held out a hand.

'Natasha.'

'Daniel.' He'd taken her hand in his and used it to pull her to one side when a loud group had descended on Jason with squeals of delight, air-kissing, and back-slapping.

It had given Natasha time to study Daniel up close. From across the room, he'd looked interesting. Ruggedly handsome, clean shaven, his hair closely cropped. Close up, he reminded her of a young Sean Connery. Later, she discovered she hadn't been the first to have thought the same. Much later, she discovered he had watched all the relevant James Bond movies and had gone out of his way to copy the man's style. It had amused her. She had thought it showed a sensitive side to the man. She became even more fascinated by him.

By the time she'd discovered that he didn't have a sensitive bone in his very fit body, that everything he said or did was generally said or done for a good reason, it was too late; she was under his spell. Dazzled as she was by his charm, charisma, and blatant sexiness, she wasn't blind to his faults. But that was okay; he was totally oblivious to hers.

A week after they met, she took him to a party at her friend Michele's house. She, Barbara, and Tracy Ann had been Natasha's best buddies since university. If Daniel was going to be part of her life, he'd also be part of theirs.

'I like your friends,' he said as they'd made their way back to his apartment in the early hours of the following day, sleepy from the late hour and the surfeit of alcohol.

'They're good people,' she said. 'Their husbands are close too, which is handy. If we go on a girly night out, they'll often go off together. Don calls it *the husband club*.' She was pleased that Daniel liked her friends, and happily answered questions about them as their taxi negotiated the rain-slicked London streets. 'Barbara is the only one of the wives who works; she's a hospital secretary. Don runs his own accountancy business. Blake's a civil servant working in Number 10, all very hush hush, you know.' She said this last part with an inebriated giggle.

Daniel smiled and held her hand more tightly. 'And Ralph?'

'He worked as a foreign correspondent for the BBC when he met Barbara, but for the last few years worked as a reporter for a newspaper. He retired a couple of months ago.'

'Interesting people,' Daniel said. 'I like them.'

She was surprised. Her friends were nice, no argument there, but they were ordinary, even a little dull. They certainly weren't the dynamic go-getters she'd met at the couple of events she'd gone to with Daniel. Maybe it was a case of opposites attracting. It didn't really matter whether he liked them or not; it simply made things easier.

When the taxi pulled up outside Daniel's apartment block, they climbed out and ran through the heavy rain to the shelter of the front door. His apartment was a three-bedroom, three-bathroom penthouse with a view over the Thames. The first time she'd seen it, she'd been staggered by the space. She knew Daniel worked in finance; it obviously paid well. Her apartment, all she could afford on a nurse's salary, was a one bed not far from the hospital where she worked as the manager of the intensive care unit. It could easily have fitted into the smaller of the penthouse's bedrooms.

After spending a few nights with him, she began to leave things behind. Casually at first. A jumper she'd taken off because it was too warm, a spare uniform so she could go straight to work from his apartment, leaving her dress hanging in his walk-in wardrobe off the main bedroom.

Over the following weeks, more and more of her belongings found a home in his cupboards and wardrobes. She didn't think he'd noticed until one morning, he came through to the bedroom holding a slinky, black dress in his hand. She was curled up in the bed, half asleep.

'I know this isn't mine.' He held the dress out.

She looked at him sleepily, unsure of his tone. Was he annoyed? 'It's for that do we're going to tomorrow night. I'm working till six so I'm going to have to come straight here to get ready. I hope that's okay.'

'Of course. I'm looking forward to seeing you in it. It's very sexy.' He sat on the edge of the bed, the dress bunched on his lap.

'We're good together. I like that you have your career and don't expect me to be available all the time. I know we've only been seeing each other for a couple of months, but I know a good thing when it appears in front of me.'

She held her breath, her fingers gripping the sheet. Was he going to propose? He'd been incredibly attentive the last few weeks and she was beginning to wonder if he wasn't the answer to all her prayers.

'Why don't you move in with me?' He waved a hand around the room. 'There's plenty of space. I know it's not so convenient for the hospital but that's why they invented Ubers.'

Not a proposal, more a proposition. It would do for the moment. 'I couldn't afford to get an Uber every day, Daniel, be reasonable.'

He shuffled up on the bed and grabbed her hand. 'You can't; I can. It'd be worth it to have you here waiting for me every day.' His mobile buzzed and with a quick kiss on her cheek, he answered it, his attention immediately on whomever had called. He tossed the dress he was still holding onto a chair and left the room.

Yes, she could see how having her there suited him. Without being vain, she knew she was attractive and her figure was good. She was intelligent too, but she wasn't sure that counted for much with him. He enjoyed having a glamorous woman to bring to the many events he attended, liked having someone to eat dinner with. He certainly liked the sex.

She climbed from the bed, picked up the dress he'd crushed, shook it out and hung it back in the wardrobe. When she opened the bedroom door, she could hear Daniel speaking in that rapid-fire way he had when he was in the middle of a deal. He used one of the three bedrooms as his office. She slipped by it and into the huge, open-plan kitchen living room that stretched the width of the apartment.

He had a top-of-the-line coffee maker, of course, and she made herself a cup, taking it to the window, to stand and stare across the city. It was a stunning view. She could get used to living there very easily. She turned and looked around the room. For this, she could be the woman of his dreams. Beautiful, charming, undemanding.

It wasn't what she'd planned for her life. She loved being a nurse, but the satisfaction, the respect, the sense that she was doing something worthwhile, had all vanished. Maybe it was time to admit defeat. To put an end to the long hours, the impossible demands, the ever-increasing workload, the struggle to make ends meet on a nurse's salary.

She'd always thought marriage and children were for other women. Now the life her married friends had was exactly what she wanted.

Daniel's offer was the thin edge of the wedge. She'd take it, and she'd hammer that wedge home to give her the future she deserved.

2

NATASHA

Moving into Daniel's apartment didn't make Natasha's life any easier – even by taxi, the commute was a bitch – but it certainly made it more comfortable. And Daniel was easy to live with. True, she saw a lot less of him than she'd expected, but when he was there, he treated her like a queen. If she was working late, they'd order a takeaway. If she was off, they'd eat out.

'I'll cook dinner tonight,' she said one morning. It was her day off and apart from going to the gym, she'd nothing planned.

He shook his head, checked his watch, and swallowed the last of his coffee. 'No, there's a new restaurant I want us to try. I've made reservations for eight. We can meet there if I get delayed, but I'll let you know, okay?'

'Fine.' She shrugged. It seemed churlish to complain that he hadn't asked her, that he never consulted her about their plans, not when he was willing to foot the bill for their always-expensive meals out and for the taxi to and fro. There was a time when she would have resented being managed in such a way, but these days, she was more willing to take the easy road.

'You're burnt out,' her friend Barbara said when she visited a few days later. 'You haven't been yourself recently. You should take time off, go on a holiday. Maybe go for counselling.'

They were sitting in Daniel's apartment drinking Prosecco and eating the canapés Natasha had bought in a local delicatessen earlier that day. She raised her glass and smiled. 'Burnt out? Do I look as though I'm burnt out?' She waved the hand holding the glass around the room. 'I mean, look at me!'

'It's fabulous, and it's great that you're happy with Daniel, but...' Barbara's voice faded away and she shook her head. 'Forget it.'

'No,' Natasha said, trying to keep a rein on her temper. 'But what?' They'd been friends for a long time, the kind of friends who felt they could say anything and get away with it. Or was that just her? Her three friends had all married within a year of graduating, almost twenty years before. Tracy Ann to an old boyfriend, Barbara and Michele to men they'd met at work. Tracy Ann and Michele had spawned undeniably gorgeous children whereas Barbara had become an enthusiastic stepmother to her new husband's young daughter. All three were conservative, middle-class women who sometimes verged on the edge of dull. Until recently, Natasha had never envied their lives, but she knew they were often envious of hers. Was that it? They didn't want her to settle down because they wanted to keep living vicariously through her? Had they fantasised about sleeping with her many boyfriends over the years when they made love to their own boring husbands?

'But what?' she said again. 'Go on, spit it out; you know you want to!' She was being unfair. Of the four friends, Barbara was the least likely to gossip or be in any way nasty. Natasha brushed a twinge of guilt aside and lifted her chin defiantly. 'I'm waiting.'

Barbara reached for the bottle and topped up her glass. Taking her time to answer or perhaps being careful to choose the right words. 'Are you sure he's the man for you, that you're not grabbing hold of him to stop you from drowning? You've mentioned, more than once in the last few months, how difficult your job has become. Always under-staffed, patients and their families more demanding. The constant pressure. I've listened to you crying down the phone to me. It's taking an enormous toll on your physical health too. You've lost weight. A stone? More?'

Since she appeared to want an answer, Natasha shrugged. 'Just over a stone.'

'You were always thin; now you're skeletal.' Barbara lifted her glass and sipped. 'But it's your mental health that worries me—'

'What?' Natasha reared back, part surprised, part bloody furious.

Barbara held her hand up. 'Hear me out, please.'

'Fine.' Irritation made her voice tremble.

'I was always in awe of your dedication, your focus, your strength of character. Of the four of us, you were the only one who seemed to have achieved what we'd all hoped for when we were in university. Tracy Ann, Michele, and I.' Barbara shook her head and gave a rueful smile. 'We fell at the first hurdle, didn't we? All our talk about careers, all our dreams for the future turned out to be just words that vanished as fast as a puff of smoke on a windy day when we fell in love. We married, and that was it; we hopped on that well-worn pathway and became housewives.'

'You have a job—'

'Yes, and I worked hours that suited me while Anna was young and needed me. I still enjoy the job, and the women I work alongside are great, but I'm a hospital secretary, not a solicitor. That had been my dream, remember?'

Natasha did. Barbara had dreamt of being a solicitor, Tracy Ann a journalist, and Michele an accountant. Only Natasha had achieved exactly what she'd wanted. The four had met at a debating society in their first year at university and, despite all reading different subjects, had become friends. How many hours had they sat talking about their futures? 'We all had big dreams back then.'

'But you made yours come true. You run a busy intensive care unit. A hugely challenging job that you were made for.' Barbara put her glass down and leaned forward, closing the distance between them. 'You never compromised; I admired that. I know Michele and Tracy Ann feel the same. It's as if you were living the dream for all of us; does that make sense?'

Natasha nodded. It had been exactly what she'd been thinking. Guessing Barbara wasn't finished, she stayed silent.

'The last couple of years, the continuous pressure of your job, it's changed you.'

'Changed me!' Natasha's laugh rang out. A false, brittle sound that seemed to echo the sentiment. 'I'm the same person I always was.'

'Are you?' Barbara waved a hand around the room. 'You moved in with Daniel after only a few weeks. You talk about eating in expensive restaurants every night of the week. You never mention work any more, when before you never shut up about your patients and how busy you were. It's like you've turned into one of us.'

This time, Natasha's laugh was genuinely amused. 'You make that sound like the greatest insult.' She reached for the bottle and poured the last of the Prosecco into her glass. 'Maybe I've had a change of heart.' She picked up the glass and raised it towards Barbara in a toast. 'Maybe I just needed to meet the right guy. We're really good together.'

'What happens when he finds out that the real you isn't as biddable and easy-going as he thinks you are though, Tash? What happens when he discovers you're an ambitious, career-driven woman, what then?'

Natasha smiled but didn't answer. She could have said that she was happy with this new version of herself or she could have told her the truth: that by the time Daniel found out what she was really like, it would be too late.

3

NATASHA

In the beginning, Natasha hadn't thought her relationship with Daniel was destined to last. Even when she'd fallen in love, not with him, but with his fabulous apartment, she'd seen an end in sight. She assumed he'd felt the same but then, and she wasn't sure when the change occurred, he became more attentive, more romantic, and she wondered if, after all, he wasn't exactly what she needed. By the time he'd asked her to move in with him, she was sure.

Over the next few weeks, Natasha met her friends a few times, but if either Tracy Ann or Michele agreed with Barbara about Daniel's unsuitability, they didn't say. And if there were knowing glances shared between them, it was easy to ignore them too. Natasha had learnt it was easier to pay no attention to things she didn't want to face.

At work, it was the only way she was coping. Luckily, as the unit manager, she was able to delegate most of the work and hide in her office with her computer switched on, her fingers resting on the keyboard so that if anyone glanced through the windows or opened the door, it looked as if she was busy. Nobody knew the screen didn't change for hours.

Following a particularly trying day, she arrived home late to find a takeaway waiting, a bottle of wine open, and a smiling Daniel waiting for her.

'You look exhausted,' he said. 'Go, get into something comfy, and I'll plate some food for you.'

She hadn't had lunch and the smell of whatever he'd ordered made her mouth water. 'Lovely, give me two minutes.'

In their bedroom, she stripped off the jeans and sweatshirt she'd changed into after her shower at work and dropped them into the laundry basket. By something comfy, she knew Daniel meant something slinky and sexy and not the cotton pyjamas she'd have preferred. There was a silk robe hanging on the back of the bathroom door. It would fit the bill.

'That smells good,' she said walking barefooted across the living room to where he'd set out the food on the table, red wine already poured. Too late to say she'd have preferred white.

'I ordered Thai food,' he said, pulling out a chair for her. When she sat, he took the seat opposite.

And way too late to say she'd have preferred Indian, or Chinese, or even a damn pizza. Thai food was his preference, never hers. She picked up her fork and stuck it into a piece of pork with more force than was necessary, sending the tines screeching across the plate.

He'd lifted a forkful of food to his mouth and stopped with it halfway, looking at her in concern. 'Is everything okay?'

She lifted her glass to take a sip before answering. 'Sorry, it's been one of those days.' He didn't need to know that every day recently had been the same. She tried a smile. 'This is great; thank you for having it all ready for me.'

He picked up his own glass, reached across and touched it

gently against hers. 'I was going to wait until we were out in some fancy restaurant, but perhaps now is the ideal time.' Putting the glass down, he took her hand in his, curling his fingers around hers. 'Will you marry me, Natasha?'

She looked down at their entwined hands. This was what she needed, wasn't it? No more worrying about the future. He'd be a good husband, and she'd be a good wife. 'Yes, I will.'

Daniel grinned, pulled her hand to him, and kissed the back of it. 'You've made me the happiest man.'

He insisted on opening a bottle of champagne to toast the occasion, making a huge fuss about popping the cork, laughing slightly manically when the bubbles foamed over his hand. He shook them off carelessly and poured into the waiting glasses. 'To us,' he said, clinking his glass against hers.

'To us.' She echoed his words and drank, tilting the glass to empty it when he did, and holding it out to be refilled. Two downed on an empty stomach wasn't perhaps the most sensible thing, the alcohol going straight to Natasha's head. Or maybe it was better that way. She was able to sit, an alcohol-inspired smile in place, and agree with everything Daniel suggested. The no-fuss, registry-office wedding as soon as it could be arranged, the short honeymoon immediately afterwards, and a longer holiday later when he wasn't so busy.

They talked about a lot of things. She wasn't sure he even noticed the one thing that neither of them mentioned, not even once.

Neither of them spoke about being in love.

4

NATASHA

Daniel left the organisation of the wedding to Natasha. If her friends were surprised at the speed it was all happening, they didn't comment. They probably had lots to say behind her back, but to her face, even Barbara remained unusually silent. They, and their husbands, came to the registry office. The only other people attending were Natasha's parents. Daniel's mother and brother, both living in the US, were, he said sadly, unable to make it.

The wedding was followed by dinner in one of their favourite restaurants. There was lots of conviviality. Natasha's parents loved Daniel. Even her friends, now that she'd become a wife rather than girlfriend, seemed to have accepted Daniel with more grace. Their husbands certainly had. On more than one occasion, in the bar they went to after the meal, she saw them huddled together, deep in conversation.

'I see you've been inducted into the husband's club,' she said, when she finally got him alone. 'They'll be dragging you out to the pub and to rugby matches soon.'

'Sounds good to me. And you can go to art galleries or shopping with the other wives.'

The other wives? Is that what she'd become? Wasn't it what she'd wanted? She struggled to keep acid from soaking into her words as she said, 'I, my dear husband, will be working.'

'But not now,' he said, pulling her into his arms. It signalled the end of the conversation, but not the end of the thoughts rattling around inside Natasha's head.

They flew to Venice for a few days the following morning and enjoyed a very luxurious stay in the Gritti Palace, one of the city's finest hotels. It was almost romantic. In fact, it was the closest Natasha had felt to being in love with her new husband.

'This is an amazing hotel,' she said, standing on their small balcony overlooking the Grand Canal.

'The only place to stay in Venice,' he said, coming behind her and slipping his arms around her waist.

She relaxed back against him. 'You come here a lot, do you?' It struck her then just how little she knew about him.

'Once or twice a year. I have a couple of clients who come to Venice on holiday so I usually arrange to meet them here. It's often easier to make a sweeter deal when they're relaxed. It'd be good if you could come too; their partners often feel a bit lost when we're talking business.'

'I'd like that very much.' She turned in his arms and kissed him on the cheek. 'It's not always easy to get the time off, though. I'd need plenty of notice, and even then, it might be difficult.' She turned again, leaning against him with a sigh. 'A shame though, I love to travel and it'd be so lovely to do it with you.' *Lovely to quit her job, to never have to cross the threshold of a hospital again.* She wanted to say it, but she wasn't sure he'd understand, nor was she certain she could explain why the career she'd loved had become so toxic.

Daniel kissed her neck and tightened his arms around her. 'It would mean a lot for me to have you with me. Do you have to work? If it's the money, you don't need to worry.'

It had been what she'd wanted and hoped to hear, but she needed to pin it down. 'And be a kept woman?' She turned again, staring into his hazel eyes with a smile. 'To have to ask you for every penny? I'm not sure I could do that. Anyway, didn't you say you liked me having my own career?'

He frowned. 'I did, didn't I? But we make a good team; I like having you around.' He kissed her gently on the lips. 'You wouldn't have to ask for money. I'd give you a credit card on my account, you could spend what you wanted. I make plenty of money, Tasha, enough for whatever you want to buy.' He smiled and lifted an eyebrow. 'As long as you don't go buying Ferraris or Porsches, that is.'

'Maybe the odd Chanel jacket or pair of Louboutin shoes.'

'I think the finances could stretch to those.' He kissed her again, more urgently this time, the kiss deepening until he groaned and pulled her by the hand back towards the bed in the room behind them.

'So what do you think,' he asked, much later, when the light that slid through the open balcony doors had faded. The distinct buzz of a mosquito made him swear softly and jump to his feet. He shut the doors, looked around for the offending insect and slapped a hand on the wall, killing it instantly.

Natasha was surprised by his expression. Normally so amiable, for a second he'd looked almost demonic. A trick of the light. She shook the thought away.

'Well?' He climbed back onto the bed beside her and ran a hand down her bare arm. The same hand that had squashed the mosquito. She couldn't hide the shiver that fizzed through her. 'You're cold,' he said with the instant concern she'd come to expect from him. He reached to the end of the bed and pulled up the sheet, wrapping it around her. 'Better?'

'Yes, much.'

'Well,' he said again. 'What do you think? Could you quit nursing?'

Quit nursing? She had loved her job: the constant challenges, the diversity. She'd been passionate about her role as the intensive care unit's clinical nurse manager, had relished the responsibility that came with the job and took great satisfaction in seeing the excellent care her team gave to every patient in their care. But in the last few years, she hadn't been able to rustle up any interest in the job. Everything seemed too much trouble, every request too onerous, every patient too demanding. She could rarely manage a full shift without hiding in one of the storerooms, or the treatment rooms, or any damn quiet place she could find to hunker down and cry.

What did she think? That for the first time, in a long time, things seemed to be going her way. 'Yes, I think I could.'

From where she lay, she could see the splotch of blood the flattened mosquito had left on the wall. Not *her* blood, she hadn't been bitten. Someone else's, in some other room, some other hotel. A stranger's blood. She shivered again.

'I hope you haven't caught a bug,' Daniel said, wrapping an arm around her and pulling her close.

No, she hadn't caught a bug. She'd caught a wealthy husband.

She couldn't take her eyes from the blood stain on the wall. It seemed to be growing, bigger and bigger, filling her eyes, until all she could see was red. A little voice inside her head screamed *it's a bad omen.*

She shut her eyes and curled into Daniel, feeling the heat of him.

This was what she'd wanted. No silly nonsense was going to stop it now.

5

NATASHA

Four days were all Daniel could spare from his job as an independent financial advisor. Even when they were away, he spent hours on his phone speaking to clients or sending and answering emails. It was during those four days that Natasha realised he never completely switched off. Even when he wasn't working, he was thinking about it.

'I'll make it up to you,' he said, kissing her cheek. 'It's just an unexpectedly busy patch. When things quieten down, we'll go away for longer. I promise.'

Perhaps it should have made Natasha consider her decision to leave her job. But it didn't, not even for a second. Barbara was right. Natasha was burnt out. Completely. There wasn't even a spark of enthusiasm left for the work she used to love so much.

When they returned from their honeymoon, she had a few days of her holiday remaining. Her decision had been made; she wasn't going to change her mind about quitting. The following morning, she rang the hospital and made an appointment to see the HR manager.

A day later, at the appointed time, she walked into the office and took a seat across the desk from the normally genial-faced manager whose expression turned sour as she listened.

It was a short, to the point meeting.

'As you're aware,' Natasha said finally, 'I've worked countless extra hours in the last few years and haven't taken even close to my full holiday entitlement, so I'll be leaving immediately.'

The HR manager conjured up a sympathetic smile. It didn't reach her eyes or make her any less sour-faced. 'I know it's been tough recently.'

Tough! Natasha didn't bother to reply. Getting to her feet, she nodded and walked from the room. She didn't stop, nor did she bother to return to the unit where she'd worked for so many years, or to say goodbye to people she'd worked with for so long. There was nothing left. Not even for that. They'd understand.

* * *

That evening in yet another new restaurant, Daniel insisted on ordering champagne when she told him. 'Great news,' he said, raising a glass. 'Here's to my beautiful wife and to our travels together.'

Natasha touched her glass to his and smiled. This was right. Good. The best thing for her. 'I'm looking forward to it. So where are we off to first?' She pictured herself jet-setting off somewhere exciting. Paris or Rome perhaps. He'd been to both in the last few months.

Daniel laughed, reached for the bottle, and topped up their glasses. 'I'm afraid the first few outings for us are going to be here in London. There are a few black-tie events coming up.'

'Oh, right.' She tried not to sound too disappointed.

'You'll need to buy something fancy for each. I'll make sure you get a credit card as soon as I can arrange it.'

From well-regarded clinical nurse manager to kept woman. It was only a short step. She reminded herself that she was Daniel's wife, that it wasn't completely unheard of for a wife to give up her career to support her husband's, but she couldn't quieten the little voice in the back of her head that was laughing hilariously at her predicament. The one that was whispering in a tone of almost manic glee, *Welcome to the 1950s.*

'I need to take this,' Daniel said when his phone buzzed. 'I've been expecting the call.' He didn't wait for her reply, pushing back his chair and striding from the restaurant, the mobile pressed to his ear.

It was almost ten minutes before he returned, minutes where she sat playing with the stem of her wine glass, taking the occasional sip, trying to look as if she hadn't been dumped. She lifted her hand to fix her hair far more frequently than the neat haircut warranted. The movement allowed the restaurant lights to catch the large solitaire nestling beside the wedding band on her ring finger. *See, I'm not simply a lonely, single woman on a blind date that hasn't worked out.* She dropped her hand when she realised how pathetic she was being.

The waiter, hovering nearby, distracted her. Seeing her quick glance, he moved in to clear the plates. 'Is sir returning?' He indicated Daniel's unfinished meal.

'Yes, but that's fine, you can take it away.' If Daniel's conversation with whomever he was talking to went well, he'd be too excited to eat. If it went badly, the cold food wouldn't appeal. 'You could bring two double espressos, please,' she said to the waiter. Whichever way the conversation went, coffee was always going to be acceptable.

When the espressos came, she sipped hers slowly, letting her thoughts wander. She'd made the right decision, hadn't she? She was thirty-eight, had been a nurse for fourteen years; it had been who she was. Now she felt adrift. She needed to take hold of her life, stop letting it run away with her. First off, it wouldn't be any harm to consider her finances. She'd always been a hand-to-mouth kind of person. Once her mortgage was paid, the rest of her salary went on bills, holidays, and socialising. These last two, curtailed by recent events beyond her control, had never really recovered. It meant she had some money in the bank, just not a lot.

She was still wondering about her next step when Daniel returned.

'Sorry about that.' His satisfied expression said it all; the outcome of the call had been a good one. He picked up the tiny coffee cup, swallowed the contents, then put the cup down and reached for his wine glass. 'Here's to more good news,' he said, lifting it towards her in a toast.

'It's a night for it,' she said with a smile. 'While you were gone, I'd time to think. I've decided to sell my apartment. It's lying empty. I might as well have the money in my pocket.' *And feel a little less like a kept woman.* 'I could pay off the mortgage and you could help me invest some of what's left.'

He'd know exactly how to make the most of her money. She had, by then, discovered the secret to his success. He had absolutely no morals when it came to making and closing a deal. Anything he needed to do, he'd do. Any rule was bent, if not smashed to pieces, as long as it resulted in a favourable outcome. He took delight in coasting close to the edge of legality, greater pleasure in crossing the line and getting away with it. What Natasha knew about the world of high finance, she'd learned from the TV; it wasn't much, but she knew insider trading was illegal.

'Aren't you afraid you'll be caught?' she asked him once. To his credit, he didn't keep his shady dealings a secret from her. On the contrary, he'd explain in great detail what he was up to. She was never quite sure if he was boasting or merely using her as a sounding board to see if a plan was feasible. It usually was.

'If I didn't take a calculated risk, I'd be sitting in a back office in a bank earning a paltry amount of money.' He raised an eyebrow and smiled. 'Notice I said a calculated risk. Everything is well planned, so don't you worry your pretty little head about it.'

He was very clever. But then so was she. Clever enough not to reach over and smack him across his condescending face when he spoke down to her. *Pretty little head.* She had both a primary degree and a master's in nursing. Her intention had been to continue studying, to have worked towards a PhD, but then she'd been offered the manager's position. She quickly discovered the role left little room for anything else. He, on the other hand, had gone straight from school to a junior position in a bank and had worked his way up.

It had been so nice to be looked after for a change, so relaxing to have someone making all the decisions. It had given her space to heal. What she hadn't taken into consideration was that he'd assume subservience was her natural state, that she had always been, and would always be, a biddable, easily guided woman. Barbara's words echoed in her head. *What happens when he finds out that the real you isn't as biddable and easy-going as he thinks you are though, Tash. What happens when he discovers you're an ambitious, career-driven woman, what then?*

She'd told Barbara that she'd changed. And she had. She was no longer career-driven, but she was definitely still ambitious. Daniel would discover that soon enough.

For now, it was sufficient to make use of his superior financial savvy in order to maximise her savings when she sold her apartment. Preferably something completely above board. He might be happy sailing close to the wind; she wasn't. She waited for him to bombard her with a list of investment opportunities and was taken aback when he shook his head.

'Not a good idea,' he said, raising a hand to catch the waiter's attention.

Natasha waited until he'd ordered another bottle of wine before asking, 'So, what? Should I just put it into a government investment scheme or something?'

When he raised his eyes to the ceiling and shook his head, she pressed her teeth together until her jaw ached. She looked at the diamond on her ring finger and wondered if it wasn't already too late to let him know she was as clever, maybe even cleverer than he.

No, she needed to pick her time for that.

'All right, so what do you suggest?'

The waiter arrived with the bottle of wine and it wasn't until Daniel was sipping a glass of it that he answered. 'Keep the apartment,' he said bluntly. 'It's never a good idea to burn bridges. Maybe rent it out if you feel it's a waste leaving it sitting empty. Near the hospital, you'll easily get someone to take it.'

It's never a good idea to burn bridges? What the hell?

He must have seen her face fall because he laughed and reached across the table to take her hand. 'That was badly said. I just mean... well, you know... who knows what the future is going to bring us; you might want a bolthole.'

They'd had a bottle of champagne and were on their second bottle of wine. She'd had a couple of glasses of the bubbly; one, or two at the most, of the first bottle of wine, and her glass was still half full. It was Daniel who'd drunk most. Unsurprising then that his eyes were glittering and he was saying things he might not have said when he was sober.

Was he already having regrets? Doubts? A case of in vino veritas? Only days after their wedding, was he already envisaging the end? They'd divorce, she'd go back to her tiny, claustrophobic apartment. Oh God, she'd have to go back to work.

When he'd brought up the idea of a prenuptial agreement shortly after they'd got engaged, she'd laughed, assuming he was joking. Prenups were for celebrities and the seriously wealthy, not for people like them. A day later, he put a document on the table in front of her. 'I think it's best if we have finances sorted before we marry. It's a changing world; we need to be prepared.'

To be prepared? For their marriage ending before it had even begun? He was standing, waiting. With a resigned huff, she'd picked it up and read it through. It was straightforward, and as far as she could see, it was fair.

If they split up within two years, and there were no children, they'd simply leave the marriage with what they came into it. If their marriage lasted longer than two years, she'd get a lump sum that would increase with every extra year they were together. If there were children, the conditions changed completely, with the family home being hers until the youngest child turned eighteen. Then it would be sold and the proceeds divided. There was also a generous monthly allowance. 'It seems very fair,' she said. She read it through a second time, wondering if she should take legal advice before signing. Or at least talk to her girlfriends about it. She smiled at the thought of their horrified faces. They'd consider a prenup so unromantic. And they'd be right. It was. But then, so was their relationship.

'It's simply as a precaution,' Daniel said, handing her a pen. 'In case you get bored married to an over-worked, busy financier and run off with the postman.'

It had made her laugh, and she'd taken the pen and signed the document with a flourish. They were going to have a happy marriage. They'd have one, maybe two children, and they'd all live happily ever after. She'd make sure of it.

And the prenup would gather dust.

That was what she'd thought. But now? *It's never a good idea to burn bridges.* 'A bolthole,' she said, nodding and smiling as if he'd said the most humorous thing. As if she was a fucking moron. And maybe she was, because remembering that damn prenup, it hit her that perhaps she wasn't quite as clever as she'd thought.

6

NATASHA

Four months later, they'd finished dinner in their favourite restaurant when Daniel pulled a slim brochure from his pocket, unfolded it, and slid it across the table towards Natasha.

'What's this?' she said, picking it up.

'I was thinking about that longer break I promised you. I saw this advertised. It's next month, so I rang to enquire about vacancies.'

'A cruise?' It was the last thing she expected.

He laughed. 'I'm not suggesting going on a barge down the Thames, Tasha. It's on the *Duchess Mary*, the newest and most luxurious of the Nobility Line fleet.' He reached out to tap the brochure. 'Have a look. It's all gourmet dining and fine wines. It's expensive, of course, but I think it'll be worth it. And even better, they have four deluxe rooms left; I thought you could ask your friends if they'd like to come along too.' He flipped a page of the brochure. 'The cruise is seven days, but you can add a variety of extensions when it's over. I thought we could go on a safari.'

'And you can take that much time off?' She looked up from the brochure, surprised. He'd always maintained it was difficult taking more than a few days off together.

He lifted his glass and took a sip of wine before replying. 'They have Wi-Fi on the ship; if I need to work for a few hours, that'd be okay, wouldn't it?'

'Of course.' She looked back to the brochure, turning the pages slowly. It looked amazing. She'd only a very vague idea where the Zanzibar archipelago was. Off the coast of Africa somewhere. 'So we'd fly into...?'

'Dar es Salaam.'

Tanzania. She'd a better idea now. Next month. That didn't leave much time. She wasn't sure her friends would be able to arrange things so quickly. 'The four of us have often talked about going on a cruise together. You know, a girlie one, maybe to New York for shopping, but this sounds more exciting.' She looked up from the brochure as a thought hit her. 'You're suggesting we pay for them all to come?' By *we* she meant him, of course.

'Why not? We can afford it. We didn't have a big wedding reception thing, so this will make up for it.'

'That's very generous.' Extremely so. Natasha was taken aback. 'You sure you want to go away for a week with them?' He seemed to get on well with her friends, but it always seemed a little forced, as if he was trying too hard to impress them. This offer certainly would.

'Absolutely. I enjoy their company.' A wistful expression crossed his face. 'I envy you your friends. I've always been too busy, I suppose, but since we got married, the guys have been great, including me in various arrangements.'

It was an unusually emotional comment from him, and once again, she was taken aback. 'They will be thrilled at the offer, but it's such short notice.'

'It was a special deal; that's why we can afford to be so generous.'

'Right, of course.' Natasha had seen enough cruise holidays advertised to understand that the companies offered price reductions on empty cabins nearer to the sailing date. Would her friends agree to go? Childcare used to be an issue, but all of her friends' children were now old enough to take care of themselves. Don was self-employed so should be able to take a week off. It only left Blake and Barbara to worry about. 'I'm sure Blake could organise to take some time,' she said, flicking through the pages of the brochure. It really did look so good. 'The biggest problem will be Barbara; I'm not sure how easy it would be for her.'

'I don't know why she keeps working. They hardly need the money.'

'She loves her job, especially the social aspect of it.' Natasha was going to add that Barbara would be bored if she stopped working, but wasn't that what Natasha had done? She blinked the thought away. It was different. She was helping Daniel with all the shmoozing that was required in his work. Plus, she was going to have a child. Maybe two. She'd given up taking the contraceptive pill before their marriage and had hoped she'd be pregnant by now. She was thirty-eight; maybe it would take time for her body to adjust. A holiday was just what they needed. Relaxation and lots of sex. She'd be pregnant before they returned.

For now, she'd concentrate on rounding up her friends for what looked to be an amazing holiday.

* * *

Natasha waited for Michele to shriek with excitement when she rang to tell her about the forthcoming cruise. *The all-expenses paid cruise.* Instead, there was such a long hiss of nothing that she thought the connection had been lost. 'Michele?'

'Yes, yes, I'm still here. Thinking. It's a very generous offer. All eight of us you said, well...'

Another protracted silence caused Natasha to raise her eyes to the ceiling. 'I know it's short notice. It was something Daniel saw and when he enquired and was told there were still cabins available, we thought it must be fate. Don will be able to take time off, won't he?'

'I've been on at him for yonks to take more holidays. Right, yes, why not, we'll come.'

Why not? An anti-climactic response if ever there was one. Was Natasha wrong to have expected a level of excitement? 'You haven't even asked where it's to.'

'Doesn't matter, we're coming.'

But again, Natasha was disappointed to hear, not excitement, but a measure of determination. As if Michele didn't really want to go but felt she must. 'Don't feel you have to come,' she said, a tinge of aggrievement in her words.

There was shuffling on the line. 'No, I want to. I've sent Don a message, told him the dates. So where's it to anyway?'

Maybe the destination would spark some enthusiasm. 'The Zanzibar Archipelago.' The words rolled off Natasha's tongue sounding suitably exotic and romantic.

'I've absolutely no idea where that is, but it doesn't matter. Wow, yes, count us in. Definitely.'

The excitement, so obviously fake, grated on Natasha's nerves. She pressed the phone painfully to her ear. 'I'll email you all the details, okay?'

'Excellent. Great, woohoo, we're going on a cruise.'

Natasha hung up before she said something she might regret. Like, *What the fuck is wrong with you, Michele?*

* * *

Michele's reaction was so unexpected that Natasha hesitated before ringing Tracy Ann. Was nothing easy and straightforward any more? With a sigh, she tapped a finger on the phone icon beside her friend's name and hoped for a better response. With Tracy Ann and Michele on board, it would be easier to persuade Barbara.

The phone was answered almost immediately and she dived straight in without preamble. 'How would you fancy going on a seven-night cruise around the Zanzibar Archipelago next month?'

'The girlie cruise we've talked about for years?' Tracy Ann was immediately enthusiastic. 'Oh yes, I'm game.'

This was the enthusiastic reply Natasha had been waiting for. 'Brilliant. It's not quite a girlie cruise, though. Daniel saw it advertised and mentioned it to me. We thought it would be great if the eight of us could go. Our treat.' Daniel's treat actually, but Tracy Ann didn't need to know that. It felt good being Lady Bountiful. 'Daniel gets on well with Don, Blake, and Ralph. They could go off and do their thing, and us wives could spend time in the spa, etc. then all meet up for drinks and dinner in the evening. What d'you think?' She expected the initial enthusiasm to continue, so was surprised when there was silence for several seconds. 'Tracy Ann, you still there?'

'Yes, sorry, I was thinking. Actually, I'm not sure Blake would be able to get time off at such short notice. In fact, I'm sure he wouldn't. You know what his job is like: all go.'

'He's entitled to a holiday. It's not as if there's an election due. I bet he'd be able to take a week easily enough. At least he will if you want to go, and you do, don't you? You were always keen to go on a cruise and this one looks fab.' Natasha gave her a rundown on the exotic ports of call, the tours that were included, the deluxe cabins. 'I'll email you the link so you can see for yourself but honestly, it'll be a dream trip. Please say yes!'

'I really don't know, Blake—'

'Would go to the moon if you said you wanted to go there.' Natasha laughed. It was a running joke between the four women that Blake would do anything for Tracy Ann. If there was a tinge of jealousy in the humour, it was never admitted.

'I'll ask him. That's all I can do.'

'Daniel and he are pally; maybe if I ask him to have a word, that'd help—'

'No!' The word came barrelling down the line quickly followed by a sigh. 'Sorry, you caught me at a bad moment. Leave it with me, I'm sure he'll agree. I'll give you a buzz later, okay?'

'Right, later then.'

Natasha hung up and sat with the phone in her hand and a frown between her eyes. From gung-ho to reluctant and reticent in the space of a few seconds. First Michele acting oddly, now Tracy Ann. What was up with her friends? Maybe inviting them had been a bad idea. Natasha would have given up, would have told Daniel she preferred it to be just the two of them, but it had been his idea and he'd been so enthusiastic about it, she felt under pressure to try to make it work.

Crossing her fingers, she tapped on Barbara's name and waited for the call to be picked up. She'd be home from work by now, probably sitting with a pre-dinner gin and tonic. Always reliable, Barbara was a creature of habit.

'Hi, Tasha.'

The faint but distinct sound of ice cubes rattling in a glass told Natasha she'd been correct. She hoped enough had been imbibed to put Barbara in an agreeable mood.

'Hi, listen, jumping straight in, could you get a week off work next month?' She wasn't surprised when there wasn't an immediate response. Of the four friends, Barbara was the most careful, always the voice of reason. Over the years, she'd be the one to hang back when the rest dived headfirst into whatever was going on. Perhaps feeding more information would help her to decide. 'There's a cruise. To Zanzibar. On the *Duchess Mary*. Mega posh. And it's our treat. What d'you say?' When the silence continued, Natasha tapped her fingernail four times on the phone. 'Hello, have you fallen asleep?'

'No, I'm thinking.'

'And?' Sometimes, trying to get information from Barbara was akin to getting blood from a stone. 'Michele and Tracy Ann are game, by the way,' Natasha added, bending the truth slightly in the hope it would encourage a decision. It didn't work and she swallowed her impatience and waited.

'Our treat, you say, so Daniel is going too?'

'Yes, sorry, I should have explained. The invitation is for you and Ralph. It was Daniel's idea; he thought the eight of us would have a great time.'

'Daniel's idea, eh? Very generous of him.'

The rhythmic clinking of ice against the side of the glass filled the silence that followed. Natasha was sorry she hadn't poured herself a drink before she started the phone calls. Stupidly, she'd thought her friends would be ecstatic at the idea of going on a cruise. There was a time when they'd all have jumped at the chance. Or was she looking at the past through ridiculously rose-tinted specs? She was damned if she was going to beg her friends to go. Despite Daniel's enthusiasm for her friends' company, perhaps it would be better if they went alone. After all, it was supposed to be an extension of their honeymoon.

'I suppose I could take a week off,' Barbara said finally.

'And Ralph would be okay with it, yes?'

'I don't see why not. He's retired, after all.'

Barbara had met Ralph in the pub after a rugby match. Natasha, Michele, and Tracy Ann had been flirting madly with a crowd of young men, but it was the older Ralph, a widow with a fifteen-year-old daughter, who had charmed Barbara. Three months later, they were married. Almost immediately, Ralph, a journalist, had taken a job as a foreign correspondent.

To her friends' surprise, Barbara gave up the idea of studying law to remain at home with her stepdaughter, Anna, taking the part-time administration job in a nearby hospital where she still worked. At the time, she talked about going back to studying when Anna was older, but that had never happened.

If Barbara regretted giving up her dream, if she regretted marrying a man almost old enough to be her father, she never said. Not one word of complaint in all the years.

'I'll email you with all the details of the cruise,' Natasha said. She hung up, and sent a message to Tracy Ann.

Barbara's game!

Hopefully, knowing all her friends were going would give Tracy Ann the ammunition to work on Blake. Not that Natasha believed there'd be a problem. What Tracy Ann wanted, she usually got.

Only a few seconds later, she had a reply.

Yes, okay, count me and Blake in too.

This time Natasha sent a message to the group WhatsApp.

We're going to have such a great time!

7

NATASHA

Usually, the four friends would have met a couple of times in the three weeks before the cruise, but every time Natasha suggested meeting up for a drink, one or the other of the women were unable to make it. Since they rarely met unless they were all free, they didn't get together until they met at Heathrow, the day of their departure. They'd chatted on WhatsApp of course and had discussed their destination, the clothes they planned to bring, the outfits they'd chosen for the gala night.

It was during one of these WhatsApp chats that Natasha finally brought up the subject of the flights that Daniel had been nagging her about for days. He was paying for the cruise, but not the flights. They were all travelling business class; he wanted to fly first. She waited until there was a natural gap in the conversation before asking, as casually as she could, if they were interested in upgrading. 'It's only a few hundred quid extra,' she said.

'Each, and each way.' Michele's voice was unusually dry. 'So probably nearer to two grand extra. I'm saying no, but you lot go for it if you like; we won't mind.'

'No, it's all or nothing; you know the way.'

It had started in college when Barbara had wanted to leave a party early. 'You three stay,' she'd said, nodding towards the exit. 'I'll be fine.'

Later, nobody could remember who'd said the words that would stick with them for ever more. *We all stay or we all go.* It wasn't quite as catchy as the musketeers' *all for one and one for all* slogan, but it had achieved the same result. Times like this, Natasha wondered if they'd not outgrown the childish sentiment. They didn't have to do everything together. But perhaps this wasn't the time to argue the point. 'No problem,' she said, although she knew Daniel wouldn't be happy. 'Business class it is.'

It was the perfect time to mention that Daniel had upgraded their cabin to a penthouse suite. As a surprise for her, he'd said, and she'd tried to look suitably delighted. It was the last available, he'd said, so it wasn't as if he could have done the same for the rest of the party. She wasn't entirely sure she believed him on either account. He'd have liked the idea of being in a bigger, posher cabin than the rest, so she guessed the upgrade was for himself, not for her. She should have told her friends then, but she hesitated and the moment was lost. It didn't matter; they'd find out soon enough.

The flight was smooth. They had seats close together, but once they were airborne, they switched so that the women were sitting together, sipping champagne, laughing and talking about nothing much, the men sinking beers, talking quietly. Daniel was huddled together with Blake, whose lips were pressed in a tight line as he nodded along to whatever was being whispered in his ear. Natasha would have to have a word with her husband, remind him it was a holiday, not a business trip.

She didn't get a chance the rest of that flight, and when they arrived, with the fuss and excitement of embarkation, it went out of her mind. She hadn't found an opportunity to tell her friends that Daniel had upgraded their cabin to a penthouse, but as it turned out, all their cabins were on deck twelve so the disclosure could wait till later. Preferably after they'd all had a few drinks to soften the blow that she'd broken their code.

They arranged to meet on deck to toast their departure after checking their cabins, and one by one, vanished into their assigned accommodation. Each of them wore a lanyard around their neck with a crown-shaped medallion hanging from it. A chip in each held their details, allowing them to charge items to their various rooms automatically, plus it opened their cabin doors as they approached. 'A magic crown,' Tracy Ann said, waving it cheerfully before disappearing into their cabin.

Natasha and Daniel, further down the long, narrow corridor, were the last to locate their cabin. 'This is fabulous,' she said, as they walked into the penthouse. It was ridiculously big. Two bedrooms. Handy, she supposed if they had a row. Two bathrooms, handy in any case. A huge living room with a full-size dining table, a great big, sprawling sofa, and sliding doors opening onto an expansive balcony. They were still exploring when the ring of the doorbell brought them to a halt.

'Maybe they've given us the wrong room,' she said with a laugh as Daniel hurried to answer it.

He returned with a bemused smile on his face, and a middle-aged man a step behind. 'This is Emilio, our butler,' Daniel said.

Their butler!

Natasha wasn't sure if she should proffer her hand or not. Instead, she offered a smile. 'Nice to meet you.'

'I'll be in charge of looking after your suite,' he said. 'There is a button on the phone with my name on it; if you want anything, press and I will come.' He pointed to the under-counter fridge. 'Every day, I will restock. If there is anything in particular you require, please ask.'

Natasha wanted to ask him to go away, but she didn't want to be rude. He was pleasant, but not particularly friendly.

'Thank you, that's great. Marvellous,' Daniel said, rubbing his hands together.

Natasha guessed he had no more idea how to deal with this man than she did. 'Thank you,' she said, hoping that was it. He'd go away, allow them to enjoy the space undisturbed.

'Would sir and madam like me to unpack their luggage when it arrives?'

God no! 'No, thank you,' she said quickly. 'We can manage.' And before he offered anything else, she walked towards the door and held it open. As hints went, it wasn't subtle. Emilio nodded and left.

'Not sure I want to see much of him,' she said, returning to where Daniel was standing. 'Come on, let's go grab the others and head up on deck to see the sail-away.'

They knocked on their friends' doors as they passed, gathering them as they continued to the lifts and down to deck six. Out on the promenade deck, they were met by smartly uniformed waiting staff with trays of champagne in souvenir plastic glasses. They weren't free, though. Each of the staff had a hand-held device to read their individual crowns, all done so discreetly they wouldn't even realise they were spending money.

'And I bet they cost the earth,' Michele said.

'It doesn't matter,' Tracy Ann said, raising her glass to the brightly lit city they were leaving behind. 'I'm so glad we came.'

Natasha glanced at her. She didn't normally sound quite so manic. And oddly, although she sounded feverishly happy, she looked anything but.

Natasha might have said something, might have whispered *are you okay?* into her friend's ear, if the air hadn't been pierced by the ship's sirens wailing a goodbye to the port. Then the moment was passed, her concern forgotten as they stood by the rail till the lights of the city became a blur on the horizon.

'Right,' Michele said. 'I'm going to unpack and get ready for dinner.'

'Good idea, I'm starving,' Barbara said. She checked her watch. 'It's almost six; what say we meet for pre-dinner drinks at seven?'

'More champagne!' Tracy Ann waved her empty glass. 'Sounds good to me.'

'Come to our cabin,' Daniel said as he led the way back inside. 'We have champagne on ice.'

There was no discussion. Natasha would have preferred to have met in one of the lounges rather than their penthouse, would have preferred to have found a good time to tell her friends that they'd upgraded, instead of presenting them with the in-your-face evidence. It was too late. Daniel had put the cat firmly among the pigeons.

'I thought you'd told them,' he said when they were back in their cabin. 'You had all the time you needed on the flight over. What were you talking about?'

She couldn't remember. They'd just been talking. 'About nothing really.'

His sigh was loud, exasperated. 'Well, they'd have had to find out sooner or later. I don't know what you're making such a fuss about. Tell them it was my fault, that the opportunity came up and I grabbed it.'

That's what she should have done, when he'd first told her about the upgrade. She could have made a joke about it then. Why hadn't she? Now, it looked as if she was embarrassed by it. As if she'd been keeping it a great big secret. When really, what she wanted to do was gloat a little about how well she was doing.

'You're right,' she said. 'I'm being silly. Let's forget about it and get sorted. It'll be seven before we know it.'

Natasha had taken great care in packing her case and it took only minutes to put everything away, shaking out the dress she'd planned to wear that evening, pleased to see it remained crease free.

With two bathrooms, she didn't need to rush to make way for Daniel. Forty-five minutes later, with her hair blow-dried and her make-up on, she slipped on the jade-green dress. It was an old one, but a favourite: her go-to dress for upmarket occasions. It swished around her bare legs as she went into the living room.

An L-shaped sofa filled one corner, with three velvet-covered chairs placed in a semi-circle on the opposite side of a large, low coffee table. Two lamps on small side tables along with a glow drifting in from the balcony lights created a relaxed, comfortable ambiance. It should have been perfect but Natasha couldn't get rid of a feeling of unease. Silly to be concerned about the upgrade. That's all it was, wasn't it? Nothing else. It was simply her imagination that her friends had been avoiding her recently, wasn't it? And when they spoke, had she imagined there was an edge to their words?

When she'd been single, there had been times when she'd felt left out. Apart. Unable to share in the moans and groans of married life, pregnancy woes, labour, child-rearing. She'd accepted it as being one of those things. They were wives, she was not. It had been their history rather than shared experiences in the intervening years that had kept them together. But now, shouldn't she be allowed in their *wife club* too?

Or maybe it was just her. It had been weeks since she'd given up her job. She'd assumed she'd feel better by now, more relaxed, more at peace. Instead, she felt on edge. Perhaps Barbara was right, and she did need to go for counselling.

She slid open the balcony door and stepped outside. It was a balmy night, only a slight breeze blowing in from the sea to ruffle the fabric of her dress. Pressing against the rail, she leaned forward and peered out to sea. There were no lights to be seen, just a vast void. A dark, empty nothingness. She shivered, wrapped her arms around herself, the cold metal of the rail sliding through her dress to brand her skin.

The balcony doors had slid shut behind her. She was suddenly conscious of the silence, broken only by the shush of the waves far below as they smashed against the side of the ship. Leaning over the rail, she looked down. There was sufficient light below to show the white horses galloping alongside but when she straightened and looked out to sea, no matter how she strained her eyes, there was no division between sea and sky.

It was like staring into an abyss and suddenly, she was back in the hospital, standing in the intensive care unit, facing the horror.

She'd thought she'd grown accustomed to death. In a high-dependency unit, you simply couldn't save everyone. But there were times, in the last few years, when they weren't saving anyone. That was the nightmare that continued to haunt her.

8

TRACY ANN

Tracy Ann did a twirl, her hands in the air, the gauzy material of her dress lifting to float around her legs. 'How do I look?'

'Gorgeous, as always.' Blake took her hand, pulled her closer and pressed his lips to her cheek. 'You'll be the most beautiful woman in the room.'

She smiled at him. 'Not that you're in any way biased of course!' It was a running joke among her friends, how much Blake adored her. Married almost sixteen years, and his love never seemed to have waned. If anything, he seemed more besotted with her than he was when they first met.

'I'm just telling it like it is.'

And that was Blake all over. He was the most honest, sincere person. The most civil civil servant.

Tracy Ann brushed a hand over her dress, frowning at a crease in the fabric she hadn't noticed till then. She pressed it down in the hope it would vanish, wondering if she had time to take the dress off and run to the laundry room. 'Look at this,' she said, pointing it out to Blake. 'I'm going to have to iron it.'

He took her hand away and gave the area his full attention. 'No,' he said decisively, 'I promise, you'd never notice.'

And that was it. Because if Blake said it wasn't noticeable, then it wasn't. She could trust him completely. *Completely.*

'What were you and Daniel chatting about on the flight?' She bent to slip her feet into the sandals she'd brought to match the dress. They'd kill her before the night was out, but they looked good. 'You had your heads buried together for ages.' She straightened and lifted her face to smile at him. 'Man stuff, was it? Golf, rugby and the price of shares.'

Blake was tying his tie. He finished and straightened it with a slight twist before answering. 'I don't remember talking to him that much. I only sat beside him because Natasha had stolen my seat beside you.'

'So he'd nothing interesting to say?'

'Some banal chat about rugby, I think. Or was it cricket?' Blake frowned. 'Sport chat of some sort anyway. You know what he's like; all I needed to do was make affirmative noises now and then and let him natter away. He likes an audience, does Daniel.'

Tracy Ann reached up to adjust the tie again. 'That's better. You look very handsome.' He was. Handsome, kind, honest, adoring. If he knew what she'd done though, she wasn't sure he would forgive her.

She'd been so incredibly stupid, and she wasn't sure if she could make things better. Coming on this cruise had been a risk she'd had to take.

Telling Blake what she'd done wasn't an option. It would destroy him. But she could tell her friends. With their help, maybe there was a way out of the mess she'd made.

9

MICHELE

Michele dragged a brush through her hair, wrapped the length of it around her hand and pinned it in place. A creature of habit, she wore her hair either loose during the day or tied back in a ponytail, but if she was going somewhere that required wearing more than chinos and a shirt, she pinned it up in what she hoped looked like an elegant chignon. But it wasn't her reflection that was keeping her attention on the mirror; it was the sight of Don standing by the balcony doors, staring out. Or maybe he was looking at his image in the glass.

What was he seeing?

The man he'd hoped to be or the one he had become. The one who'd made a stupid fucking decision that might destroy them.

Or perhaps he was looking at her reflection, and wondering how he could make it up to her.

She wasn't sure he could.

'Did you get a chance to speak to him?' *Him*. Don didn't need to ask who she meant. Daniel Vickery-Orme had been the sole subject of their conversation for weeks. If only Don had spoken to Michele about him before he'd taken him on as a client, before he'd allowed himself to be swayed by vague promises and even more vague assurances that everything would work out.

If Michele had known, she'd have stopped it before it began. She'd started to train as an accountant. It was how she'd met Don. The shared experience had drawn them together, and despite a heavy workload they'd found time to fall in love. They'd unfortunately also found time to fall pregnant. *We're pregnant*, he'd said, she remembered. But much as he'd wanted to share, it was she who carried the child, and she who'd breast-fed – because she'd wanted what was best for their baby. What was best too was for her to shelve the studying to look after their child when it turned out it was a cheaper option than trying to pay for childcare.

The second pregnancy came as a surprise to Don, and a shock to her. They'd been careful but obviously not careful enough. They spent a weekend discussing their options. He thought there were some. She knew there wasn't. Anyway, she'd always wanted two children; it was probably a good idea to have them close together. She could go back to her studies in a couple of years.

They got married before her first pregnancy had started to show and moved into a small, terraced house. Before she knew what was happening, she was a housewife with two small children, a husband who worked long hours, and never quite enough money to do more than get by. Any thought of getting back to her studies vanished as she lived in what seemed like an endless circuit of breastfeeding, weaning, potty training, teething, baby groups, toddler groups, kindergarten, junior school and on and on.

Michele never regretted the choices she'd made. She adored their two children, loved her husband and when he decided to start up on his own, she'd been there for him, supporting his decision every step of the way.

It had paid off. They'd moved to a larger house in a better

area. There was money for extras. Foreign holidays, nice clothes, private schools for the children.

'You could train to be an accountant now,' Don said one night. 'Now that the kids have gone off to university.' He lifted his hand, spread them out to make a banner in the air. 'I can see the sign now. Turner and Turner Accountancy.'

Why hadn't she grabbed the opportunity? Fear, perhaps. It had been years since she'd left university and although she'd tried to keep abreast of changes in technology, she knew she was lagging behind. She imagined training with youngsters who'd come straight from university, stars in their eyes, enthusiasm oozing from their pores. The thought of competing with them made her shiver.

'I don't think so,' she said. 'I'm happy with my volunteer work now.'

'Suit yourself.'

Michele had looked at him with sharp eyes. He'd made the suggestion so why did it seem to her that he was satisfied she'd turned it down? She should have seen the signs that things weren't quite right. If she had... if she'd asked the right questions back then, maybe they wouldn't be in this pickle.

She snorted at the choice of word. *Pickle*. What a prim and proper word for the fucking mess they were in.

Don hadn't answered so she asked again, raising her voice, allowing acid to creep around the words. 'Did you get a chance to speak to him, Don?' He turned around then and her heart dropped. It was a strange sensation. She could feel it like a cold, heavy weight pressing her down. Maybe it was the over-bright light of the cabin that was throwing strange shadows on his face, making his cheeks look hollow, his skin a pasty grey. She knew he'd lost weight. Always a trim man, she'd seen from his belt that he'd had to tighten it one hole recently. Odd how the stress was having the opposite effect on her. She'd been comfort eating. She could feel the result in the dress she was wearing; it clung more tightly to curves that had grown more voluptuous in the last couple of weeks. *Voluptuous, a much better word than fat.*

There was no point in pressing him for an answer. No point in forcing him to make excuses as to why he hadn't spoken to Daniel. She knew why. There was nothing to say. Don had entered into the agreement of his own accord. He was a grown man, a professional. He'd had all the information needed to make a correct choice. He hadn't been pushed.

Michele sighed, walked over, and put her arms around him. He had tried to explain weeks before when it had all come out. She'd been too angry to listen to his excuses then. She wasn't angry now. After all, she'd seen exactly how charming Daniel could be. How charismatic. How everything seemed to come so easily for him. Could she really blame her incredibly hard-working husband for wanting a little of the glitter Daniel seemed to sprinkle about so carelessly?

Had it been her fault? Had there been a deep-seated, unacknowledged resentment behind her refusal to look after their finances? She wasn't the accountant, Don was, so she'd left it all to him, and she had to admit, she enjoyed being the wife of a successful businessman. Enjoyed all the trappings of the high income after years of counting the cost of every damn thing. There was never any indication of trouble. No sign that those early lucrative years were followed by years of dwindling profits. There had never been any discussion of cutting back, of watching the pennies. He'd never said; she'd never asked.

Not even when he'd seemed unusually irritable or when she began to smell alcohol on his breath when he arrived home late from work. It was this last that had made her wonder if something was going on. Made her open her eyes for the first time in a while and really look at him. Had the furrow between his eyes always been so deep? His complexion always so pale, and unhealthy? When had he begun to look so... old?

Finally, she'd asked the question she should have asked months before. 'Is there something wrong, Don?'

And it had come spilling out, as if he'd been waiting for permission to spew.

'Daniel offered me an investment opportunity. A sure thing.' Don threw his hands up and shook his head. 'I can't believe I fell for it, but you know what he's like. Mr Charm. And the business... I should have told you months ago. I was barely scraping by. We're in arrears with the mortgage. Our credit cards, even ones you don't know about, they're all maxed out.'

Michele had wrung her hands together and looked at him in dismay. 'Why didn't you tell me!'

'I didn't want to let you down.'

'Well, you'd better tell me now. Everything.'

And he had. The sure thing investment was indeed a *sure thing*. What Daniel hadn't told Don was that the details of it came as a result of insider trading. 'I made a killing.'

'Right.' Michele frowned, trying to piece together the information in her head. Insider trading was illegal, but if Don hadn't known where the information came from... 'If you didn't know, then it's not your fault. You were just lucky.'

'Daniel said he told me.'

'Did he?'

Don shrugged. 'We'd been drinking. It's possible but I don't remember.'

'Okay.' Michele sat beside him. Her initial dismay was quickly turning to anger. She knew there was more to come. 'So has someone found out?'

'No, that's not it.' He reached for her hand. 'Daniel has been very... kind... about it all. He says it won't get out.'

Michele braced herself for what was to come. 'But?'

'He has a huge amount of capital. He wants me to help him hide it from HMRC.'

Michele guessed he wasn't talking about tax avoidance, which was legal if somewhat morally reprehensible, but tax evasion, a crime which could result in a prison term for those involved. Anger spilled over then. At Don for being so stupid, because if they were caught, Daniel would lose money, he might even go to prison, but Don would be destroyed. His career, his reputation, would be in tatters. More anger was directed at Daniel for being the manipulative bastard he was. She'd do what she should have done from the beginning. She'd take charge.

A week later, Natasha rang to ask her if they'd like to go on the cruise.

A cruise! To be stuck on a ship with Daniel? *When hell freezes over!* Michele was trying to think of a good excuse for not going when an idea came to her. A cruise. Stuck together for days on end. Wouldn't it be the perfect opportunity to deal with Daniel? 'Wow, yes, count us in. Definitely.'

She'd watched Daniel on the flight to Dar es Salaam, chatting to everyone, flirting with the hostesses, being Mr Big. The same on the deck as the ship pulled out of port. He'd been the first to raise his glass in a salute, the first to cheer, exuding charm and bonhomie to all. But this time, she'd seen under the charm, behind the act; this time, she'd seen the monster that slithered under his skin, the glint of darkness in his eyes, the cruelty in the curve of his lips.

And she knew there was no point in talking to him. To fight a monster, they needed more than words. They needed to come up with a different plan.

No, not they – Don would crumble at the first obstacle. He was the brains, the planner and dreamer. It was Michele who got things done.

She would this time too.

There was only one way to deal with monsters.

Cut off their heads.

10

BARBARA

She wondered if the new lipstick she'd bought suited her. Tom Ford's Scarlet Rouge. It had cost her over forty pounds. Usually, she shopped in Boots for her lipsticks, paying less than a tenner. She wasn't sure what had possessed her to go all out this time. A victim of clever marketing, perhaps. Wear this dramatic lipstick, become a dramatic woman.

If that's what she'd hoped, it had been an epic failure. She looked like a damn clown. Pulling a tissue from a box, she blotted her lips then applied one of her older, paler lipsticks. She nearly cried at the result. A mess. She looked like a fucking mess. Squirting cleanser into her palm, she rubbed it roughly over her face, removing all the carefully applied make-up.

'Are you nearly ready?' Ralph's voice, sounding irritated. 'You've been in there forever. If we don't get a move on, it'll be too late for these pre-dinner drinks.'

She should go as she was. Mascara and eyeshadow smeared around her eyes. Her lips bruised with a mix of pink and red. Wouldn't that give them something to talk about? The sensible, restrained Barbara, losing it. Maybe, at last, she could tell them all... all of them, her friends, their partners, anyone who cared to listen... that she was fed up being the sensible one, good old dependable Barbara. She wiped her face with her creamed hand, dragging the mess of colour over her cheeks. She wondered what they'd say? Wondered if Ralph would even notice.

'I'm almost ready,' she said, pulling tissues from the box and wiping her face. 'Just give me a minute.' It was all it took to clean her face. Ignoring the new make-up she'd purchased, she reached for the old, reliable stuff she'd used for years and slapped it on. In less than the allotted time, she was done.

When she looked in the mirror, once again she wanted to cry. The new dress was gorgeous. Low cut, spaghetti straps, full length. A rich red, it cried out for that stupid Tom Bloody Ford lipstick to balance it. In her pale make-up, she looked lost, invisible, a ghostly, bland figure wrapped in red. Too late to change, she lifted her chin, turned, and opened the door.

'About time,' Ralph said, reaching for the remote to switch off the TV. 'Come on, let's go.'

He didn't comment on her dress. She wasn't surprised. If she'd come out as she'd been minutes before, with her face a mess, he probably wouldn't have commented then either.

It didn't matter.

She wasn't wearing the new dress for him; she hadn't bought that ridiculously expensive lipstick for him either.

11

NATASHA

Natasha listened out for the cabin doorbell to ring. She wanted to be the one to answer it. Wanted to be the one to usher her friends into their penthouse suite and have time to give a quick explanation before Daniel took over. She planned to lie. The upgrade was totally unexpected. They weren't aware until they'd opened the door. When they'd asked, they were told it had been a complimentary upgrade. And weren't they so lucky! Daniel, she knew, would be amused. He'd go along with it because it didn't matter to him. He didn't understand that it mattered to her. She'd tried to explain their code but he'd laughed uproariously and told her she was talking nonsense.

'It's not like they could have upgraded, even if they'd wanted to. This was the last suite and we got it. I don't know why you're making such a fuss. Your friends will be able to enjoy it too. As they are tonight.' He waved to the generously stocked bar, and to the canapés they'd ordered. 'Perks of the penthouse,' Daniel said. 'To be enjoyed by all.'

Natasha wasn't sure if he simply didn't understand or wasn't

bothering to try. It didn't matter; she had the lie ready to
churn out.

Tracy Ann and Blake were the first to arrive. 'Come in,'
Natasha said, opening the door wide and waving them through.
'Look at this, we were upgraded. How lucky were we!'

'Upgraded!' Tracy Ann followed Natasha, taking in the space
with wide eyes. 'Wow, this is fabulous; I'm thrilled for you.'

'Probably upgraded you because you arranged it all,' Blake
said, accepting the glass of champagne handed to him.

'Yes, probably.' Natasha was annoyed that she hadn't thought
to say that. It would have made perfect sense. 'Anyway, we can all
enjoy it.' She waved at the trays of canapés. 'Help yourselves.' So
far, it was going okay, Tracy Ann didn't look in the slightest bit
suspicious. Perhaps Daniel had been right and she had been
worrying without cause.

But when Michele and Don arrived moments later, she knew
she'd been too optimistic. 'It's probably because we arranged it
all,' she added when her spiel about being upgraded unexpectedly was met with blank stares. 'It was such a lovely surprise.' She
linked her arm through Michele's and led her towards where the
canapés were laid out. 'But we can all share in our good fortune,
eh? Have one, they're delicious.' She knew she was trying too hard
to convince when her friend pulled away with a shake of her
head.

'I don't want to spoil my appetite,' Michele said. 'I'll have a
drink though, if there's one going.'

'A drink, ha, of course.' She waved to attract Daniel's attention.
'A glass of bubbles needed.' She was sounding like a maniac.
Taking a deep breath, she let it out slowly. It didn't help. Neither
did the second glass of champagne. Or perhaps that was the problem. How much had she had to drink that day?

'This really is nice,' Michele said, looking around.

'It was such a lovely surprise.' The story about having been upgraded had become cemented in her brain so that it no longer felt like a lie.

'Barbara's late,' Tracy Ann said as she joined them. She picked up one of the canapés and popped it into her mouth. 'These are really good. I'll need to do a few laps of the deck to get an appetite for dinner if I eat any more.'

'Two laps of the ship makes a mile,' Michele said. Relenting, she picked up a canapé, peered at it as if trying to decide what it was, before shrugging and putting it into her mouth. 'Or maybe it's four laps. I can't remember.' She tilted her glass in Tracy Ann's direction. 'Many more of these and walking on deck won't be advisable. We don't want you falling overboard on our first night.'

'I'm not planning on falling overboard any night,' Tracy Ann said calmly.

Natasha checked the slim, gold watch that circled her wrist. 'Maybe I should give Barbara a ring, see if they're okay.'

'They'll be here,' Tracy Ann said dismissively. 'We're on holidays, relax.'

It was another twenty minutes before the cabin doorbell rang. 'Here they are,' Natasha said, hurrying to answer it, her lie primed and ready to be delivered again. 'Hi, come in, we were starting to worry about you.' She gave Barbara a hug. 'Come and have a look! We've been upgraded. I assume because we organised the trip; isn't it great!'

'Lovely.' Barbara smiled and raised a hand to wave to the others. 'Sorry we're late; I don't know where the time went.' She crossed to join the group gathered on the far side of the cabin. Tracy Ann and Michele were sitting on one end of the sofa, Blake in one of the velvet chairs. Don and Daniel were standing to one side, Daniel with his hand resting on the neck of the champagne bottle, as if prepared to lift it to fill their glasses at a moment's notice.

Natasha frowned as she watched Barbara ignore the empty chairs to join the two men, giving each a kiss on the cheek in greeting. Had she lingered just that little bit more as she kissed Daniel? He was an incorrigible flirt and Natasha had noticed Barbara lapping up his compliments and attention as if they meant something more than they did. Perhaps she should have a word with him. He didn't realise the impact he had, didn't realise how charming he could be. Barbara should know better. Other women's men were off limits. Wasn't that an unwritten code?

He'd obviously complimented her on her dress. She was looking down at it, running her hand over the fabric.

Natasha had to admit, it was very pretty. A shame she hadn't spent a bit of money on some new make-up instead of wearing the same pale colours she always wore.

It was a real shame she was flirting with Natasha's husband. Anger surged through her. All evening, she'd been worried about the blasted upgrade, and now, suddenly, here was something much more important to concern her. Barbara, her oldest friend, was trying to seduce her husband, and Natasha could see it. Barbara's stupid, over-the-top laughter at Daniel's quips, the fluttering of her eyelashes, her hand touching his arm. Oh yes, Natasha saw it all.

Picking up a plate of canapés, she approached the group. 'You should try one of these,' she said, holding the plate out to Barbara.

'They do look nice.' Barbara's fingers hovered over the selection before choosing one. She looked at it dubiously before taking a tiny bite, almost immediately screwing up her face in distaste.

Natasha managed to hide a smile. 'You don't like it?'

'It's a bit too fishy fishy for my liking.'

'Give it here,' Daniel said, reaching to take it from her. He popped it into his mouth. 'Fishy, indeed.' He smiled at Barbara. 'Very nice.'

Natasha stood between them with the plate of canapés. She'd like to have raised it and brought it down on one of their heads but she was unsure which of them deserved it more.

12

NATASHA

Alcohol had a lot to answer for. Natasha was sure it was the reason her brain felt so befuddled. Or perhaps it was the barely perceptible rocking of the ship.

They'd drunk too much. The glass of champagne as they left Dar es Salaam. More bubbly before dinner, wine with the meal, cocktails afterwards. They were all slightly buzzing when someone, one of the men probably, suggested they go to the casino.

Tracy Ann was quick to second the idea, with a loud, 'Yes! Brilliant idea!'

Eyeing her friend, Natasha thought she'd become even more manic with every drink. But there was something discordant in her expression. Whereas her eyes were now glittering, almost feverish, her lips were trembling as if, any moment, she was going to break down in tears. Once again, Natasha promised herself to have a word with her when she got the chance.

'Oh yes!' Michele and Barbara spoke at the same time. They giggled stupidly as if this was the funniest thing they'd said all evening.

The initial excited agreement turned to headshakes as, one

after the other, the women stood and felt the impact of the alcohol they'd consumed.

'Oops,' Michele said. 'I think maybe the sea has got rougher because the floor is moving.'

In a ship as colossal as the *Duchess Mary*, it was easy to forget you were at sea, but Natasha didn't think Michele was swaying gently to the rhythm of the waves. Not drunk enough to challenge a friend who could be sharp-tongued at times, Natasha looked around with a wavering smile. 'On second thoughts, I think I'll leave the casinos to another night. It's been a long day and I think I've had a little too much to drink.' It was a gross understatement. She'd had a *lot* too much.

Tracy Ann lurched wildly before jabbing a finger towards the ceiling. 'Maybe a nightcap in your fancy suite?' The sneer in her words said quite clearly that she hadn't believed Natasha's story about being upgraded unexpectedly.

It was Michele who answered. 'That's a marvellous idea.' She linked her arm through Tracy Ann's. Whether to support her friend or because she herself needed someone to hold on to, wasn't clear.

Barbara shook her head. 'Not for me, I think I've had enough.'

'Nonsense.' Natasha slid an arm around her waist. 'We'll have a final drink to finish the night.' And maybe she'd get the opportunity to drop a hint to Barbara about her flirting with Daniel.

He was hovering, getting obviously impatient with the delay. 'Good idea,' he said, leaning forward to kiss Natasha on the cheek. 'You take the girls back for a drink; I'll take the guys to the casino for an hour.' He draped an arm around the nearest two men and led them away, leaving the third to follow.

Girls. Natasha shook her head. It was just a word. It didn't have to be seen as a derogatory one. He hadn't meant to belittle her, make her feel small, reduce her to a dependent child. It wasn't him. It was her. The adjustment from career woman to wife was harder than she'd expected it to be.

'Looks like we've been abandoned,' Tracy Ann said. 'Let's get to this suite of yours, Natasha.'

There would have been room to have met up in the deluxe balcony cabins her friends had, but only the suite allowed the space to sit in comfort. 'Sounds like a plan,' she said, hoping she wasn't setting the stage for the way it would be every night. There was space to entertain her friends, but it didn't mean she wanted their company every day of their seven-night cruise.

They took the lift to the twelfth deck and walked along the narrow corridor to the suite, the door unlocking automatically as they approached.

'Such a brilliant idea these,' Barbara said, her hand going to the silver crown that dangled on the lanyard around her neck. 'No need for keys or money.'

'No need to even remember who you are,' Tracy Ann said with a snort of amusement. 'I bet that'll come in handy.'

'Plus, it connects to that app on your phone so we can follow the guys when they go sneaking off without us.' Michele swung her crown. 'That'll definitely come in handy.'

'You think Don's going to carry it, if he's going to places you'd prefer he didn't?' Tracy Ann said. 'You should have asked him to embed it under his skin if you don't trust him.'

Natasha sighed. It was always this way when they met up, going back to when they'd met in university almost twenty years before. They'd all drink too much. The only difference these days was the quality of the alcohol they consumed. They'd come a long way from cheap beer and two-for-one cocktails in dodgy pubs. Usually, it would be Tracy Ann who'd get hammered, messy, and often obstreperous. That hadn't changed.

And it would be she or Michele who'd say something stupid

or hurtful or both and they'd fall out, only to tearfully make up in the morning when they'd sobered up, neither remembering what they'd fallen out over. Natasha and Barbara would sit back and let their squabbling drift over them, Barbara because she was the most even-tempered of the foursome and never got involved in their arguments if she could help it, and Natasha because she knew there was no point in trying to intervene.

Natasha hoped that Tracy Ann's snarky remark wasn't going to launch a series of arguments or disagreements. It would easily happen. They all seemed a little on edge these days. Nothing Natasha could put her finger on. A note of tension in a word, a tightness in an expression, a sliding away of eyes.

A few days being spoilt on this fabulous cruise liner and they'd all feel better.

Much later, Natasha wondered if she hadn't tempted fate with that thought.

Luckily, Michele hadn't taken umbrage and the atmosphere remained relaxed, optimistic, and comfortable as they entered the cabin. Tracy Ann and Michele retook the seats they'd had earlier, Barbara dropping into one of the velvet chairs. She regaled them with details about their first port of call in two days' time as Natasha opened a bottle of chilled white wine and poured each of them a small glass. Perhaps she should have refused when Tracy Ann knocked hers back in a series of quick, almost frantic gulps and held her glass out for more. Natasha poured her a tiny amount and put the bottle down. All of her friends had seemed in an odd mood recently, but none more than Tracy Ann.

Natasha definitely shouldn't have left the bottle on the table within her friend's reach. There wasn't much wine left in it, but Tracy Ann reached for it and emptied the last of it into her glass. Even for her, this was knocking it back a bit. Behind her, the curtains hadn't been pulled on the balcony door. They hadn't switched on the outside light, the darkness behind the glass turning it into a mirror, the inside scene reflected perfectly, although oddly, as if the action had been suddenly frozen. As if they were all waiting for something to happen. Natasha shivered. She wasn't normally given to flights of fancy, but in the reflection, it looked as if something was bubbling under Tracy Ann's skin. Something that was waiting to ooze out like pus, nasty and rank. Worse, Natasha knew, with a clear certainty, it was something to do with her. *Her*. She stood to cross to the light switch, to flick it on and dispel the unsettling image, but before she could take a step, Tracy Ann swallowed the last of her wine almost dramatically. Then she put the glass down onto the marble-topped coffee table with such force that the stem broke, the bowl shattered, sending several vicious-looking shards flying across the surface.

Natasha wanted to grab one, wanted to hold it against Tracy Ann's neck to stop whatever it was she was going to say, because she was going to, Natasha could see it in her suddenly resigned expression, the wide-open, intent eyes that seemed to be saying there was no way back.

And then, before anyone could react or say a word, before Natasha could find a way to beg her to stay quiet, to keep whatever secret she was hoping to dispel, Tracy Ann spoke. 'I kissed Daniel.'

Only three words, but they fell heavily into the silence and stayed there shimmering in the air as if each had a life of its own. Neon-lit words that widened eyes and dropped jaws and could never, ever, be taken back or erased.

Whoever had said confession was good for the soul had no idea what they were talking about. Confessions should be for dimly lit confessionals in old churches that stank of incense, not for the lavishly decorated, spacious penthouse suite of the *Duchess Mary*. Confessions should be for death-bed passages in Shakespearean plays, or for the final scenes in bad movies, not for a gathering of old friends on their first cruise together. Natasha sat back down. Confessions, she decided, should be banned.

She almost laughed to see the expressions on her friends' faces. Tracy Ann wearing a look of self-congratulatory contrition as if the mere act of confessing had come with a guarantee of forgiveness. Michele, looking gobsmacked, her mouth hanging open. Barbara, blinking, a half-smile on her lips, as if she was waiting for the punchline of a joke she was sure was going to follow.

Then, as Tracy Ann continued to stare straight ahead, Michele and Barbara turned their heads like automatons to face the woman whose husband Tracy Ann had admitted to kissing. The uneasy silence was broken by the occasional sigh that rippled over them like a Mexican wave.

And still Natasha didn't speak.

She could have done. Could have unleashed a torrent of angry words. Sharp, cutting ones, wielded like a rapier to slice and wound until Tracy Ann was laid out in harmless pieces, incapable of kissing another woman's husband ever again. But the words that squeezed from her were sad rather than angry. 'Why would you do such a thing?'

'It was a moment of madness. He'd said something funny, made me laugh and I just...' Tracy Ann was staring straight ahead as if mesmerised by the blankness beyond the patio door. 'It was only a kiss.' She reached a trembling hand up and smoothed it over her head, tucking a curl of hair behind her ear.

Had Daniel done that, Natasha wondered? Had he run a finger down Tracy Ann's cheek? Brushed her hair back before closing in for the clinch? Did their tongues dance together? Did he run a hand down her back and over the cheeks of her bottom as the kiss deepened? *Only a kiss.* Had she wanted more? Had Daniel?

Tracy Ann finally turned to look at her with big, tear-filled eyes and painted lips, the same ones that had pressed against Daniel's.

'I'm sorry, Tasha,' she said.

She'd made her confession, offered an apology; now she was waiting for forgiveness. She'd wait till hell froze over. Wasn't it an unwritten rule of friendship that thou shall not screw around with your girlfriend's man? Friends! Barbara flirting with Daniel, Tracy Ann kissing him.

But it seemed even Barbara thought Tracy Ann had crossed the line, her voice scathing as she said, 'How could you do such a thing?'

'Were you drunk?' Michele asked.

As if that would make everything all right. Natasha glared at her. 'That's not a good enough excuse—'

'I didn't mean—'

'Plus, if she was drunk, what are you implying? That she came onto my husband, and he's the sort of guy who swoops in and takes advantage of inebriated women? Is that what you're saying? It was really all his fault for not beating a hasty retreat?' *But why hadn't he? For goodness' sake, why hadn't he pushed her away and run for the hills?* 'Are you implying Michele, that Tracy Ann was the innocent party? Her mouth just happened to land on my husband's mouth by accident. Is that it?'

Michele's eyes widened and she held her hand up in surrender. 'I was trying to help!'

'Well, don't.' Natasha stood. She'd planned to storm off in what her late grandmother would have classed as *high dudgeon*. It might have been effective if she hadn't stood too quickly, immediately felt dizzy and been forced to sit again. Hanging her head, she allowed a long sigh to escape. Anger seemed to float away on its tail. 'Honestly, Tracy Ann, you're such a fool. Why didn't you simply keep your mouth shut?' She straightened and looked at her friend. 'Unless it was more than a kiss. Is that it?'

'No, I swear,' Tracy Ann said, holding her hands together as if in prayer. As if that would make her denial more believable.

Natasha held her gaze for several seconds before nodding slightly. 'Right, well let's forget about it then, shall we?' She pushed to her feet again, more slowly this time. 'I think we all need to get to bed. Put this night behind us.'

Normally, they'd have all hugged before parting, but by unspoken consensus, they didn't, merely muttering goodbyes and heading from the cabin to find their way to their own further along the corridor.

Alone, Natasha crossed to the balcony door, pulled it open and stepped outside. Standing at the rail, she shut her eyes and listened to the shush of waves. It was a balmy, almost sticky night. The first of seven. Two full days at sea before their first port of call. Two days shut in a tin-can with Tracy Ann. A big ship. It wasn't big enough.

Because despite Tracy Ann's words, despite her tear-filled eyes, her piously joined hands, Natasha knew the bitch had lied.

13

TRACY ANN

Tracy Ann's room was the furthest away from Natasha's suite. Neither of her friends bade her goodnight as they disappeared into their cabins. In fact, there wasn't a word said as they swayed along the corridor. Or was she the only one who was swaying? Perhaps. She knew her friends thought she drank a lot, that she was a lush. She didn't, or at least not any more. In fact, she was probably the one who drank the least. Blake didn't drink apart from beer and the odd whisky, so she'd gone from buying half-bottles of wine, to not buying any at all. As a result, her tolerance had decreased over the years. These days, two drinks made her merry, three and she was tipsy, four... then she was a bloody idiot.

That night, she'd drunk extra in the hope it would give her courage for what she'd planned to do. False courage, of course, but she'd needed it. Perhaps she should have stopped at the one or two extra drinks, not the several she'd had. The extra alcohol had wiped the rehearsed words off the blackboard in her head. The clear, concise explanation she'd planned to give. The one that would make her friends understand, perhaps even sympathise.

She came to a halt and rested her hand on the wall as she looked along the length of the passageway. It was so long, longer than she remembered. And so empty. She turned and looked back to where she'd come from. Had she missed her room? Walked past it in a daze?

Her fingers crept to the crown that swung from the lanyard as she swayed. It was linked to an app on her phone. If she had that, she'd be able to find out where she was. But she'd left her mobile in their cabin. *Stupid woman.*

She turned to go back to Barbara or Michele's room, then unable to remember what number they were in, turned again and leaned against the wall. What number cabin was *she* in? Panic set in as she realised she couldn't remember. She looked both ways with no idea which direction to go.

Why hadn't she kept her mouth shut?

Natasha had been understandably angry, and her question had been reasonable: *why would you do such a thing?* Tracy Ann's answer had been written clearly on that blackboard in her head and she'd stupidly... stupidly... washed the words away with copious amounts of alcohol. All she'd been left with were those three bare words: *I kissed Daniel.* It said so much. It said nothing at all.

Stone-cold sober, she might have had a chance of cobbling an explanation together. Drunk as she was, there'd been no hope.

She'd wanted to confess before the damn cruise, but the opportunity hadn't arisen. She'd tried, hadn't she, to arrange a meeting with her friends, but for one reason or another, it hadn't happened. Perhaps it would have been better to have left it till the final night, then they could disembark the following morning and never need to see one another again. But that would have meant seven nights pretending, and she wasn't that good an actress.

She'd convinced herself that her friends needed to know, that Natasha needed to know. Had Tracy Ann been right or was it simply a case of misery wanting company?

If only she hadn't drunk so much. If she hadn't, she'd be sitting with her friends around her, basking in their sympathy, their understanding. Not leaning against the wall, lost and alone.

That kiss. That one brief moment of weakness. It was a shallow scratch in the surface of what had happened. She'd wanted to tell them everything... everything... but in the face of the fury that had rolled over her with a ferocity she could almost taste, she couldn't tell them the rest.

How could she?

If this was their reaction to one kiss, what would they say to the rest of her sad tale? How she'd been willing to betray her friend, betray her husband, everything she had believed in. *So willing.* The memory made her heave and she slapped a hand over her mouth. She needed to find her cabin. It had to be here, somewhere among all these identical doors.

Keeping one hand over her mouth, she trailed the other along the wall and waved the damn crown at each door she reached, willing it to give the beep that told her she'd arrived. When it finally did, she fell through the door and staggered across the room to the bed.

She dropped onto it, flopping backward. Hopefully, Blake wouldn't return until she'd pulled herself together, maybe sobered up a little. Coffee would help. There was a posh machine on top of a cabinet with a supply of pods. She'd get up and make herself a cup. It would help.

Idiot, nothing was going to help. Tears ran down the side of her face into her hair. She couldn't tell anyone what had happened after that one kiss. She'd learnt her lesson. Regardless of the consequences, regardless of the little voice that was screaming inside her head telling her that she had to finish what she'd started, she would stay silent from now on.

She was on her own. There was no choice except to keep everything a secret and do what needed to be done.

14

NATASHA

Natasha was in bed by the time Daniel returned almost two hours later. She'd left a light on in the separate dressing room. The bedroom was in darkness and she was curled on her side, her eyes shut, her breathing slow and regular in a good pretence of being asleep. The sound of his ablutions drifted through followed by a clunk as he dropped a shoe, the rattle of hangers on the rail as he hung up his suit.

Even with her eyes shut, she could tell when the dressing room light went out and the bedroom was plunged into the kind of darkness that was rare for city dwellers. Straining to hear, she thought she could make out his footsteps as he crossed the room. Then there was light again, but dim; he wasn't trying to wake her. The bed was super-king-size. She was curled on one side of it and waited to feel the bed shift under his weight. When it didn't, she was afraid to open her eyes in case he was standing over her, looking down, waiting for her to stir. Then it did shift, just a little. But it was a long time – several minutes, maybe even an hour – before she heard the soft snore that told her he was in a deep sleep. It would take a lot to wake him at this stage. Only then could she relax enough to sleep.

She'd already told him that she'd be leaving the cabin early the following morning. She and her friends had been determined to make the most of what the ship had to offer and there was an exercise class in the main piazza at seven thirty.

After the night before, she guessed it was unlikely the others would turn up. She'd little interest in going herself but she needed more time before she faced Daniel. The debate in her head – to confront him with what she knew or to let it go – was ongoing. Sleep as a result, had come in short bursts. Awake, she felt the sway of the ship rocking her gently. It should have been comforting, should have ensured a comfortable night. Her thoughts shouldn't be twisting in an attempt to make sense of what Tracy Ann had done.

What Tracy Ann had done. Perhaps Natasha should have forced her to tell the full story. The problem was, she wasn't sure she could handle the details. What was it that Jack Nicholson had said in *A Few Good Men*... oh yes, *you can't handle the truth*. Tom Cruise had been able; Natasha wasn't sure she was. Not if the truth was that Tracy Ann and Daniel had had an affair. No matter how brief it had been. Assuming it was over... oh God, was that it, was the full truth that it was still going on? Maybe they were in love. Maybe he was going to leave her. And thanks to that prenup, she'd be left with what she had before she'd met him.

She'd have to go back to living in that tiny apartment. More scary, more stomach-churning, she'd have to go back to work.

The thought made her heart thump so loud that she imagined it echoing around the room, surprised the sound didn't wake Daniel.

If he sat up now, alarmed at the noise, if he asked her what was wrong, then it would come out in a torrent. She'd be unable to hold back. And like Tracy Ann's words, once hers were out, there was no putting them back.

She allowed the rocking of the ship to calm her. To comfort her. Like a baby. Only then was she able to see how foolish she was being. Tracy Ann had admitted to kissing Daniel. Maybe that's all there was to it, and Natasha's suspicion that Tracy Ann was lying was wrong. Blake adored her. Their marriage had always seemed happy, secure. She had probably given in to a drunken moment. Yes, that would have been it. Like tonight, she'd probably had too much to drink and gave in to a moment of lust. Just as Michele had suggested before Natasha had shot her down. Because Daniel wasn't the type to take advantage of a drunk woman. She was sure of that. He had no morals when it came to business, but this was different. *Wasn't it?*

When the bedside clock showed seven fifteen. Natasha threw back the sheet and slipped from the bed. In the dressing room, she pulled on a pair of leggings, sports bra, T-shirt, and trainers. Her lanyard was hanging on a hook on the back of the door. She grabbed it and left.

The main piazza, a central meeting space, was accessed from the fifth deck but could be viewed from galleries on the two decks above. Natasha took the lift to the seventh floor and walked to the balustrade to look down. People were already gathering for the exercise class. She was surprised to see Barbara there. No sign of Michele or Tracy Ann. Relieved, she walked down two curving flights of stairs to the piazza.

'Hi,' she said, crossing to join Barbara. 'I wasn't sure anyone would make it.'

'Did you really think Michele would come?' Barbara smiled. 'I swear she's allergic to exercise.'

Neither of them mentioned Tracy Ann.

The music was loud enough to prevent further conversation and soon they were all following a lithe, tanned, ponytailed woman with a big, toothy smile as she bent, stretched, and danced in front of them, extolling them through her mic to follow as best as they could. It wasn't difficult, the movements simple and relatively undemanding for both Natasha and Barbara, who regularly attended fitness classes. At the end of the half-hour session, neither had broken into a sweat.

'There's Zumba later,' Natasha said as they walked towards the stairs. 'Plus if we walk rather than taking the lift every time, it should counteract all the food we're going to eat.' When there was no comment, she turned to look at her friend. 'Everything okay?'

Barbara stopped; her fingers curled around the handrail. 'We're avoiding the elephant in the room, aren't we?'

Natasha would have preferred to keep avoiding it too. Not mention Tracy Ann's kiss, or Barbara's flirting. 'What's to say,' she said, continuing to climb the stairs.

'So you're going to do nothing?'

'What do you expect me to do?' Anger coloured Natasha's words. 'Challenge her to a duel?' She moved to one side to allow a group to pass and stood looking down on Barbara a step below. 'It was a kiss. Hardly the crime of the century. Right, she shouldn't have done it, but she confessed, apologised. It's over. Now we should just forget about it.'

'And you think you can. Just like that?'

What did Barbara want from her? To say that she was gutted by her friend's behaviour? To say that she wasn't sure she could forgive her? Or did she want to hear that Natasha had spoken to Daniel about it and had got his version of what had happened? Maybe this was the opportunity to explain that she couldn't risk

Daniel leaving her, that the marriage had to last, otherwise she'd be left with nothing.

Or did Barbara really want to hear that Natasha was going to teach Tracy Ann a lesson she wouldn't forget? Tracy Ann, Barbara, and even Daniel. Make them all pay.

She wasn't sure Barbara could handle that.

15

BARBARA

Ralph had already left for breakfast when Barbara returned to their cabin. She was relieved. Since his retirement two months before, he'd changed. After years talking about what he was going to do when he finished work, the reality was far different. Instead of taking up golf, going to afternoon recitals, visiting museums, he spent the days sitting around watching TV.

He'd started to let himself go. Most days, he didn't bother shaving. Or showering. Barbara tried to be patient. Encouraged him to get out of the house. To meet her after work. Go somewhere. Anywhere. But as days passed, he sank more and more into the doldrums.

'You're retired, not dying,' she'd said to him one evening, when she arrived home after a busy shift to find him slouching around in a raggedy dressing gown, a sour, unwashed smell coming off him in waves. 'For goodness' sake, go have a shower, shave, get dressed. We'll go out for a meal. Cheer ourselves up.'

'You go out to work every day,' he'd grumbled. 'What do you need to be cheered up for?'

Because she was only forty-one years old but recently felt a hundred.

She'd never regretted marrying an older man. Age didn't come into it when you fell in love. But in the last few weeks, her handsome silver-fox of a husband had turned into a surly, grumpy old man. He didn't want to go out, and complained when she did. Complained when she, as he called it, tarted herself up.

The last time they'd met up with her friends and their partners, she'd looked at their more age-appropriate husbands and felt a pang of envy. More than a pang when she looked at Ralph slouched in a chair, looking bored and down in the mouth.

'Ralph finding it hard to adjust to retirement?' Daniel had asked quietly, his sympathy welcome.

He'd stood close enough that she could smell his aftershave, an expensive, oaky scent that made her nose quiver like a rabbit. 'He's had such a dynamic job for so long, it was always going to be difficult to adjust.'

'Hard for him,' Daniel said, then smiled. 'Harder on you, I'm guessing.' He put a hand on her waist. She felt the heat of it through the silk of her dress, felt the glow of it spreading. And then, she looked into his eyes and saw desire, and for the first time ever in her long marriage, she knew she was going to cheat on her husband. Almost as bad – or was it worse – she was going to cheat on her best friend.

Just once, she reasoned. That was all she wanted. To be desired again. Then she'd happily stay with the grumpy, ageing husband she loved.

It was Daniel she'd been thinking of when she bought the dress and that ridiculously expensive lipstick. At night, he'd haunted her dreams; during the day, he invaded her thoughts, and she found herself smiling inappropriately, drawing odd glances from work colleagues. How could she explain? She hadn't seen him since that night. In fact, for one reason or another, she hadn't seen any of her friends for the weeks before the cruise.

When she'd seen Daniel at the airport, she'd felt weak with longing for him.

And when she'd walked into the penthouse suite, with Natasha muttering on and on about how lucky they'd been to be upgraded, all she could see was him. And like a moth to a flame, like the stupid cliché that she was, she crossed to him, simpering and smiling. She might even have batted her eyelashes.

And then to discover that Tracy Ann had kissed him. Only kissed him, she'd said, the lie screamingly blatant. Or maybe only to Barbara, who'd struggled to control the seething anger that had shot through her with such speed, she'd almost fainted.

Because she could see it in Tracy Ann's eyes. She'd fucked him.

And suddenly, Barbara had felt seedy, dirty and so very, very small. She'd been willing to cheat on her husband and on her best friend for Daniel. Now it seemed his interest in her wasn't exclusive. Thinking back to the previous night, hadn't Michele been a little off with him too? Was that it? Was Daniel making his way through the group of friends, seducing them one by one with his undeniable charm?

She could almost feel his hand on her waist. The heat of it.

God, she was such a fool. She'd almost fallen for it.

Daniel, the bastard, she'd make him pay.

16

NATASHA

Daniel was waiting for Natasha when she returned from the exercise class. 'I'm starving,' he said as soon as she came through the door.

'And a good morning to you too.' She planted a kiss on his cheek then crossed to the balcony door and slid it open. 'We could have breakfast out here if you like,' she said, stepping outside. There was nothing to see except the ocean for miles. She leaned over the rail and looked down.

'Don't fall in whatever you do.' Daniel came up behind her, placing a hand on the rail on either side. 'I can swim, but I'm not sure I'd be able to save you.'

'If I fell in here, I'm not sure I'd be saveable.' She turned to him with a smile. 'Saveable? Is that a word?'

'If it isn't, it should be; it makes absolute sense.'

She raised a hand and rested it on his cheek. 'You always say the right things.' She took a step closer and laid her cheek against his chest. His heart was beating loudly. Budum, budum, budum. Slow and steady despite her proximity. She wondered vaguely if he loved her at all. If he ever had. And her own feelings? Apart from a desperate desire to hang on to the lifestyle he'd introduced her too, she wasn't sure. 'You and Barbara were looking very cosy last night.' Still no increase in his heart rate. Maybe he hadn't realised Barbara had been flirting with him. It had been obvious to Natasha, probably to everyone else too. 'What were you chatting about? I hope she wasn't boring you; she can be a little intense at times.'

'She's fine. I feel sorry for her with Ralph being the way he is.'

Natasha pulled away from him and leaned back against the railing. 'Ralph's just having a hard time coming to terms with retirement. He'll get his act together soon and they'll go on as they always did. Be careful with Barbara though; she's a bit of a flirt.'

'Barbara!' He laughed as if it was the biggest joke ever. 'I'd have said a bit prim and prissy myself.'

Prim and prissy! Natasha felt a dart of anger on her friend's behalf. Barbara had obviously made an effort wearing that new dress. Suddenly, her flirtatiousness seemed harmless. It wasn't as if she'd done a Tracy Ann on it and had kissed Daniel. *Or more.* That thought darted into her head. Perhaps now was the time to ask Daniel exactly what had gone on between them. He'd tell her the truth, wouldn't he? That Tracy Ann had come onto him and there had been one kiss. Nothing more. If he did, would she believe him any more than she'd believed Tracy Ann? Thinking back to the previous night, had it been a good or bad sign that she'd appeared to avoid being in Daniel's vicinity?

She was giving herself a headache. 'Barbara's neither prim nor prissy, and she's my friend so don't be mean.'

'I'm always mean when I'm hungry.' He jerked his thumb towards their cabin. 'Let's go for breakfast and I promise I'll be better.'

In the restaurant, Natasha was relieved to see that none of her friends were there. Michele was probably still asleep. Tracy Ann in hiding. But she was surprised, and grateful, that neither Barbara nor Ralph had made an appearance. Her flirting might very well be harmless, but it didn't mean Natasha wanted to see it. 'They've probably gone to the buffet,' Daniel said when she commented on their absence.

'Perhaps.' She doubted it. None of them were fans of the help-yourself buffet, not when their deluxe cabins and penthouse allowed them to eat in the more rarified surroundings of this restaurant. She looked around the beautifully furnished, spacious room with pleasure.

The menu was extensive but she wasn't a big eater so early and settled for a plain omelette. 'And coffee, please,' she said, handing the waiter the menu.

'I'll start with the fruit and yoghurt, then the fried octopus.' Daniel shut the menu. 'And toast, a croissant, and coffee too, please.'

When the waiter left, Natasha raised an eyebrow. 'The fruit is jackfruit and soursop. Neither sound very appetising.'

'I like to try different things,' Daniel said.

She liked that about him: that he was adventurous. Even in bed, he was an exciting lover. She wondered now if his need for something new made him bore easily with the old. The prenup welled in her head. Was that it? He'd never been married before; maybe he was afraid two years was as much as he could commit to, that he'd be bored by then and want to move on. She wanted to ask him. Wanted to ask why he'd bothered to marry her in the first place. She hadn't put any pressure on him, had she? *Had she?* She couldn't really remember. There were so many gaps in her memory in the months before she'd stopped working. Hours when she'd retreated into herself to get away from the dreadful stresses of her working days. Maybe she had pressed him to marry her. *Or maybe he had his own reasons for marrying her.* The thought came out of nowhere and she batted it away. There was no point in drifting into conspiracy-theory territory.

'Try some,' he said when his fruit and yoghurt arrived a few minutes later.

She had to admit, it did look good. Taking a teaspoon, she poked at a piece of creamy white fruit, then picked up a tiny portion. She looked at it suspiciously before putting it into her mouth. 'Oh, it's nice,' she said. 'Sweet and tangy.'

'Better than that.' He pointed his spoon at her omelette.

He was right. There wasn't much excitement about it. It was boring. *Like her? Is that why he had taken to flirting with other women, kissing other women? Was it all her fault?*

She sat up straighter in her chair. Her self-criticism was getting ridiculous. She was fine. Their marriage was fine. So, he was a bit of a flirt; there was no harm in that. Tracy Ann had kissed him, not the other way around. It was gentlemanly of him not to have mentioned it. *Gentlemanly*, she insisted to the little voice that was screaming inside her head, the one that kept insisting she was being a fool.

'Have you looked at the programme for the day?' she asked, reaching into her handbag to pull it out. 'There's a talk about Zanzibar's colonial history at eleven that sounds interesting. Shall we go to that?' She handed the programme over for him to have a look but he shook his head.

'I'll have a look at it later; I don't want to be too corralled by talks. I'll go to that one at eleven, though.'

'I'm going to a Zumba class at twelve. I'm guessing you won't want to go to that.'

'Definitely not! I can meet you back here for lunch at one thirty.'

His fried octopus arrived. Natasha looked at the plate of tentacles in horror. 'I thought it would be round circles like calamari;

that's, that's...' *Disgusting* was the word that was popping into her head but she couldn't say it.

'It's octopus.' He sliced his knife through it, stuck his fork in and lifted it to his mouth. 'It smells good,' he said, before eating it. 'Crunchy, yet tender.' He nodded, satisfied. 'It's really good; you should try some.'

She imagined the suction cups on the tentacles attaching themselves inside his stomach. Maybe growing there. 'No, thanks, I'll give it a miss.' He looked to be enjoying it, shoving the lumps into his mouth with gluttonous speed. It made her feel nauseous. She poured more coffee into her cup, added the half spoon of sugar she took, stirred slowly, all the time keeping her eyes on what she was doing rather than watch Daniel eating. Not till she heard the clatter of his cutlery hitting the plate did she look up.

'Where's our first port of call then?' he asked, buttering a slice of toast.

She'd given him the itinerary the previous week. Hadn't he bothered to look at it?

'We're currently sailing north. Then the ship turns and we have our first stop on the north of Pemba Island.' He looked blankly at her. 'It's the second biggest island in the Zanzibar Archipelago. We stop at Kigomasha Peninsula. We have a couple of hours free to wander around, then we've booked to go on a coach trip to Makangale Beach ten kilometres away. The drive is supposed to give us a good feel for the island. After lunch in a hotel, we have another couple of hours to wander around before a coach takes us back to Kigomasha for the tender back to the ship.' All of which he'd have known if he'd read the information she'd given him.

She checked her watch. 'If you're done, I'd like to go back to our cabin before we go to that talk.'

He drained his cup. 'All done,' he said, getting to his feet. 'Let's go.'

* * *

The talk was held in the Gallery, one of the three theatres on the ship. Seating reminded Natasha of the lecture halls in university. With more comfortable seats. They were early enough to get central seats close to the front which she liked but Daniel complained about. He'd have preferred to have sat nearer to the entrance for a quick getaway when it was over, or to be able to sneak out if it wasn't interesting.

Luckily, it was, the speaker making the history of Zanzibar both colourful and interesting.

'That was really good,' she whispered to Daniel as the applause at the end died away. 'Right, I'm going to have to hurry if I want to make the start of my Zumba class.'

'I told you we should have sat closer to the exit.'

He was right, of course he was. The line of people trailing out in front of them wasn't in any hurry, all of them in holiday mode. She should have anticipated this and taken seats nearer the door.

'Relax,' Daniel said into her ear. 'If you're late, it's not the end of the world. Why don't you give it a miss? We could go back to our cabin, do some alternative exercise.'

They could. It was probably a good idea. If she wanted to get pregnant, they should be at it like rabbits. But Zumba was only held in the morning. 'If I don't keep up my exercise routine, I'm going to be like a hippo by the end of the week.' Some people, she'd heard, put on almost a stone on a week-long cruise, she was determined not to be one of them.

'Hmm,' he said, 'good point, we wouldn't want you putting on weight.'

It was tempting to say that she wasn't the one who was stuffing her face. *Or flirting, or being kissed by other people.*

In their cabin, she quickly changed into her exercise clothes. 'Right,' she said, pulling her hair back with a band. 'Do you want to meet me here and we'll go to lunch together?'

'No, I'll meet you there. I'm going to have a ramble, see what's happening.'

'Okay, but don't forget we said we'd meet the others for lunch, so look out for them.' She kissed his cheek. 'Don't fall overboard!' She grabbed her lanyard, slipped it over her neck and hurried from the cabin.

The Zumba class had started by the time she arrived, but the instructor simply gave her a friendly wave and that was it. In fact, several more people arrived minutes after she did. She really needed to stop stressing. They were on holidays, not at boot camp.

It was a good class, the instructor motivating and almost irritatingly positive, cheering them all on as if they were beginners. Some were, of course. Natasha looked around and saw some struggling, a few dropping out before the class officially ended. None of her friends had turned up. She wasn't surprised. Of the three, Tracy Ann was the only one to have done Zumba. Natasha guessed she was keeping her distance.

It would be impossible to keep doing so even if she had told Blake what had happened the night before, which Natasha doubted. He adored Tracy Ann; her revelation would have destroyed him. Why she'd told anyone was a puzzle. What had she hoped to achieve by it? Forgiveness? *Not bloody likely.*

It was an energetic Zumba class. She should feel relaxed and good after it. Not stressed and confused.

With a wave of thanks to the instructor, she left the exercise room and headed to the lift. The class hadn't been as long as she'd expected. Only thirty minutes, not an hour. She must have misread the programme. Checking her watch, she saw it was only twelve forty. She'd plenty of time to have a shower and get ready for lunch. She wondered where Daniel had gone, then smiled and pulled her phone from her pocket. The app would be able to trace his crown medallion and tell her where he was; she could go and surprise him.

It was easier than she'd expected; he was in their cabin.

There was time before lunch to have that alternative exercise he'd wanted earlier. The thought put a bounce in Natasha's step as she took the stairs to deck twelve. The cabin door unlocked as she reached it and she pushed the door open. 'I'm back,' she called. 'And I still have plenty of energy to spare.'

But the suite was empty. She checked the app on her mobile again. She must have just missed him. But no, it still said he was in their cabin. She looked out to the balcony, wondering if he was sitting outside. He wasn't but her seeking eyes did find something. Daniel's crown medallion lying on the coffee table.

What an idiot to forget it!

Or had he left it behind so that Natasha couldn't locate him? She never used to jump to such negative conclusions; she shouldn't now. He'd simply forgotten it. It was easily done. She was still telling herself that as she showered and dressed for lunch. She took the band from her hair, shook it out and ran a brush through it. It was only a little after one. Daniel might come back before going to lunch. She should wait there for him. She could ring his mobile, of course, but she'd already been warned about the roaming charges. It seemed an unnecessary expense when she could simply go and look for him. She grabbed her bag and headed out. Where would he have gone? Maybe he was sitting out by the pool, topping up his tan.

She headed up to the pool deck. It was a bustling, busy space. The pool was full, sun loungers mostly occupied. She took the stairway up to the viewing deck above and leaned against the rail to look down, scanning the crowd for Daniel's handsome face. She didn't see his, but she did see Don stretched out in garish orange swimming shorts. There was no sign of Michele but no doubt she was lurking somewhere. Dragging her eyes away, Natasha moved on, looking out to sea as she walked, before turning to stand at the rail once more.

With no expectation of seeing her husband, it was some time before she realised he was there, in the hot tub. She smiled. She should have guessed really; he loved lounging in the hot, bubbling water.

Her smile froze before fading completely. It wasn't unusual for there to be five or six people in the tub but Daniel was the only man, and the only woman, with a strange, almost euphoric expression on her face, was Tracy Ann.

As Natasha watched, battling with betrayal and gut-wrenching, bitter anger, Daniel stood and climbed out of the tub.

But Tracy Ann stayed, her eyes following him as he hauled himself from the water, a simpering smile on her stupid, treacherous face.

Natasha wanted to go down, creep up behind, and push her head under the water. Keep it there until there was no more struggling. Until the lying, cheating bitch was dead.

17

TRACY ANN

She barely slept that night. Guilt and regret were not good bedfellows. Luckily, Blake slept the sleep of the honest and her restless shuffling didn't disturb him. At one stage, she'd levered herself onto one elbow and stared down at his face. Even in the darkness, she could make out the curve of his cheek, that Kirk Douglas dent in his chin. Lying to him was the most difficult part of all of this. *She'd never done so before.* Their marriage, their whole relationship, was built on the bedrock of honesty, mutual respect, and love.

But sometimes, just now and then, it had all felt so dull, so staid, as if their future was neatly mapped out for all the years to come. Even their lovemaking had become a comfortable routine of co-ordinated, unchanging moves that frequently left her feeling unsatisfied. Not that Blake ever guessed her orgasm was occasionally faked. She'd never lied to him before. She'd truly believed that, but wasn't every one of those fake orgasms a lie? Which meant she'd been lying to him for years.

A liar and a cheat. If he knew, he'd never forgive her.

She'd really thought her friends would understand and

maybe they would have done if she hadn't stupidly drunk so much and been unable to explain. Now, she had six more days, stuck in this goddamn tin can trying to avoid her friends, and especially Natasha, without Blake being any the wiser.

She certainly couldn't face any of them that morning. 'How about we go to the main restaurant and try their buffet breakfast?' she said as they prepared to leave the cabin that morning. She wasn't keen on help-yourself meals, much preferring to sit and be waited upon, but Blake loved them.

He raised an eyebrow in surprise. 'The buffet? Are you sure?'

'It's good to try it.'

'I bet it'll be fantastic.' He picked up their crown medallions, hung his around his neck and handed her the other.

The buffet was as ghastly as Tracy Ann had expected. A huge space, the full width of the ship, windows on both sides flooded the space with light. Tables and chairs lined the area in front of the windows. The middle of the room held row upon row of food stations. At first glance, it seemed to her that there were hundreds of people milling about holding plates piled high with food.

'There's nowhere to sit,' she said to Blake. This was a bad idea. They should go to their dedicated deluxe restaurant. She'd have to face the music sometime. And at least they'd have a decent breakfast.

'There's one.' Blake pointed to an empty table several feet ahead. 'Come on, let's grab it before someone else does.'

She had to smile at Blake's excitement. He was like a child at Christmas. 'Go on,' she said, once they'd claimed the table. 'You get some food; I'll find where the coffee is hiding and get us both a cup.'

By the time she'd located the drinks station and returned with two mugs of coffee, Blake had already returned. She put the drinks down and sat, looking at the mountain of food on his plate in disbelief.

'The food is amazing,' he said. 'They have absolutely everything you could want.' He looked at her in surprise. 'You not eating?'

'Yes, I'll go now.' She searched the room for any of her friends, not really expecting to see them. She definitely wouldn't see Daniel. Mixing with the hoi polloi wasn't his scene at all. She wasn't hungry but if she didn't get something to eat, Blake would worry. 'Back in a tick.' She crossed to the nearest station, relieved to see it was one for cereal. Filling a bowl with cornflakes, she added milk and returned to the table. How ironic, that here when there was an array of exotic, exciting food to try, she was choosing something as mundane, as downright boring, as cornflakes. It appeared her one grasp at excitement had been enough for her.

'Cornflakes?' Blake shook his head. 'Trust you!'

She wanted to ask what he meant by that. Was it that he thought she was a boring, dull woman who, when faced with such a vast choice, decided to stick to what she knew? If only she had, she wouldn't be in this shitty, fucking ridiculous mess. She dipped her spoon in the cereal and lifted the dripping mess to her mouth. Drops fell to mark the front of her T-shirt. She looked down, saw the stains, like tears.

Oblivious to her dilemma, Blake finished the food on his plate and stood. 'Off to get some more. You want anything?'

'Some more coffee, please.'

Once he'd gone, she put her spoon down and pushed the bowl away. Seconds later, it had vanished along with Blake's empty plate. She smiled a thanks at the waiter but he'd already moved on. With a sigh, Tracy Ann took the printed programme of the day's events from her bag. The friends hadn't planned to be tied to each other all day, every day. They had mentioned meeting up for lunch, and for dinner, of course, but otherwise they were all doing their own thing. She glanced through the list, mentally crossing out anything Natasha might like.

'That talk about Zanzibar's colonial past looks good,' Blake said, putting a plate of some indefinable food on the table. 'I'll be back in a sec with the coffee.' And he was gone again.

'I think I'm going to chill today,' she said when he'd rejoined her. The coffee he'd brought was hot; she took a sip and sighed. 'I'm thinking of the pool and the hot tub. I might leave more intellectual stuff for another day.'

'You don't mind if I go?'

'Of course not. You can tell me about it later.'

She was relieved he made no comment on her lack of appetite. But then he was considerate like that. A good man, he deserved better than her.

'I think I'm done.' He put his cutlery down and sat back, patting his belly. 'I'm not sure if I ever need to eat again.'

'We can skip lunch.' That would suit her fine. The longer she could leave before bumping into any of her friends, the better.

'Won't you be hungry? You didn't eat much.'

A mouthful of cornflakes and she'd struggled with that. 'I can get a snack by the pool. They do pizza by the slice. That'd suit me perfectly.' A few glasses of wine too. Maybe that's what she should do: get drunk, and stay drunk until the cruise was over.

'You want to walk up?' Blake asked, nodding toward the stairwell.

They were on the fifth deck. It was a long walk to the twelfth. A lot of turns where she'd be holding her breath for fear of seeing Natasha appear.

'Let's take the elevator.'

It was still a case of holding her breath as they waited for one of the lifts to ping and announce its arrival, waiting for the door to open, afraid her friend would be there, a look of disgust on her face, in her eyes, in the twist of her mouth. But when the lift did arrive, when the doors shushed open, the woman inside was a stranger.

Their cabin was a long way along the narrow corridor. They walked side by side, Blake chatting about something or other. Tracy Ann wasn't listening; she was peering ahead, hoping none of her friends would pop out from their cabins, like those figures she'd seen in that clock in Prague. The ship should have felt huge; it felt tiny. Claustrophobic. Speeding up, she caught a surprised glance from Blake and shook her head. 'I need to wee,' she explained.

Back in their cabin, she hurried into the bathroom, locked the door, and sat on the toilet seat with her face in her hands. She needed to pull herself together. Blake wasn't a fool. He'd know there was something wrong if she didn't get a grip.

Flushing the toilet, she washed her hands and splashed water onto her face. She'd find a way out of this mess. Drastic times called for drastic measures. She dabbed her face with a towel and caught her reflection in the mirror. She barely recognised the set, angry face. Barely recognised the emotions that sizzled through her. Because suddenly, she faced the truth. If she wanted to keep the secret from Blake, she had to shut Daniel up.

18

TRACY ANN

With a colourful kaftan over her swimsuit, and a raffia bag holding everything she might need for a lazy morning by the pool, Tracy Ann left Blake watching the news and headed off. Outside their cabin, she stood for a moment pressed against the door, and stared up and down the corridor. An unease had settled into her after struggling to find her room the previous night. The corridor stretched a long way on either side. Blake was the one with the good sense of direction, she the one who always got lost, so once again she was confused as to where her friends' rooms were. Any one of the doors she passed could open and she'd be faced with them. Perhaps it was better to stay in their cabin. She could relax on their balcony with a book, lean over the rail and cry into the sea below.

But Blake wouldn't understand. It would worry him. He might even tell her friends he was worried, then they might tell him what she'd said... what she'd done.

What a mess! Pushing away from the door, she kept her head down and walked, almost ran, down the corridor to the elevators. She hammered on a call button, as if by doing so it would make one appear more quickly. It was tempting to take the stairs, but it was four decks above and she was wearing flip-flops. Anxious as she was, she was afraid she'd trip and fall. Fall, break a leg, be flown home by helicopter. God, it was almost worth it, but the way her luck was going, if she fell, she'd probably sprain her ankle or bruise her face, neither of which would get her out of her current predicament.

The elevator door opening took the decision away.

The sixteenth deck where the pool complex lay was already bustling when she arrived. It was well-equipped with tables, chairs, and sun loungers. She was relieved to find one free and set a little apart under a parasol. Putting her hat and bag down, she crossed to grab a couple of towels. It was already warm, the sun a fiery disc in a crystal-clear, blue sky. She spread the towels out, pulled off her kaftan, tossed it on the end of the sun lounger, and lay down. With her eyes shut, and the sun warming her skin, she could almost believe all was right with her world.

Unfortunately, the sun's rays did nothing to calm the worries that were rattling around her head. Sitting up, she took out one of the paperbacks she'd brought. It was probably very good, but the words kept blurring. She shut it, put it down, lay back and closed her eyes again, begging herself to relax. It didn't work, of course, because in the darkness, Daniel's face appeared with that smile she'd once thought so sexy, so enticing. *So dangerous.* That was it, really: a scarily exciting injection of danger into her rather dull life. It had all felt unreal. As if she was acting in a seedy movie, playing a part polar opposite to the settled, happily married wife and mother she was. And now she was counting the cost of her complete and utter stupidity.

With a sigh, she gave up the attempt at relaxing and got to her feet. It was tempting to head to the bar, start drinking. Maybe getting and staying plastered was the best idea. She grimaced at the thought and instead turned to look at the pool. It didn't tempt her, but the hot tub on a raised platform at the end did. It was currently empty. She grabbed her hat, hurried to it and stepped into the warm, churning water. With her hat in place to shade her from the sun, and her body massaged by the bubbles, she could finally feel some of the stress easing.

Maybe she could stay there for the duration. Refuse to come out. Have all her food brought to the side. Blake could join her. It was such a tempting thought.

With her hat tilted over her eyes, she was aware of someone getting into the tub. There was room for several people; she didn't expect sole occupation. She also didn't expect to feel someone touching her bare leg.

'What?' She pushed her hat back with a dripping hand and turned to glare at the person beside her, ready to launch into an attack for this violation of hot-tub etiquette.

'Hello, Tracy Ann.'

Of all the hot tubs in all the world, Daniel Vickery-Orme had to climb into hers. She'd known it would be difficult to avoid him. They'd be together for dinner every night. But she'd hoped to avoid being alone with him. Had never dreamt to be in such close, almost intimate proximity. Not again. Once was enough. That one moment of weakness that was going to destroy everything. If she let it.

'Daniel.' It was all she could manage. She should leave. Would have done if his fingers weren't suddenly coiled around her wrist. Like the snake that he was. 'I was just getting out; I've been here a while.' She laughed and tried to tug her hand away, feeling his grip tighten. 'I'm beginning to feel a little overcooked.'

'A few minutes longer won't do you any harm. I wanted to have a quiet word.'

She'd have liked to flutter her eyes innocently and say, 'What

about?' But playing games had got her into this mess; it wasn't
going to get her out. She knew exactly what he wanted to have a
quiet word about. To know if she'd managed to open her
husband's private files to get Daniel the information he wanted.

'I didn't get a chance,' she said. It was the truth. Sort of. She
didn't get a chance because she hadn't tried. How could she? Open
Blake's computer, look through private, confidential files to find
information to help Daniel succeed in some dodgy scam. *Betray
her husband. Again, don't forget the again.*

'You didn't get a chance.' His fingers tightened further. Hurting. There'd be bruises to explain away with more lies. 'It's a
shame I don't have my mobile with me, so I could show you what
you're capable of when you do get the chance.'

'I made a mistake.' She tilted her head back and met his eyes,
hoping to see some modicum of pity in his. Stupid woman, of
course there wasn't.

'Listen,' he said, releasing her hand. 'You know what I want.
Get it for me, I'll delete that video, we'll forget it ever happened.'

'Blackmail is a crime.' Pathetic words, as if he didn't know, as if
it was going to make the slightest difference.

'Yes, it is.' He smiled. 'But it isn't as if you were the innocent
party. Oh no,' he said with a sneer twisting his mouth. 'I've
watched that video many times; there was nothing innocent
about it.'

She wanted to sink into the water, stay there till every breath
in her body was gone. End it all. She'd watched the video. It had
made her throw up. The thought of Daniel watching it made
her want to turn and scratch his eyes out. Hurt him. Make
him pay.

'If you play ball, it'll be deleted and Blake will never have to
know what a slut his wife is. And don't worry, nobody will find out
where I got my information from. I can promise you that.'

She tried to find a slice of gumption. 'You can promise me! You really think I believe you?'

He grabbed her thigh under the water and squeezed painfully. More bruises she'd find difficult to explain away. 'Believe me, don't believe me, I don't care. You have till the end of the month to get me the information I need.'

He left then, and if anyone was watching, they'd see a handsome, fit-looking man with the water sluicing from his tanned, toned body. They might look at the woman he'd left behind too. Tracy Ann fixed a smile on her face, just in case. A smile that hid what she'd liked to have done – reach forward, grab his ankle, and pull him back in, force his head under, hold it there until he stopped struggling. He was bigger, stronger than her, but she could do it; she had righteous anger on her side to give her strength.

Did she move? Of course not. That would require doing something. Being proactive. Not waiting for some miracle to happen to get her out of the absolute mess she was in, or hoping someone would come to her rescue. Not sitting there with that silly grin on her face, looking up at Daniel as if in thrall.

If anyone was looking, they'd assume she was in love with the man, not that she was sitting there, being slowly par-boiled as she wondered how she could kill the bastard and get away with it.

19

MICHELE

They had breakfast on their balcony delivered by an almost irritatingly cheerful young man with unnaturally gleaming white teeth. Neither Michele nor Don had wanted to go to one of the many restaurants. Michele because she really didn't want to meet any of her friends and Don because he was hungover.

He held a bottle of water to his mouth and drained it in a few frantic gulps. 'I was drinking some goddamn awful cocktail last night. It was easier to keep ordering another rather than talking to Daniel or losing money on the slot machines.' He tapped the crown that was hanging on the lanyard around his neck. 'You just use this, you know; it makes it so easy to gamble.'

'I bet he was gambling though, wasn't he?'

Don nodded, then groaned and held a hand over his forehead. 'My head! Of course he was. Playing the big I am, chatting to the croupiers, laying on the charm.' He picked up his fork and poked at the cold meat on his plate. 'Blake, Ralph, and I, we gave up after a couple of goes on the slots. We're not the gambling type.'

He wasn't the drinking type either. Michele smiled, went back into the cabin and took another bottle of water from the fridge.

'Here you go. Once you've got enough fluids back inside you, you'll feel better.'

She reached for a croissant and tore a piece off, sending flakes of pastry flying into the air to drift out to sea. When Daniel had burst into their small social circle, they'd been so pleased that Natasha had met someone nice, and had welcomed him in, prepared to like him for her sake. He'd charmed and dazzled them, so at first it was easy. The women liked him, so did their husbands. When Natasha and Daniel married, when the four friends met up, the husbands did too. Often, they'd arrange to join up together later in the night. And it was good. Wasn't it? Or had they all imagined they were characters in *Friends*? Was it not all a bit fake?

Michele no longer knew but somewhere in the intervening months, even before she discovered what a manipulative bastard Daniel was, she'd decided she didn't much like him.

She wondered if Natasha knew the truth about Daniel's financial dealings. If she knew he was putting the squeeze on Don. Michele didn't want to believe her friend could be that treacherous. But money was an evil master, and love could make a person stupidly blind.

Money, love, and lust, they had a lot to answer for. Michele put the piece of croissant into her mouth and looked across the table at Don. 'While you were getting sozzled in the casino, Tracy Ann was getting blotto in the penthouse.'

'Nothing new there.'

'No, but this time, she was sober enough,' Michele frowned, 'or drunk enough, I'm really not sure which. Anyway, whichever she was, she told Natasha she'd kissed Daniel.'

Don spluttered on the mouthful of coffee he'd taken. 'What? Shit, I'm sorry I missed that. Did Tasha go ballistic?'

'Actually, she didn't.' Michele took another mouthful of the croissant. 'She was remarkably calm about it. If Tracy Ann had said she'd kissed you, I'd have torn her head off.'

'Would you really?' He looked pleased.

'Yes, but it wasn't ever likely to happen, was it?'

He reached for her hand and planted a sloppy kiss on it. 'No, I'm not that stupid.'

Nor would the slightly nerdy-looking, chubby-cheeked man have tempted Tracy Ann, but Michele loved him too much to tell him the truth. 'I did suggest that she might have had too much to drink, you know the way Tracy Ann can knock them back, but Natasha bit my head off for suggesting that her precious Daniel would have taken advantage of an intoxicated woman.'

As Michele knew it would, that made Don laugh. 'Daniel would take advantage of his own mother if there was something in it for him.'

'*You* know that, and *I* know that, but I'm not sure anyone else sees beyond his Mr Charm façade.'

'Barbara looked to be getting quite cosy with him last night, didn't she?'

Michele had noticed. She wasn't sure what was going on there. Of the four friends, Barbara had always been the sensible one, the one who'd kept them out of too much trouble in their student days. It was almost as if she'd been flirting with Daniel, but that wasn't possible, was it? Unless... 'You've seen how low Ralph has been recently. I don't suppose they're in the same kind of trouble as we are?' When Don looked puzzled, she huffed and shook her head. Sometimes, her beloved husband could be slow on the uptake. 'With Daniel, I mean?'

'Don't be daft! What would a washed-up columnist have to offer Daniel?'

'Don't be mean, he wasn't washed up—'

Don held a hand up to stop her. 'He told me in confidence, so you can't go blabbing about it, okay, but he didn't retire. He was made redundant in that last shake-up at the paper. That's why he's been so low.'

'No!' Michele was horrified. She wasn't sure what shocked her more. Ralph being made redundant, or Barbara lying to them, saying that he'd retired. No wonder she'd been acting so oddly recently.

Michele's head couldn't take any more. She needed to clear her mind so that she could come up with a plan for getting Don out of the mess he was in. 'Right, if you're finished, let's go and explore the ship.' She pushed back her chair and stood. 'Unless you want to go to one of the talks?'

'Not this morning,' he said, draining his cup and putting it down. 'I wouldn't mind a wander, see what this old tub has to offer.'

'Okay, but let's get into our swimsuits; we might get the opportunity to sunbathe.'

The *old tub* had plenty to offer but by the time they'd walked the three decks that encircled the piazza, Don was beginning to wilt. Taking pity on him, Michele linked an arm through his and guided him towards the elevators. 'Let's go to the pool deck; we'll find somewhere shady to sit, you can sleep and I can explore what the deck has to offer. Okay?'

He didn't argue, allowing himself to be led along like an overgrown puppy. Nor did he argue when Michele found the perfect spot, in a quieter space away from the melee around the pool, and pressed him to lie down on a sun lounger. 'Honestly, an hour's snooze and you'll be feeling far better. You might even be able to go for lunch at one.' She tilted her head and smiled. 'You do remember we made an arrangement to meet the others for lunch, don't you?'

'Vaguely,' he said. He stripped down to his swimming trunks.

Balling up his shirt and shorts to use as a pillow, he lay down on the lounger with a sigh. 'You're right: a rest and I'll be perfect.'

'Or as close as you ever are,' she said, bending down to kiss his cheek. 'I'll have a wander and come back. I'll bring you some more water too.'

'You're the best wife.'

'Just you don't forget it,' she said, but he was already asleep.

With a smile, she turned to continue her exploration. The buffet restaurant was one end of this deck. She had a walk through, promised herself they were never going to eat there before being tempted by a station devoted entirely to cakes and pastries. She couldn't let the opportunity pass. Choosing one, she found where she could get coffee then took both to a seat by the window. This was peaceful and relaxing. For a moment – and possibly a thousand calories – she could pretend that their life wasn't in freefall.

A few mouthfuls, and the cake was gone, and with it went her feeling of relaxation. She could walk off the calories; she wasn't sure she'd be able to walk off the worry.

Back outside, she was passing the pool bar when she remembered the promise to bring some water. There were several people waiting to be served. The wait staff were efficient and friendly but most of the orders were complicated cocktails and she guessed the wait would be long. Nobody appeared to be in any hurry, everyone chilled out in holiday mode.

She might as well chill out herself and enjoy the view. People-watching, it was always fun. Her eyes widened as a family of four passed by, parents and two preteens, all wearing matching Hawaiian shirts and shorts. They'd certainly be able to find each other even without their crown medallions. There were several slim women in bikinis soaking up the sun. And more women her shape, thank goodness. Perhaps she should have changed into her swimsuit, maybe had a dip. She was still wondering, and waiting to be served, when her sweeping gaze was caught by the hot tub on a raised dais at the far end of the pool.

It was too far to see her face, but she recognised the hat; she'd been with Tracy Ann when she'd bought it. And she certainly recognised the man who was climbing out of the tub. Daniel! Was Tracy Ann out of her mind? Michele's eyes darted around the deck. No sign of Natasha. Then she looked upwards, to the deck above, a walkway surrounding the pool and leading to the gym on the far end. There were several people standing there, either looking out to sea or down at the mass of people in and around the pool. And then she saw her. Natasha. Staring down at the hot tub. Even at a distance, Michele could see the anger that kept her body rigidly flattened against the rail, her lips pressed tightly together. She'd almost swear she saw sparks fly from her eyes.

Natasha may have been calm and composed last night, but she certainly wasn't now. She looked as if she was going to kill someone.

20

BARBARA

Assuming Ralph had gone to breakfast without her, Barbara had a long shower, then pulled on one of the incredibly soft bathrobes and went out onto the balcony. It was mesmerising to stand at the rail and look down at the water. Fascinating to look out and see nothing but the ocean. There was an interactive map on the TV; she could switch it on and see where the nearest land was. There may even be land in sight on the port side. She should go and have a look. But she didn't move.

All she could do was stand there and think of how foolish she must have looked the previous night. All decked out in that stupidly unsuitable dress, fluttering her eyelashes at Daniel. *Flirting with him.* What a fool she was.

What a silly, pathetic fool.

Had her friends noticed?

Probably not Tracy Ann, who was fighting her own demons, probably not Michele, who seemed to be preoccupied these days, but Natasha? Yes, Barbara guessed, she'd have noticed but would have brushed it away. Daniel wasn't likely to be tempted to cheat on his gorgeous wife with someone as dull as Barbara. But

Natasha wasn't privy to the looks Daniel shot Barbara's direction when nobody else was looking; nor had she seen the way his fingers brushed against her thigh or her backside. She hadn't imagined it all, or the spark in his eye when he'd looked at her.

Now she realised he'd been playing with her and it made her gut curdle. Oh God, she'd been such a fool.

Her face was buried in her hands so she didn't hear the balcony doors sliding open.

'Are you all right?'

No, she wasn't bloody-well all right. 'Yes, I'm fine, just looking down at the waves below.' She turned and hoped the smile on her face didn't look as scary as it felt. 'Have you had breakfast?'

'No, I was waiting for you. I was just having a wander.' He pulled at the belt of her robe. 'We can go as soon as you're dressed. I'm not sure they'd appreciate you going like that.'

She didn't want breakfast but it seemed easier to go along. 'No, probably not. Give me a few minutes and I'll be ready.'

The Malfi Restaurant, where they'd eaten the previous evening, looked different in the daylight. Still elegant, but less glamorous. Despite the late hour, Ralph was surprised to find none of their friends there. 'I wonder where they all are,' he said, more than once, in an irritating whine as if he felt let down by their absence.

Barbara bit her lip and concentrated on the menu.

'They've hardly gone to the buffet,' he said, waving a hand around the room. 'Not when they can eat here.'

Desperate to change the subject, to talk about anything apart from their friends... not Daniel, and certainly not Tracy Ann... Barbara shut the menu. Because they were late, they'd managed to get a table by the window. The drapes were tied back to allow light to stream into the room and to give those seated a perfect view of the sea. Once again, she was mesmerised, and almost unnerved, by the rolling water. Turning away, she focused on the room. It really was very elegant. 'I'm puzzled by their choice of name. I know they've called all their restaurants after famous duchesses, but the Duchess of Malfi is hardly an appropriate choice, is it?'

Ralph looked up from his menu and frowned. 'Since I, and probably most of the people here, have no idea who she is, I doubt if it matters.'

'She was a tragic, fifteenth-century Italian woman who, after the death of her first husband, fell in love with a steward her family didn't approve of. She was eventually murdered, probably by her brother, as were the two children she bore the steward. John Webster wrote a play about it called *The Duchess of Malfi.*'

'Sounds like something that should be on Netflix,' he said dismissively.

A waiter appeared at the table. 'Good morning. Are you ready to order?'

'I'll have the Malfi special,' Ralph said, shutting his menu and handing it back. 'And a large pot of coffee, please.'

'Coffee for me too,' Barbara said. 'And I'll have the muesli with mixed fruit and yoghurt.'

A steaming pot of fragrant coffee came almost immediately. It was exactly what she needed and she sat back sipping it, her thoughts fixed on the sad tale of the duchess whose only crime had been to fall in love with someone unsuitable.

'Barbara?'

There was a querulous tone to Ralph's voice. Had she missed something important? She needed to get a grip, stop daydreaming, imagining things, fantasising. 'I'm sorry, did you say something?'

'I was asking if you wanted to go to one of the talks later?'

'Yes, that'd be good. There's one on colonialism in Zanzibar and one on the history of it as a trading hub. I don't mind which.'

'The trading hub one should be interesting.'

As Ralph ate his Malfi special – an assortment of food, none of which was recognisable – they chatted about the various talks and entertainment on offer over the week. Or at least she chatted; Ralph mostly muttered a word now and then whilst poking at the food on his plate as if wondering what the hell he'd ordered.

'I'm looking forward to the tour tomorrow,' she tried again. 'I've been reading up about Pemba Island. Kigomasha Peninsula, where we disembark, is supposed to be beautiful.' She obviously wasn't doing a great job of selling it because he looked bored. But then he always did these days.

The talk they went to was interesting. At least she thought so but when she turned to ask Ralph if he was enjoying it, she noticed his eyes were shut. Asleep or pretending to be. She wasn't sure. She wasn't sure she cared.

They went back to their cabin afterwards. A silent ride to deck twelve, a quiet walk along the corridor to their room, the door opening automatically as they approached so they didn't even need to ask who had a key.

There was a vague arrangement to meet the others for lunch at one thirty. Barbara hoped Ralph would forget about it but as soon as they were inside, he kicked off his shoes, lay down on the bed and said, 'I'm going to have a nap. Call me in time for lunch, will you?'

'Right,' she said, looking down at him. For a strange moment, it was Daniel she saw lying there and she felt a dart of lust that dissipated quickly when Ralph opened one eye and stared up at her. 'You going to sit out on the balcony and read?'

It's what she could have done, what she should do. Sit down, have a rest, conserve her energy. 'No, I think I'll have a walk around. Explore. There are a few shops I want to have a look at too.'

'Okay, I'll see you back here before one.'

She stopped in the bathroom, pulled a brush through her hair, and reapplied her lipstick. The Tom Ford red one was sitting on the side, taunting her. It was tempting to slick some on. Tracy Ann wore red lipstick. Had she always done so or was this a recent change? Barbara couldn't remember ever noticing before. What did her friend have that she didn't? They were the same age but Tracy Ann was smaller, slighter. Was that it? She turned side-on to the mirror and grimaced. She'd let herself go, hadn't she? Ralph had done, so she'd kept him company.

That was her excuse. A sad, and not entirely truthful one. She'd nobody to blame but herself.

Ralph was snoring lightly by the time she'd finished in the bathroom. She shut the door quietly, stood looking at her husband for a while, reminding herself that she did love him, before turning to open the cabin door to leave.

There were a few shops she wanted to explore but, the mood she was in, nothing caught her fancy apart from a diamond and ruby pendant that she drooled over for a moment but shook her head when the assistant asked if she would like to try it on. She'd seen the price tag; she didn't have thirty-five thousand pounds to spare.

She saw a scarf she quite liked, fingering the silk, wondering if it would go with a dress she had, then walked away from it because she couldn't remember. Maybe she'd come back later. It wasn't as if she'd forget where it was. Wasn't as if she was moving on to a different town and had to decide. She was going to be there all week. What a crazy idea it had been to come on this damn cruise. Suddenly, she had to get out of the shop. Outside, she crossed to the rail. She could look down on the piazza, and up to the deck above, but the open space didn't alleviate the sudden, unexpected attack of claustrophobia. Hurrying back to the elevators, she pressed a call button and shuffled from foot to foot, turning one way and then the other, waiting for any of the eight elevator doors to open. When it did, of course it was the one furthest away and she ran towards it as if it was going to vanish in a puff of smoke. Inside, she pressed the button for deck sixteen. She was alone, but the space was small, and closing in on her. Feeling panic build, she clamped a hand over her mouth to stop a scream from erupting and hammered on the lift buttons to get it to stop. When it didn't, when it kept going, she tried to claw open the doors to get out wherever she was. It wouldn't open, of course, and seconds later, the lift stopped and the doors opened to deck sixteen.

With her eyes wide, and her mouth trembling, she must have looked like a crazy woman, because the people waiting for the elevator backed away when she stepped out.

Someone put a hand on Barbara's arm. 'Are you all right?'

The tone and the words were kind, but the last thing Barbara needed was sympathy. She pulled her hand away and hurried through the doors to the pool deck and the open sky, ignoring the muttering she left in her wake.

Outside, there was a horde of people milling around the bar. Sunbeds surrounding the pool were draped with people, the pool itself home to several more, mostly standing about chatting. Pushing through the crowd, Barbara took a stairway upward, her eyes fixed on the blue sky above. That was what she needed: sky and a bit of space.

There were fewer people on this deck. The midday sun was too strong to be wandering around without a hat or sunscreen. She had neither and immediately felt the heat soaking into her skin. But there was also a hint of a breeze, an unhindered view over the rail to the sea, and the space to breathe.

After a minute with her face held up to the sun, she felt a little calmer. It was this ship, this damn floating hotel. Too many people everywhere, the air heavy and cloying, thick with secrets, angst, lies, and lust. She wiped a hand over her face and moved along to a shady spot. What must those people outside the lift have thought of her? They'd looked startled. Had she looked that wild, that crazy? What the hell was wrong with her these days? Maybe she was premenstrual. Or maybe, and her heart sank at the thought, she was menopausal. She'd always been irregular; it was hard to know.

With a sigh, she moved to the railing overlooking the pool deck and looked down. It was a melee of people moving about, availing themselves of all there was to offer. With the sun high overhead, even the people in the pool had given up and were climbing out to seek shade.

She was about to turn away, when she caught sight of Natasha standing on the opposite side. She was Barbara's closest friend; perhaps chatting to her would help ease her mind. She couldn't mention her silly infatuation with Daniel, but they could discuss Tracy Ann's confession and what Natasha was going to do about it. It would be good to focus on someone else's problems rather than her own.

She was about to raise a hand to attract Natasha's attention when she was struck by the expression on her face. Even several feet away, she could make out the lines of anger. What was she staring at so intently that would have had such an effect?

Barbara turned to look and drew a sharp breath. At the far end of the pool, on a dais slightly raised above it, there was a hot tub and Tracy Ann was in it, but it was Daniel rising from the tub that made Barbara's breath come out in a sigh of longing. Broad shoulders tapering to narrow hips, the water streaming down his back. Then he stood at the top, like a Greek god, and ran a hand through his hair before turning to face the pool. He squinted slightly in the sun, then took a few steps and dove into the water, barely making a splash.

Barbara held her breath until he reappeared, then let it out in a gush of desire. She watched as he swam a length, turned and swam back. She'd have watched him all day if she hadn't felt eyes on her and stupidly looked up. Across the gap, she could feel the heat of Natasha's eyes staring straight at her.

For a moment, neither of them moved, then Barbara dropped her gaze and shuffled away.

21

NATASHA

Natasha was pacing their cabin, furious irritation in every jerky step, when Daniel returned. He'd pulled a shirt on, but it was open, showing off his bare chest and his firm six-pack. She wondered how many admiring glances he'd acquired on the way. Because, dammit, he was an impressive-looking man.

She stopped pacing and glared at him, folding her arms defensively across her chest as he moved towards her. 'I saw you.'

'You did?' He smiled and reached for her, pulling her close. 'You don't seem too pleased by that, so am I to take it you saw me doing something you don't like?'

He seemed so casual, so damn pleased with himself, it made her even angrier. 'How about flirting with Tracy Ann in the hot tub. I'm not terribly keen on that, Daniel.'

He laughed and kissed her cheek. 'You came down to the pool? Why didn't you join us? We were having a laugh; you'd have enjoyed it.'

That wasn't the way it looked or the way it was. She was sure of it. She wanted to bring up Tracy Ann's confession of the previous evening, of the lie she'd seen in her face. Or had Natasha imagined it? Was all the stress and strain of the last few years finally too much to bear? *No*, a little voice screamed in her head, *you know what you saw.* She sought for something more concrete to accuse him of. 'Barbara was there, staring down at you too. You've been encouraging her, Daniel; that has to stop.'

He held her away from him, his fingers circling her arms. 'Have you lost your mind?' He shook his head. 'First, I'm flirting with Tracy Ann, now it's prim and prissy Barbara. Next you'll be bringing Michele into the equation. What have I done to make you so suspicious, so jealous?' He sounded disappointed with her.

What had he done? Been nice to her friends. Was it his fault he was so charismatic, so charming? It was why she'd been attracted to him, after all. She was tempted to tell him about Tracy Ann's confession and ask what had happened. Ask for all the gruesome details of her friend hitting on her husband. *The same friend he just happened to be sharing a hot tub with the following day.* Natasha didn't know what to think. For the moment, it seemed better to stay silent.

'I promise you,' he said, pulling her closer again. 'I do not fancy any of your friends. They're nice women, but not my type, and anyway, I have you; I don't need anyone else.'

Then he kissed her. 'We have time before lunch,' he said, drawing her towards the bed. 'Let's make the most of it.'

And put all thoughts of Tracy Ann from her head, just like that? But Natasha didn't argue. The more times they had sex, the better the chance she'd have of getting pregnant. She'd been a career woman, and a husband and children were something other women needed, not her. All that had changed. Now she had a husband, and she wanted the children. With the terms of that prenup preying on her mind, she *had* to have children. She wasn't going to lose the happy ever after she'd finally achieved. It wasn't too late to have it all.

* * *

They went down to lunch, hand in hand, a beaming smile on her face to tell anyone who wanted to know that they'd just had mind-blowing sex. It was as fake as the orgasm she'd had, Daniel too caught up in his own pleasure to notice.

She half-expected that they'd be on their own for lunch so was surprised to see all three of her friends and their partners at the table when they arrived. Both Tracy Ann and Barbara looked as if they'd rather be anywhere else, whereas Michele was sitting back with a strange smile on her face as if she was waiting for everything to explode. Or for Natasha to lay into Tracy Ann with some biting comment about keeping away from her man. Like an escapee from a country and western song.

'Hi,' Natasha said, pulling out the chair and sitting with what could only be described as a flounce. 'I hope we haven't kept you waiting.' She threw Daniel a look from beneath her eyelashes. 'We got delayed.' *See, everyone, see how happy we are together.* Was she rubbing it in a bit too thick?

There was a time when her *we got delayed* remark would have caused hilarity, when her friends would have jumped in with ribald comments about the kind of things that could possibly have delayed them. There was a time when they were that comfortable and relaxed with one another. She wasn't sure where that time had gone. After all these years, had they just outgrown one another? Or was it something else? She didn't miss the sharp, knowing glances directed her way from Tracy Ann and Barbara. As if they could see right through her fakery. Even Michele was looking at her oddly.

It was Blake who broke the uncomfortable silence. 'I went to that talk this morning about Zanzibar's colonial past. Great speaker, very interesting lecture.'

It was enough to start talk flowing. Between the men at least, the four women adding a brief comment now and then but none of them instigating conversation. Perhaps Natasha should ask Tracy Ann if she'd enjoyed sitting with Daniel in the hot tub, or if Barbara had enjoyed watching him as he climbed from it a short time later. Or maybe she should ask Blake and Ralph if they minded their wives lusting after another man.

'That's a nasty bruise on your hand.' Michele pointed to where Tracy Ann's hand was resting on her glass. 'It looks painful.'

Whipping her hand away, Tracy Ann shook her head. 'It's fine. I stumbled getting out of the hot tub and hit it on the railing.'

'And her leg too,' Blake added. 'She has a whopper on her thigh.'

Natasha opened her mouth to question the lie. She'd stayed staring as Tracy Ann had eventually climbed from the tub a minute after Daniel. She hadn't stumbled as she pulled herself almost wearily from the water. *How very interesting.* She definitely hadn't acquired those bruises getting out from the tub, so where had she got them? And why lie? Natasha's eyes widened as she looked from Tracy Ann to Blake. Was it possible that he was responsible? Had anyone asked, she'd have said he was the last person she'd suspect of domestic violence. But wasn't that the way it was, how it stayed hidden? Poor Tracy Ann, maybe that was why she was looking elsewhere for love.

A shame she'd chosen Natasha's husband though. She'd thought there was something preying on Tracy Ann's mind, now she knew what it was. Not all of it though. There was more. Natasha was sure of it. Sometime over the next few days, she'd tackle her. Find out the truth of what had occurred between her and Daniel, and the truth about those bruises. It was the perfect opportunity; they'd be stuck in close proximity for several days to come.

Several days. The thought was suddenly horrifying. Cracks had already appeared in their relationships. More might occur, and all the secrets they didn't know they had would come tumbling out.

22

NATASHA

There was some discussion about the afternoon's activities but, apart from Blake, who said he fancied going to a talk, nobody showed any interest in going to anything.

'We're just going to chill by the pool,' Michele said. 'So that's where we'll be if anyone's looking for us.'

If anyone else had plans, they weren't discussing them.

'Dinner at seven?' Natasha said, looking around the group. 'And then the show afterwards?'

There were nods of agreement to the plan. She wasn't inviting them to their penthouse for pre-dinner drinks that night. Despite what she'd said about them making the most of what their suite had to offer, she wasn't sure it had been a good idea. Cracks had appeared; she wanted to prevent them turning into crevasses. They were already spending a lot of time together. And the following day, on the excursion to Pemba Island, they'd be together all day. *All bloody day.*

'I might go to the casino,' Daniel said, just as they were all getting to their feet. 'Anyone else fancy it?' He shrugged when there were no takers. 'How about you?' He looked at Natasha. 'You fancy a flutter?'

'Yes, why not,' she said, still glowing from their pre-lunch love-making. She had a good feeling about it. Maybe even now, that brave spermatozoan was introducing himself to her eagerly waiting egg. As she stood, she ran a hand down her flat stomach. Perhaps she should cut down on the booze, even cut it out. If anyone noticed, or commented, she'd cite the calorie content. Her friends had often accused her of being obsessive about staying slim so it should do the trick.

A late convert to the idea of motherhood, she was now eager to get on with it. She'd like two. Then, if Daniel left her – she didn't know why this idea constantly appeared in her head, but she didn't seem able to stop the doubt – but if he did, then she'd have her children. And with two children, a protected income from him to support them.

The casino was loud and brash. She watched Daniel at the roulette table until she got bored. The noise and colour of the slot machines drew her but after playing on a few without winning anything, she gave up. Gambling held no allure for her. 'I'll leave you to it,' she whispered to Daniel, getting a nod in return, his concentration on the ball that was spinning around the roulette wheel. She didn't wait to see if he won or not.

Deciding to get the elevator rather than walk up to the twelfth floor, she pushed the button and waited with a few other people, exchanging a few pleasantries as was the way. Inside, they all pressed for their various decks. About to press twelve, her finger moved to hit sixteen instead.

She'd been so angry earlier to see Daniel and Tracy Ann looking so cosy. This time, the hot tub was empty and there was nobody in the pool she recognised. It was good to be outside in the fresh air. There were several people at the bar waiting for drinks. She could get one. A non-alcoholic cocktail perhaps. She never used to be so indecisive, but these days, everything seemed difficult. Everything – Daniel, the prenup, her friends – all had developed into a seething tangle in her head.

Unable to decide what to drink, she'd turned to retrace her steps to the elevator when she saw Barbara, sitting on her own. She was staring into the glass she held as if the answers to her problems were floating with the ice. Natasha's earlier anger at both Tracy Ann and Barbara drifted away. These women, with all their spiky edges, their annoying habits, were her friends. Part of who she was. They couldn't outgrow each other.

'Do you want to be alone, or can I join you?' Natasha waited, unsure whether Barbara was pleased or annoyed to have her reverie interrupted. A mix of both, she decided, when Barbara sighed, shook her head, then waved to the chair opposite.

Natasha had no desire to harp on her friend's fixation on Daniel. It was so unlike the normally sensible woman that she had to think it had something to do with Ralph's depressive mood since he'd retired. Or maybe something else was going on. She'd liked to have asked her what she thought of the bruises on Tracy Ann's hand, and if she was right about Blake being responsible, but Barbara looked so miserable, she didn't have the heart. Instead, she told her news that might be true. Cheerful, life-affirming news.

She leaned across the table, closing the gap between them. 'Daniel and I, we're trying for a baby.' She smiled and hunched up her shoulders. 'I know it's stupid, that I couldn't possibly know already, but we had sex earlier and I'm convinced it did the trick.' She expected a surprised reaction, maybe even a pleased, excited one. What she didn't expect was for Barbara to throw her head back and laugh.

Natasha sat back, eyes wide in shock. 'I don't understand—'

'Of course, you don't, because you're a stupid, stupid woman.'

Barbara lifted her glass, took two gulps, a breath, then tossed back the remainder. 'Right, I need another drink; you want one?'

Natasha opened and shut her mouth, unable to utter one word. There weren't any. That Barbara, her oldest friend, would greet her news with such vitriol was as unexpected as it was shocking.

'Oh please, don't tell me you're not drinking because you think you're pregnant.' Barbara laughed again: an exaggerated, false sound. To add to the act, she wiped a hand over her eyes and flicked her fingers to shake away imaginary tears. 'Funniest thing I've heard in ages. I'll get you your usual. Believe me, you're going to need it.'

Natasha sat, unable to move, stunned by her friend's viciousness. Perhaps a storm was brewing, because suddenly she felt the deck rocking. She gripped the edges of the table and looked around in alarm. Nobody else appeared affected by this localised storm. Just her. And maybe Barbara who, minutes later, was returning with a glass in each hand. She too was swaying.

'Here, drink this,' Barbara said, putting the glass down on the table, then sitting with her own.

Rather than argue, Natasha took a sip, then pointedly put it down. 'Now, how about telling me what the fuck is going on, Barbara?'

'You said you and Daniel were trying to get pregnant?'

'Yes. I'm not sure why that's a cause for such hilarity though. I'm only thirty-eight; it's not too late.'

Barbara swirled her drink, sending ice rattling. Her expression was suddenly serious. 'No, of course it's not. Ignore me, I'm just being a bitch.' She lifted a hand to her forehead and rested it there. 'Life has been a bit difficult recently. Ralph has been...' She shook her head. 'Well, you can see for yourself; he's depressed and won't see anyone, won't listen to me. I'm not sure what to do.'

Natasha frowned. She'd already guessed this. It was why she was giving her friend so much leeway over her obsession with Daniel. But this didn't explain her reaction to Natasha's news. 'There's something else you're not telling me, isn't there?'

Barbara shook her head. But her eyes filled with tears. 'I shouldn't have said anything.'

Famous last words. 'Perhaps, but you did, so now you'd better tell me what it was you were going to say before you got cold feet.'

'Daniel...'

'What about him?' Natasha said when nothing more was forthcoming.

Barbara put the glass she'd been holding down and reached across the table for Natasha's hand. 'I know something I shouldn't. Something you, however, should know and obviously don't.'

How many drinks had her friend had? She wasn't making any sense but the feeling that the ship was rising and falling as it hit wave after wave returned. 'Something I should know. You'd better tell me.'

'If it gets out that I told you, I'd be in serious trouble. Fired, maybe even prosecuted.'

'Right, then I'd better promise not to tell anyone that you told me, but if you don't tell me what the hell is going on, I swear to God, I'll throw you overboard.'

'You're trying for a baby—'

'Yes.' Natasha's voice was raised, loud enough to draw curious glances from other passengers.

'Try all you want, but you won't get pregnant by Daniel. He's had a vasectomy.'

23

BARBARA

Barbara watched as the irritation on Natasha's face was replaced by amused disbelief.

'Don't be ridiculous,' she said. 'Of course he hasn't had a vasectomy! He's as eager to have a child as I am.'

It was too late for regrets, too late to wish Barbara had kept her mouth shut, way, *way* too late to wish she'd never looked at Daniel's medical records. 'I'm so sorry, Tash, but he's lying to you. He's had a vasectomy.'

'That's ridiculous!' But there was less force in the words now and Natasha's expression was no longer amused. 'I don't understand, how would you know such a thing?'

Barbara shouldn't, of course. It was completely against every policy, every rule, to access Daniel's medical records. 'I remember when you met him, you were telling us how amazing he was. Honestly, you painted such a picture that we thought—'

'We? So Tracy Ann and Michele know about this too?'

Barbara shook her head. 'No, I never told them. There was no reason to. But we did think Daniel sounded too good to be true. Tracy Ann thought he had to be married. Michele that he was

some sort of con artist. The following day, I was in work and...'
She groaned and ran a hand through her hair. 'I don't know what
possessed me, but I searched the system to see if he had medical
records.' A flush of colour flooded her cheeks. 'I was being protective of you. I wanted to find out if he was married, or if there was
anything dodgy, but there wasn't. I did see the note about the
vasectomy, but I didn't think that would matter. I thought you'd
probably see it as an advantage actually. You'd always said you
weren't interested in having children; how was I to know you'd
had a change of heart?'

Barbara looked towards the bar. She'd like another drink. In
fact, she'd like to line several up and drink them one after the
other. With a sigh, she looked back to Natasha who was sitting
rigidly, eyes wide, lips pressed so tightly together it must have
hurt. Barbara had done this. Caused this pain. Not Daniel. His
secret wasn't hers to tell. Worse, Barbara wasn't sure about her
motive for telling – was it because Natasha was her friend and
deserved to know the truth, or could it be that Barbara hoped it
would damage their marriage, and maybe Daniel would need
consolation? Was she really that desperate? That wicked and
pathetic?

Natasha peeled her lips apart. 'When did he have it done?'

Barbara wasn't sure why it mattered. 'Two years ago. I don't
remember the exact date.'

'Before he met me.'

'Yes. He probably didn't think it was worth telling you. You've
always been adamant you didn't want children.'

'You don't understand.' Natasha stared down at her clasped
hands.

Barbara would add it to the list of things she didn't understand: why she'd become so stupidly obsessed with her best
friend's husband, why Ralph's retirement was proving to be a

nightmare, why she felt so damn miserable every day. But Natasha was her friend, and she'd caused her pain; now it was time to stop being so self-obsessed and try to help. 'Maybe not, but if talking about it would help, why don't you try me?'

Natasha was still staring at her hands, fingers clasping and unclasping. She pulled them apart and looked up.

Barbara was taken aback. She'd seen her friend irritated, annoyed, upset, but she'd never seen her angry. And it was directed at her. It seemed the messenger was indeed going to be shot.

24

NATASHA

She wanted to reach across the table and tear Barbara's eyes out. No, on second thoughts, maybe tear those loose lips from her face, her tongue from her mouth. Cause her as much pain as she'd caused Natasha. So much easier to blame her than to face the truth about Daniel, about her marriage. Anyway, Barbara was right, Natasha had always said she didn't want to have children, and when she'd reconsidered, when she'd decided she no longer wanted to be a career woman, when she looked at her friends with their children and thought their lives looked better, she'd never told them. Only Daniel knew about her change of heart.

They'd been going out a few months, he'd met her friends and seemed to fit into her life so well. She remembered looking across the table at him and thinking this was what she wanted. And then he'd proposed, and everything was looking rosy. She'd mentioned children. 'I was thinking I'd like two and if we're lucky, it'll be one of each.'

She remembered he'd smiled.

The bastard had smiled. He hadn't taken the opportunity to tell her the truth. Not then, not later when he insisted on a prenup that would leave her with nothing if the marriage ended within two years and she was childless.

The drink Barbara had brought Natasha was sitting untouched. Picking it up, she took a sip, then tilted and gulped a few mouthfuls. 'It appears I have no need to cut out the booze.'

'I'm so sorry. I should never have told you; it wasn't my secret to tell.'

'Perhaps you could have told me more kindly.' *Not to have spat it out with such viciousness, not to have almost gloated in the telling.* 'You're my friend; you were looking out for me.'

'I'm sure Daniel would have told you if he had known you had a change of heart about having a child.'

'He did know. I told him, before we got engaged, that I wanted children.' Natasha almost smiled at the look of shock on Barbara's face. 'Yes, it's hard to believe the eminently charming, charismatic Daniel could be such a liar, isn't it?' Natasha drained her glass and got to her feet. 'I need a refill. I'll get another for you too; you'll need it when I tell you the rest.'

There was only one other person at the bar, but they were ordering a couple of finicky cocktails so Natasha was forced to wait. She turned to look across the open pool deck. So many people. They looked as if they were enjoying themselves, but perhaps they were all lying. Perhaps every single person lounging on the sunbeds or lazily swimming in the pool was harbouring a secret. How would anyone know? Liars didn't have horns or forked tongues.

'Two large chardonnays,' she said, when it was her turn to order.

'There you go, Mrs Vickery-Orme, enjoy.'

The magic of the crown medallion. No need for money or credit cards. The chip in the crown easily read by the staff's equipment. No secrets here. Perhaps that's the way it should be. If

Natasha ruled the world, everyone would have a chip, updated automatically by some higher power. Although what would hers say? She wasn't sure.

'Here you go,' she said, putting the glass on the table beside Barbara's now empty one. She was being unusually quiet, maybe worried about the ramifications of what she'd done. If the hospital found out, she'd be fired at the very least. If Daniel found out... well, that wasn't going to happen. The time for truth had passed. 'I won't tell him that you told me,' she said now. Expecting to see Barbara look a little relieved, she was surprised when her expression stayed tight as she reached for her wine and swallowed a couple of mouthfuls. 'There's no point really,' Natasha said finally.

'You were always so clear. You didn't want children. Maybe Daniel—'

Natasha frowned. 'You think *I'm* lying? That I never told him I wanted children. Is that it?'

'I can't see why he wouldn't have told you about the vasectomy if you had. It doesn't make sense.'

'No doubt he had his reasons. Daniel is good at that. He doesn't do anything without a good motive.' She picked up her glass, swirled the wine, took a sip. 'There's something else, something you don't know.' She quickly spelt out the terms of the prenup.

Barbara looked appalled. 'So if the marriage ends before you reach your second anniversary, you both leave with what you came into the marriage with.'

'Yes. I'd move back to my tiny apartment. I'd have to go back to work.' She put her glass down and wiped a hand over her face. 'I can't go back to nursing, I just can't, but I'd need to work to pay the mortgage on the apartment.'

'But that's if your marriage doesn't last,' Barbara said. 'There's no reason to think it wouldn't, is there?'

Was she for real? 'You've just told me that he's had a vasectomy and has been lying to me for months. God!' She shoved her hand into her hair and yanked as anger sizzled through her. 'Even earlier, we had sex and I told him I thought this might be it. And do you know what that bastard did? He fucking smiled at me. Smiled!' He'd made a fool of her. She'd make him pay for that.

'So what are you going to do?'

'I don't know.' The flash of anger faded, leaving her feeling weak. 'You'll think I'm foolish, but I had my heart set on this, you know: having a child, maybe two. Being a mother rather than a career woman.'

Barbara pushed her glass to one side and leaned forward to grasp Natasha's hand. 'Are you sure? You loved your job. The last couple of years have been tough, but they were the exception, not the rule. Things will go back to how they were—'

'No! They won't.' Once again, Natasha's voice had risen and attracted sideways glances from other passengers. She glared at them till they turned away. 'It's like being in a bloody goldfish bowl.'

'The cruise was your idea,' Barbara reminded her. She looked around. 'I have to admit, I'm finding it all a bit too claustrophobic for my liking. I'll be glad to get off tomorrow and the following few days and I'm relieved we only have one more full day at sea.' She waited a beat before saying, 'I know I've said it before, Tasha, but I'm saying it again: you should get help. Talk to someone. All the stress of your job, especially the last couple of years, I'm sure you have PTSD or something like that. It'd help to talk.'

Natasha pulled her hand away and sat back. 'I don't need to talk to anyone. I've made my decision; I'm never going back to nursing.'

'Well, you might not need to, if you can get over this—'

'Get over this! Can you hear yourself!? Daniel deceived me; how can I possibly forget, let alone forgive that?'

'Well, then you need to face it. If you leave him, you'll have to go back to work.'

Natasha laughed. The sound wasn't pretty and once again drew glances from people sitting nearby. This time, there was an element of fear in their response. Ignoring them, Natasha leaned forward. 'You think that's the only option for me, do you? Shut up and put up with my marriage as it is, or return to that nightmare job?' Her voice dropped to a whisper. 'You don't know me at all.'

25

MICHELE

There was only one way to deal with monsters. Cut off their heads.

When she saw Don's hunched shoulders and hang-dog expression, she'd almost have done it. Taken a very sharp knife, sneaked up behind Daniel – maybe when he was showing off his tanned, muscled body on a sun lounger – crept up, sliced quick and hard across his throat. Chopped his head right off, grabbed it by the hair, and held it aloft in triumph.

She and Don were on the jogging track – walking, not running – seven laps were equivalent to a mile. They were going to do two miles, then go down to listen to a lecture on the flora and fauna of Zanzibar. At 3 p.m., there was afternoon tea, following which Don was going to a lecture on the political history of the country, and she was going for a facial in the spa. Each of them was determined to get the most from the cruise. 'We're not going to let that bastard ruin this holiday,' she said, tucking her hand into the crook of his elbow. 'We're going to enjoy every moment.' Her joie-de-vivre was forced, but necessary. If Don knew how dark her thoughts were, he'd be even more depressed than he was. He was a good man.

Decent, hard-working. A good husband, great father. The kind of man who'd say, *yes, of course*, as soon as he was asked to do something. And that bastard Daniel had taken advantage.

But he'd messed with the wrong person, because Don was married to her, and she wasn't nearly as nice as he was. There was a streak of ferocity lying deep inside her. She felt it stir when either of her children were threatened and used the edge of it to right a wrong against them. For Don, the man she'd loved for so long, she was happy to allow it completely off the leash.

'Two more laps,' he said as they passed by the marker. 'I'm looking forward to that afternoon tea already.'

'Because you didn't eat enough at lunch?' She laughed and linked arms with him tighter. 'Don't forget we've dinner in only a few hours.'

'No problem.'

No problem. If only everything were so easy. She'd searched the corners of her mind for a solution to their dilemma and had been unable to come up with anything that didn't require taking a massive step. Usually, she'd turn to her girlfriends for advice. Not this time. She obviously couldn't talk to the loved-up, besotted Natasha about what a shit her husband was. Barbara, too, looked to be under Daniel's spell. That only left Tracy Ann. Michele had thought about asking for her advice but... She frowned... She couldn't put her finger on it but there was something off with Tracy Ann. It wasn't just that misguided kiss. She was convinced she'd been right there, and Tracy Ann had been drunk when that happened. It was something more. She was all smiles, as ever, but there was something sad behind her eyes. If she didn't know Blake adored her, she'd have thought there was something wrong there, but they were rock solid. Weren't they? *Weren't they?*

She thought about those bruises on Tracy Ann's hand. They looked painful. Had Tracy Ann really fallen getting out of the hot tub? It was unlike the nimble woman to be so clumsy. Blake hadn't seemed worried, had remarked that she had a bruise on her thigh too, before carelessly brushing them away. *Too carelessly?* Why had he mentioned the bruise on her thigh at all? Was it so that the friends wouldn't question it if they saw Tracy Ann by the pool or in the spa? The friends had, after all, talked about going into the sauna at some stage.

They'd see the bruise and not question its provenance.

Michele's grip on Don's arm tightened as a terrible thought hit her. It couldn't be true, could it? Blake wouldn't hurt Tracy Ann.

Maybe there were still more secrets to be revealed...

26

TRACY ANN

She hated lying to Blake. Hated it more when he believed her so easily, and almost cried when he'd taken her hand and kissed the bruises that marked her skin. It had almost broken her heart when he then bent to kiss the bruises on her thigh. When she'd seen them, she'd been horrified. They looked exactly what they were. Bruises made by fingers. She used the rounded end of her hairbrush and slammed it into her thigh, over and over. The pain was agonising, and yet almost satisfying. As if the self-flagellation was some sort of atonement for her stupidity. She didn't stop till she was certain she'd covered the glaring reality of what Daniel had done.

'It was my fault,' she said, when Blake threatened to complain to the staff. 'I wasn't paying attention to where I put my stupid feet and I should have been holding on to the rail.' She ran her fingers over the bruises on her hand. 'They look more dramatic than they are because I bruise so easily and I'm so pale.'

'They're not painful?'

'Not in the slightest.' Another lie. The self-inflicted bruises hurt like a bitch. She lifted her leg and pointed her toes. 'See, I can still dance!' Pleased to see him smile, she lowered her foot to the floor, swallowing the pain the movement caused. 'Right, if you're going to get the start of that lecture, you'd better hurry.'

'You won't come?'

'No,' she said, pressing a kiss to his cheek. 'I'm going to sit out on our balcony with my Kindle and work my way through all the books I've been promising to get to when I had the time.' She waved her hand in the air. 'At four, I have a manicure booked. Maybe I can ask her to match the colours to the bruises, what d'you think?'

'I think you're one crazy woman,' he said, pulling her close. He kissed her, then moved his lips down her neck. 'Maybe I don't need to go to that talk after all.'

She laughed and pushed him away, feeling, as she often did these days, guilty for having been tempted by that worthless piece of garbage, Daniel. 'Go, we've time for that nonsense later.'

'Promise?'

'I promise.' And she did, she promised to love him, to make it clear he was the only man she'd ever love, to prove that she was a good, faithful wife, that what she'd done was done in a moment of madness that would never happen again.

If she could believe Daniel – if she could trust him – then she'd be tempted to do what he asked. She could. Easily. Once they were back home. One of their spare bedrooms was used by Blake as an office. Tracy Ann had a laptop, of course, but when she'd had trouble with it the previous year, she'd used the office desktop computer. Blake had given her the password then. There was no reason for him to have changed it. When the two boys were home on holidays, they never went into the office, having learnt at a young age it was out of bounds to sticky fingers.

But it was never out of bounds to Tracy Ann. Blake trusted her absolutely. He shouldn't have done.

She could wait until he'd gone to work, open his computer, search his files for the information Daniel wanted. And that would be it. He'd delete that incriminating video, and that would be the end of it.

She was stupid, but she wasn't gullible. If she did what was asked, if the information she provided proved successful and made Daniel a shitload of money, he'd be back for more. She couldn't trust him, couldn't believe a word out of his lying, cheating, devious mouth.

But she'd seen it in his eyes. If she didn't do what he asked, he'd send that awful, awful video to Blake. And that would be the end of them. She knew her husband; it would break him, and he'd never be able to forgive her.

There was no space between the rock and the hard place. It was crushing the breath from her. Soon she'd have to make a choice.

Kill or be killed.

27

NATASHA

Barbara and Natasha were still sitting by the pool. Their glasses were empty but neither woman suggested ordering another drink.

Neither spoke for a long time, Natasha still reeling from Daniel's deception, Barbara wishing she could turn back time and keep her mouth shut.

It was Natasha who finally spoke. 'Come on, let's investigate the cakes in the buffet.' She didn't wait, getting to her feet and walking towards the double doors leading to the twenty-four-hour buffet. It took a few minutes to locate what she wanted. A station serving only pastries. Enough to satisfy any taste.

Picking up a plate, she stood undecided for a moment before choosing a small chocolate profiterole, a strawberry mousse slice, and just because they were there, a macaroon.

'You'll never eat all that.' Barbara reached for a fruit tartlet.

'I will, plus this,' Natasha said, adding a tartlet to her plate. 'Coffee and tea are over there.' She nodded to a station a little further along.

With their plates and drinks, they searched for somewhere to sit. Luck was with them; a couple were about to leave a cosy seat by the window. 'Perfect,' Natasha said, moving to take it with a smile for the departing diners.

Eating delicious pastries, sitting looking out at the sea, being completely spoilt, it was almost hard to believe her life had suddenly descended into chaos. And yet, despite what were probably the best pastries she'd ever tasted, here she was. Chaosville. She truly didn't know what she was going to do. Confront Daniel? Tell him she knew about the vasectomy? He'd ask how. Natasha had no compunction about dropping Barbara in it. Would have done if it had made any difference. It wouldn't. There was no way he could lie his way out of this.

Better that she kept quiet until she could figure out what to do. If she left him before two years, she'd get nothing. Barbara was right. She'd have to go back to nursing. She didn't know anything else. The thought made her skin crawl. It wasn't an option, but what was the alternative? Staying with the lying bastard to fulfil the conditions of the prenup?

She looked across the table to where Barbara was nibbling at the fruit tartlet she'd chosen. She didn't know Natasha at all. Or rather, she didn't know the woman she was now. Life changes alter people; dramatic life changes alter some people completely.

She picked up the chocolate profiterole and bit into it, sending cream dribbling down her chin. She scooped the leakage into her mouth with her finger, then popped the remainder of the profiterole in on top.

'You look like you're enjoying that,' Barbara said.

'It's lush. I might be coming back here every day.' She picked up the tartlet and took a bite. 'Seriously good, you should get some more.' When Barbara shook her head, Natasha shrugged. 'Suit yourself.' She finished everything on her plate, then sat back cupping the mug of tea in her hand. 'What did you think of Tracy Ann at lunchtime?'

'Tracy Ann?' Barbara sounded surprised by the change of direction. 'What do you mean?'

'The bruises on her hand, and on her thigh according to Blake.'

'She said she fell getting out of the hot tub.'

'Yes, that's what she said. But she didn't, did she?'

Barbara lifted her mug and took a sip of her tea. 'I don't remember... I don't think... Maybe she stumbled.'

Natasha shook her head. 'I forgot, you weren't looking at Tracy Ann because you were staring at Daniel swimming up and down. Well, I was, and I saw her stepping from the hot tub. She didn't fall or stumble. Not once. She got out, grabbed a towel, wrapped it around herself and walked away.'

'Right.' Barbara shrugged. 'I'm not sure what you're getting at, Tash.'

'Tracy Ann has bruises on her hand. According to Blake, she also has one on her thigh. If she didn't fall getting out of the tub, how did she get them?'

'Maybe she slipped on her way back to her cabin.'

'Then why would she lie about it?'

'No idea.'

Barbara was sounding a little bored, as if Tracy Ann's bruises weren't of any importance. Maybe they weren't, but maybe they were. Natasha wasn't sure why she cared. Was it because she preferred to think of Tracy Ann as a victim, rather than the woman who kissed Daniel? Maybe she really wanted her friend to have an excuse for behaving inexcusably. 'Have you noticed she's been a little quieter recently?'

'Not really, but then I have other things to worry about.'

Like ogling and flirting with your friend's husband? For one horrible moment, Natasha thought she'd said the words aloud but Barbara's expression never changed. Natasha stifled a giggle, then took a breath. She was sure she was right about this. It made sense and explained Tracy Ann's recent behaviour. 'There's one reason a woman lies about bruises.'

Barbara looked at her, then snorted a laugh. 'Is that what you're getting at? You think Blake is hitting her? Come on, Tasha, he adores her, always has, always will.'

'Domestic violence is more complex than loving or not loving someone. You know that, Barbara.'

'Of course I do, but I still think you're adding two and two together and getting the wrong answer.'

'He was quick to add that she had a bruise on her leg too, wasn't he? Why did he want that out there, eh? So that if we saw her by the pool, or in the spa and saw the bruise, we wouldn't question it.' She nodded, as if realising how clever a move that was. Because they wouldn't, except maybe to commiserate or ask if it was painful. They wouldn't query the cause.

'Now that you mention it, I did think he was being very careless about her bruises. He's normally so protective of her.' Barbara's eyes widened. 'You really think he could be hitting her?'

'He always seems so calm, so laid-back, but he has a very high-powered job, doesn't he? Maybe with the changing political scene in London, his job is at risk.'

Barbara shook her head. 'He's a civil servant; his job doesn't depend on who's in power.'

'Okay. Well maybe it's something else. But I think we should keep an eye on Tracy Ann.'

Barbara suddenly sat forward. 'Maybe he knows about the kiss! Or maybe the stupid cow told him; after all, she told you!'

Natasha groaned. 'She wouldn't be that stupid, would she?' She lifted a hand. 'No, don't bother answering that. If she was stupid enough to have told me she kissed my husband, she'd possibly have been stupid enough to have told Blake.'

'Doesn't excuse him for hitting her though.'

'No, of course not!' Natasha sighed. 'They might have had a row that got physical. Maybe we won't say anything just yet but keep an eye on them.' She met Barbara's eyes. 'What do you think?'

'I wasn't planning on saying anything anyway. I mean, what could you say? Is Blake beating you up? If she says yes, what do we do? If she says no, do we believe her?' Barbara shook her head. 'Anyway, I'm not sure why you're so bloody concerned about her. She kissed Daniel, remember?'

'It's not exactly something I'd forget.' Natasha's voice was as sharp as the thoughts that were jabbing inside her skull. How could she explain to Barbara that she took pleasure in the bruises that she saw marking Tracy Ann's skin? Her only regret was that she hadn't put them there. Natasha mightn't love Daniel, but he was her husband and should have been off limits. But Tracy Ann was her friend. It was the conflicting thoughts that were causing her such anguish. 'Maybe Michele was right: Tracy Ann had too much to drink and behaved stupidly. I'm not going to hold it against her forever. And anyway, since I heard about the...' Her voice faded away.

'The vasectomy?'

'Yes, that. Everything is changed now.' *And behind all the conflicting thoughts, it's that damn prenup drilling a hole in her head, in her life, making big holes, letting the water in. She could drown.*

28

NATASHA

There was no drama at dinner that evening. In fact, everyone was subdued and the conversation came in fits and starts rather than flowing as it usually did. That night, even the men were quiet.

Natasha kept darting glances between Blake and Tracy Ann, but it wasn't obvious that their relationship was cracked any more than it was obvious hers was. *Cracked*. She squeaked a laugh, turning it quickly into a cough. Her marriage wasn't cracked; it was shattered, the shards ground down to dust and blown away.

Once again, the food was excellent. And as expected, Daniel ordered the most unusual item on the menu: a Zanzibar seafood dish. When it arrived, they all looked at it in horror.

'I think some of it is still alive,' Michele said.

Maybe it will climb from the plate and eat him. That would be a solution to her problem that Natasha hadn't considered. It was good to be able to see the funny side of things. She tried to relax and eat her dinner, a filet steak that was probably delicious. Unfortunately, her appetite seemed to have gone the same way as her marriage.

Looking around the table, she saw she wasn't the only one

struggling. Tracy Ann had barely touched her meal, Barbara was pushing food around her plate but didn't look to be eating anything, and Michele, although she appeared to be eating, didn't finish even half what was on her plate before she put her cutlery down, positioning her knife and fork neatly together and muttering a barely distinguishable, 'Very nice.'

Very nice. Such a nothing compliment. Was Michele referring to the cutlery, the plate, or the food?

Tracy Ann, Barbara and now Michele – in varying ways they'd all succeeded in upsetting Natasha. Tracy Ann's kiss, Barbara's revelation, Michele's irritating personality. Natasha knew she was being unreasonable and perhaps it was simply that being in such close proximity for an extended period of time was too much. The ship, although big, wasn't big enough. She glanced across the table to where Tracy Ann sat, the bruises on her hand more prominent in the glow of the wall lights. They looked painful; Natasha hoped they were. She glanced at Blake. Was he really capable of such violence?

Tracy Ann had definitely lied about falling.

And Barbara... Natasha was watching her surreptitiously and had seen the sideways glances she'd given Daniel, the softening of her eyes, her mouth, the longing that was written clearly... Why had she chosen to tell Natasha about Daniel's vasectomy?

Even Michele was hiding something. She possibly wasn't even aware, but every time she looked at Daniel, her expression hardened. As if she hated him. But she'd no reason to, had she?

Her friends. Natasha had thought they were good women who were ever so slightly boring, dull even. Now she wondered if she knew them at all. It appeared they were all keeping secrets of some sort and now, thanks to Barbara, so was she.

She saw Daniel looking at her questioningly and turned to beam a smile at him. Years of dealing with the patients in her care and their relatives had taught her how to switch on a reassuring façade.

It had splintered and fallen away in the last couple of years so that she was no longer able to offer the lies that were expected of her. That was the final nail in the coffin of her career. She could no longer pretend.

But now, she had to. Until she could figure out a course of action.

It would be a relief to get off the ship.

It didn't seem big enough to contain all their secrets.

29

TRACY ANN

After dinner, they went to a variety show in the main theatre.

'Do you know the way?' Tracy Ann asked as they left the restaurant together. She was looking at Blake, but it was Daniel who replied with the certainty of a man who always had an answer.

'It's one deck up. Deck seven, forward.'

She waited for him to explain which direction forward was and almost smiled when he turned and did just that in the supercilious way he had.

'The front of the ship, in case you're wondering.'

How had she ever considered him charming, charismatic and irresistible? He was evil incarnate. 'I wasn't,' she said, sharp enough to attract a puzzled glance from Blake. She slipped her hand into his and gave him a reassuring smile. 'This should be a good show; I'm looking forward to it.'

They were later than they'd wanted to be though, and the theatre was already filling. To Tracy Ann's relief, they weren't able to sit together. She and Blake slipped into two vacant seats in the middle of a back row. She watched the others finding spaces in different parts of the large theatre. It would be easy for herself and Blake to make a quick exit at the end; her friends would be caught up in the crowd. She could relax knowing she'd not have to see them again that evening.

She slid her hand into Blake's and felt his warm fingers close over it. He leaned closer and whispered, 'You having a good time?'

Sitting there with him, as the lights dimmed and the spectacle unfolded on the stage in front of them, she could believe she was having a good time, that everything that was happening outside could be dismissed. In the half darkness of the theatre, she felt cocooned. But when Blake took his hand away to applaud the cast, she felt bereft.

Taking her hand back, she pulled away from him and from the large woman who sat on her other side, curling in on herself, suddenly wary of the darkness that surrounded her. It suddenly felt less friendly, as if it recognised something in her it could identify with. On the stage, the cast were wearing masks. She was in the wrong place. She should be on the stage with them. After all, she was wearing a mask too. The one of the loving, faithful, supportive wife.

Daniel should be up there too. Maybe he'd take his mask off and show the world what an evil bastard he was.

He wouldn't, of course. If she was brave, she'd do it. Walk up to him in a public place and expose him for what he was. And she'd do it, she would if it was only herself to consider, but there was this man beside her. A man she loved, a man the truth would destroy.

No, she'd not expose Daniel. But one way or another, she'd put a stop to him.

30

NATASHA

When they returned to their cabin after the show, Natasha switched on the TV and located the channel that gave information on Kigomasha where the ship would drop anchor the following day. It was their first excursion. All of the friends and their husbands were going.

'It looks fabulous,' she said, nodding to the screen as Daniel crossed to the bar.

He opened the bottle of whisky and poured a healthy amount into a glass. 'You want one?'

'No, thanks, I've had enough.' It was tempting to say, she didn't want to drink more in case she was pregnant but she couldn't bring herself to utter that lie. She wasn't sure she'd be able to get it out without running over and tearing scratches down his handsome face. 'You should watch this,' she said, her eyes fixed on the screen.

'Why?' He tilted the whisky into his mouth and swallowed noisily. 'We're going to see it tomorrow and no doubt there'll be someone droning on when we're in the coach to the other place.'

'Makangale Beach.' She sighed, reached for the remote and

switched the TV off. Since Barbara's disclosure, everything seemed soiled. Spoilt. Meaningless. She wished she were at home. There, maybe she could make sense of everything and come to a decision about her future. But there were five more days and nights on this ship. Trapped. She crossed to the balcony door and slid it open, suddenly needing to be outside, to breathe fresh air rather than the air-conditioned, heated, stinking fug of the cabin. She gripped the railing, leaning forward to stare down into the water far below. In the light cast by the ship, the sea was a dark nothing topped with white crests. Nothing. Wasn't that exactly what she needed. The calmness of nothing.

'Are you okay?'

Daniel's voice pierced her thoughts almost painfully. She turned to shout at him. To tell him she knew everything. But before she could, he was there, his arms wrapped around her, holding her, making her feel... what? Loved? She didn't think he loved her and was sure she didn't love him. But he made her feel safe. *Him or his money?* It wasn't as simple as that. She thought he'd keep her safe and give her the children her life needed. Thought he'd protect her from all that could be dragged up from the deep nooks and crannies of this hideous world. Thought he was one of the good guys.

It seemed she was wrong on all accounts.

She couldn't meet his eyes; he'd see the truth written in them. Instead, she rested her head on his shoulder. 'I'm tired, that's all.'

'You feel tense,' he said. Reaching behind, he opened the door that had automatically slid shut behind him. 'Let's go to bed; I know what'll help relax you.' He must have sensed her reluctance because he added, 'Maybe this will be the time we get you pregnant, eh?'

And finally, *finally*, she could admit it. She hated the bastard.

31

THE WIVES

It was an early start the following day. They had to be at the embarkation point on deck six by eight o'clock. Staying in the penthouse suite, Daniel and Natasha had priority boarding of the water shuttle, but to his annoyance, she insisted they join their friends. 'We're doing the excursion together,' she said, in a tone of voice that said she wasn't going to argue about this.

When they arrived at the general disembarkation desk, Ralph and Barbara were standing nearby.

'I tried to get shuttle tickets for all of us,' she said, greeting Daniel and Natasha with a smile. 'But unfortunately, they said we have to wait until we're all together. When we get them, then we have to wait till our group is called.'

Natasha saw Daniel glance towards the sign pointing towards priority disembarkation and waited for him to make some comment. She linked her arm through his. 'It doesn't matter; we're in no hurry. They're so well organised, we'll all be off in a few minutes.'

She would have been right had their friends arrived at the agreed time, but although Michele and Don arrived a minute later, it was another ten before they saw Tracy Ann and Blake hurrying towards them.

'We're so sorry,' Blake said, holding his hands up in surrender. 'You should have gone ahead without us. I couldn't find my crown medallion and you know we can't disembark without it.' There had been a warning on the TV information channel and a similar one highlighted in red on the day's event guide. 'I thought I'd hung it on the hook on the back of the door as always but we were about to leave and it was nowhere to be found.'

'It was in the pocket of his robe,' Tracy Ann said with a shake of her head. 'Of course, it was the last place we thought to look.'

'Well, let's get our tickets and get on the damn shuttle.' It was probably the longest sentence Ralph had made for some time. His tone raised eyebrows and made Barbara's face take on the pinched look she'd worn more and more recently.

'You're the last!' The cheerful crew member holding the tickets sang the words out, as if being last was a badge of honour. 'You don't need to bother with tickets now, just make your way towards the gangway where the crew will guide you onto the shuttle.'

'Last,' Daniel muttered to Natasha. 'We could be ashore by now.'

Ignoring him, she tapped her crown medallion on the monitor as they left and stepped onto the short gangway to the water shuttle. Daniel insisted on climbing up to the outside deck. 'We'll get a good view,' he said, urging Natasha to follow.

She shook her head. 'I'll sit inside, you go, enjoy.' *Maybe fall in and end all her problems.*

Only Blake joined Daniel on the outside deck, the rest of them taking seats inside.

It was a short, bouncy trip to the wharf at Kigomasha. From where they sat, there was little for the inside passengers to see, the gap visible around the helmsman giving only a tantalising glimpse of blue sky, nothing of the island ahead. The rhythmic bounce of the shuttle hitting the water wasn't loud enough to prevent conversation yet they sat quietly.

Natasha was staring straight ahead. Suddenly, above the sound of the shuttle's engine and the rush of the sea, she heard Daniel's booming laugh roll down the steps from the upper deck. A totally free, unconcerned sound of amusement. She wondered what had caused it. Was he thinking of her, and how he'd deceived her? Was he laughing that she was so easily fooled?

Before the sound of his laughter died, she knew what she had to do.

* * *

Tracy Ann was dreading a full day in Daniel's company. Blake wasn't the most observant of men, but even he was likely to see how uncomfortable she was every time she was in Daniel's vicinity. Her ruse to prevent their departure had failed when Blake insisted they could go to the disembarkation desk and explain that he'd lost his crown medallion.

She'd tapped her wrist watch. 'We've probably missed the last shuttle anyway. They won't have waited for us. It doesn't matter; we can have a relaxing day on board.'

Blake had looked at her in surprise. 'But you were looking forward to seeing Kigomasha.' He shook his head. 'No, come on, we'll go and explain. I'm sure it happens all the time.'

There didn't seem to be any point in continuing the lie. She pointed towards the closed door of the bathroom. 'Have you checked the pockets of your robe? Remember, you put it on last night to go out on the deck.'

He had, and later while her beloved husband was sleeping the sleep of the innocent, his cheating, lying wife snuck over to the door, took the lanyard down, curled it around the crown medallion and looked around for somewhere she could hide it. Deciding on the pocket of the robe he rarely wore, she slipped it inside, then crept back to bed and lay staring at the ceiling wondering how many more lies she'd be forced to tell.

On the shuttle, she was seated between Barbara and Natasha. Both were ignoring her. In fact, none of her friends had addressed her since her ill-judged confession. An ill-judged confession of an ill-judged act that wasn't even half the story. The lump that seemed to be constantly lodged in her throat these days felt bigger, heavier. And then she heard it. That bastard's laugh, tripping down the short stairway from the upper deck. She imagined him up there, head thrown back, mouth open to show his over-whitened teeth. What was he finding so amusing? Was he thinking about her, and her pathetic attempt to delay the inevitable? God, how she hated him. And as the last note of his laugh grated on her nerves, she knew there was only one thing she could do.

* * *

Michele had fallen asleep late and slept through her normal waking up time to discover they only had an hour to get ready and have breakfast before the agreed meeting time at the disembarkation desk. She poked Don in the side. Twice, harder the second time, getting a grunt in response. 'Do you really want to go on this excursion today?'

That woke him faster. He pushed up onto an elbow and looked at her with sleepy eyes. 'Of course, it's going to be amazing.'

She'd seen photographs. It did look stunning. Was she really going to allow Daniel to spoil what might prove to be the high-light of the trip? Hadn't he done enough damage.

'Right, well we'd better shower together to save time.' She grinned at her husband's expression before jumping out of bed and running into the bathroom. She was in and out of the shower before he'd dragged himself from the bed. She stood with a towel wrapped around her and stared at him. 'You missed out,' she said with a shake of her head. 'But we'd better not miss out on break-fast. So get a move on.'

They had a buffet breakfast for speed but it was still a few minutes after the agreed time when they reached the desk. Barbara and Ralph were standing to one side, Natasha and a visibly annoyed Daniel on the other. Michele had read the daily event page thoroughly. She was aware that Natasha and Daniel could have gone for priority boarding. She guessed the choice not to hadn't been his and dared to give Natasha a conspiratorial wink that was returned with an accompanying smile.

Almost as soon as Tracy Ann and Blake arrived, several minutes later, they were shooed towards the disembarkation point. She listened to Tracy Ann and Blake's story of the missing crown medallion and laughed appropriately even as she saw unease cross Tracy Ann's face. Something is definitely not right with her, she thought.

It was the last shuttle to head across, and they were the last passengers to board. A few others were already inside, waiting patiently.

'Upstairs,' she heard Daniel shout. Only Blake followed him. She headed to the one empty bench at the rear of the inside and slid along to the end. Barbara cosied up to her with a smile. Tracy Ann reluctantly sat beside her, staring straight ahead when Natasha took the last space. Don and Ralph sat separately. And then they were off.

Michele wondered if she shouldn't have insisted that they stay behind. Maybe had a relaxing day on the ship. Almost like having it to themselves. She'd noticed they were doing special offers in the spa; she could have had a massage at half the price it usually was. The thought made her shiver with longing. A nice, relaxing massage to smooth away the stresses and strains. Maybe if she relaxed enough, a solution to the mess their life had become would come to her.

She was still thinking about the joy of a full-body massage when she heard something that sent a shiver of pure hate darting through her. Daniel laughing, the sound curling in the air, almost hanging there malevolently. Was he up there thinking what a fool he had made of Don? Thinking how to use him in future? Because men like him, they never stopped.

She stared up the flight of steps, wishing she could see him falling down, breaking his neck, ending their awful dilemma. And before the thought finished, she knew exactly what she needed to do.

* * *

Barbara relaxed into the sway of the shuttle, rubbing arms with Michele on one side, Tracy Ann on the other. It would be good to be on land, even for a few hours. Cruising, she'd decided, wasn't for her. Or maybe it was just this cruise... with these people. It should have been perfect. Four good friends and their partners. But everyone seemed to be on edge. Maybe being in such close proximity for an extended period of time had been a mistake. They were all rubbing against each other, causing abrasions. *Bruises*. She glanced down at Tracy Ann's hand where it lay resting in her lap. The marks had turned a lovely shade of green. It was hard to believe Blake had been responsible, but if Natasha was to be believed, Tracy Ann had lied about falling. *If Natasha was to be believed. If Tracy Ann was lying.* She suddenly wondered if she knew these women at all. Or just the face they had shown her for all these years.

She regretted telling Natasha about Daniel's vasectomy. What had she been thinking? Had she really believed that if they'd split up, he'd have turned to Barbara for consolation? She almost laughed out loud at the absurdity of her obsession. *Stupid old woman.* With a sigh, she looked to where Ralph was sitting, wearing the hangdog expression he'd taken to wearing recently like a favourite coat. She'd loved him almost from their first meeting. She still did, but... That made her give a weary smile. It had come to that, hadn't it: she loved him, but... but she wished he hadn't suddenly turned into a grumpy old man.

When they got home, she'd insist he went to see a doctor. She'd go too. It wasn't only Ralph who was feeling out of sorts recently. Some days, she barely recognised the woman she'd become. This obsession with Daniel, for instance: what the hell was wrong with her? It was totally out of character for her to behave so irrationally. She was forty-one. Getting old. Feeling older. It mightn't be any harm for her to have a chat with her doctor too. Get a blood test, see if she could blame everything on the approaching menopause. It would almost be a relief to have a reason for how she was feeling. Nice to know she wasn't simply going crazy.

At least she hadn't acted on any of the erotic thoughts she'd had about Daniel. Not like Tracy Ann. What a fool she'd been to have confessed to kissing him. Was that all she'd done? They'd looked awfully cosy in the hot tub together. Had he flirted with her the way he'd flirted with Barbara? Because she wasn't imagining the little smiles, the accidental brushes of his hand against hers, the way his eyes would linger on her cleavage then rise to meet her gaze and open his mouth, just a little. He'd played with her. Like a cat with a particularly stupid mouse. Had it been fun for him? Make dowdy old Barbara fancy her chances with him? He'd made her value her base desires higher than her friendship with Natasha. What a fool Barbara had been. What a fool he'd made of her.

Her head jerked upwards when she heard the distinct sound of his laughter coming from the top deck. She pictured him with his handsome head thrown back, mouth open, a lock of hair falling over his eyes that he'd brush away with a flick of his strong fingers. And she hated him for the lick of lust she couldn't prevent from darting between her legs. As the laughter seemed to peal again and again, the lust died and only the hatred remained.

32

NATASHA

There was a welcoming party waiting on the wharf when the shuttle pulled up. Those inside were first off, the four friends walking together, with a distance between them that wasn't counted in space. The excursion organisers bustled about, welcoming them to the island, handing them each a map of their location with strict instructions to return to the wharf in three hours. 'It will,' they insisted, 'give you plenty of time to walk along the beach and to have a look around the market that runs between it and the town.'

Tracy Ann raised a hand. As if she were in school. Had she raised a hand to ask if she could kiss Natasha's husband? She shut her eyes on the mean thoughts that were rattling around her brain, the one where she hoped Blake would bash his wife's head in.

Oblivious, Tracy Ann kept her hand up until one of the excursion organisers smiled in her direction. 'Madam?'

'Are we going by coach to Makangale Beach?'

Natasha's laugh was cuttingly sarcastic. 'It's ten kilometres away; I don't think they expect us to walk in this heat.'

Colour flared in Tracy Ann's cheeks. 'I meant was it by coach or taxi, that's all. A coach means we have to wait till everyone is back. If it was by taxi, we wouldn't have to hang around.'

'Right.' Natasha shrugged. She was being a bitch but should Tracy Ann expect anything different? That she was having problems in her own relationship didn't excuse her for making moves on Daniel.

Oblivious to the sudden tension in the little group, the organiser beamed a smile which managed to include them all. 'The journey will be by coach, madam. It will take us to the hotel where we will have lunch. After, there will be more free time to wander about.' He gave a slight bow, this time an individual one directed at each of the group. 'Enjoy your stay in this beautiful spot.'

It was indeed beautiful, Natasha thought, as they turned to walk towards a row of tall palm trees framed against a gentian-blue sky. It looked almost unreal. But then recently, she'd felt disconnected from everything. She'd hoped this cruise would help to restore some peace in her head. Slim hope of that happening now.

Lost in her thoughts, she was startled when Daniel grasped her hand. 'Let's go,' he said, tugging her along. 'Three hours isn't long enough to be standing around in a daze.'

'It's better if we split up, don't you think?' Michele said. 'I want to mosey around the market. We can meet back here for the coach.' Without waiting for an answer, she linked her arm through Don's and the two walked off towards the palm-thatched stalls of the market.

'She's right,' Barbara said. She nodded towards a denser patch of trees at the far end of the beach. 'We want to investigate the mangroves.' She walked off, leaving Ralph to shrug and follow.

The awkward silence in their wake was broken by Daniel's impatient, 'Come on then, I want to dip my toes in the Indian Ocean.'

'I think I'd like to go to the market first,' Tracy Ann said, tucking her arm into Blake's. 'See you back here in a few hours.'

'That's worked out perfectly,' Daniel said, linking an arm around Natasha's shoulders as they walked towards the beach. 'Nice to get some private time in this beautiful spot just for us, eh?'

Natasha couldn't bring herself to reply. Instead, she took in the view. The sea was that shade of turquoise usually only seen in travel brochures, the beach a golden fringe that curved towards the dense woodland that Barbara had insisted she'd wanted to see. Natasha guessed that desire had been an excuse to break away from the others.

Within a couple of steps, the fine sand had worked its way into her flat sandals. Daniel had already taken his off and was heading to the edge of the ocean to dip his toes. She wished he'd keep going, walk into the sea, and never come back. Take the decision about their future from her. The sand was hot under her feet; she curled her toes, feeling it crunch as she watched him wade further out, the water now mid-calf. She found herself humming the theme music from *Jaws*. Smiling, she sat to wait for his return.

'Come in, it's warm,' he shouted, kicking his foot up to send a stream of water into the air.

She shook her head, sending the broad-brimmed hat she was wearing tilting forward. Suddenly, she was in darkness. He was gone and she was alone. And then, without warning, she was back there in the intensive care unit, helpless as one after the other of the patients in her care succumbed to a virus nobody had antici-pated. Maybe, after all, the cruise had had a benefit, because for the first time, she understood that she needed help. When she got home, she'd seek it out and hope that coming to terms with her past would enable her to face the future.

She tilted her hat back to stare out to where Daniel had moved along the beach, looking smaller now, still kicking the water. Like a child.

Like the child she'd never have if she stayed with him.

33

NATASHA

When they arrived back at the meeting point almost three hours later, they were all looking a little more relaxed. All of the women apart from Natasha were carrying bulging cotton tote bags and were eager to catch up with their friends and share the results of their foray through the market.

Barbara took out a string of beads she'd bought for her step-daughter. 'Anna will love these. See,' she held them out to show Natasha, 'they're made from coconut shell.' She reached back into the tote bag. 'And these ones are made from the seeds of some plant whose name I've already forgotten.' She laughed. 'It doesn't matter; I'm sure I'll be able to find out.'

Michele and Tracy Ann showed similar purchases along with some garishly coloured scarves and exquisitely carved wooden animals.

'You sorry you missed out?' Daniel said, resting a hand on Natasha's waist. He leaned closer, his mouth brushing her hair as he whispered. 'It looks like a lot of tat to me.'

'It's handmade and supports local people,' she said sharply, pulling away from him. 'I'm hoping there'll be more for sale when we arrive at the hotel, or that we have a few minutes to spare when we return here. There'll be a queue for the shuttle back to the ship. I might get a chance to go back to the market then.'

'What've you been doing?' Michele said, overhearing her. 'There isn't that much else to see here.'

'We walked to the Ras Kigomasha lighthouse.' Natasha pointed to where a structure jutted from the ground in the distance. 'It's fascinating. We thought it was a relic but it's still operational and we were able to climb to the top and get a look at the view.' She pulled her phone out, clicked to get the photos to show them.

'Very nice,' Barbara said, peering at the screen.

'They mentioned it at one of the lectures I went to,' Ralph said. 'The lighthouse is made from cast iron and was built in 1904 by the Chance Brothers of Birmingham.' He frowned at Barbara. 'We should have gone there instead of going to the market.'

Natasha caught the flicker of annoyance on Barbara's face and hurried to stop it escalating into a row. 'It was great, but I'm sorry I missed the market. Those beads you bought are gorgeous. Show them to me again.'

By the time the coaches arrived, moments later, peace had been restored. The excursion manager did a head count as they climbed into the air-conditioned interior.

'In case any of us were eaten by sharks,' Daniel said, taking a seat.

Barbara took the seat behind. 'You were the only one foolish enough to go into the water. We saw you splashing around; don't you know that attracts them?'

He turned to smile at her. 'Would you have been heartbroken, Babs?'

Natasha heard the come-on flirtatious, teasing tone of his

words and wondered how she'd ever fallen for him. He was so damn obvious. She slapped a hand against his thigh. 'Stop.'

'What?' He looked at her innocently.

'You know exactly. Stop flirting with her. She isn't finding it amusing.'

'Really.' He folded his arms and shuffled down in the seat. 'I thought we were having a bit of fun.'

She wanted to ask him if that's what he'd been having with Tracy Ann, but she couldn't bring herself to ask the question for fear of what she might hear. Not the words – she knew he'd never admit to any wrongdoing – but the lie she'd hear in them. Because there was something going on, something simmering between her husband and her friend. She needed to get Tracy Ann on her own to find out exactly what it was.

As soon as the coach pulled onto the road, the driver began what seemed like a well-rehearsed spiel about what they were seeing. Not that there was much, the road cutting through dense woodland. Natasha tuned his words out and retreated inside her thoughts. She wished they could finish the cruise here. Pack up and head home. How far was the nearest airport? She hadn't a clue. She turned to stare out the window, pretending an interest in the passing scenery as her eyes filled. Stupid woman, she wasn't going to go anywhere. Not yet.

The drive, although only ten kilometres, seemed to last forever. The driver had a curious monotone voice and between it and the rocking of the bus, she drifted off to sleep, jolted awake only when the bus arrived at their destination.

Opening her eyes, she had to smile at the view from the window. If you were asked to describe the perfect exotic hotel, this would be it. Thatched roofs, palm trees, gushing fountains, smiling staff waiting to greet them with trays of drinks that sparkled in the sunlight. They hurried off the coach, then stood around in the shade of huge parasols, laughing, sipping their choice of alcoholic or non-alcoholic drinks, the friends separated by other travellers, the conversation general, unexceptional. Even Ralph was looking less curmudgeonly than of late.

Lunch was a buffet affair in a massive dining room overlooking the vast gardens.

'Thank goodness for air-conditioning,' Michele said, sidling up to Natasha as they walked inside.

'I agree,' Barbara said, attaching herself to them. She pointed to an empty table. 'Let's grab that one.'

Natasha supposed it was inevitable that they'd end up together. Although, with a glance towards an unhappy looking Tracy Ann, she guessed it was Blake who'd instigated the dash across to join them.

Buffet-style eating wasn't Natasha's favourite but she guessed it was a convenient way for the hotel to serve lunch to such a large gathering at the same time. Sticking to what she knew, she helped herself to a small amount of rice and chicken curry and headed back to her seat.

'That's all you're having?' Daniel commented when he returned to sit beside her with his well-laden plate.

'I can always go back for more,' she said reasonably. She wouldn't, but she could. She was surprised when Barbara returned, took the seat opposite and put down a full plate. 'You feeling both hungry and adventurous?'

'It all looked interesting,' Barbara said picking up her cutlery, 'but I couldn't decide so took a little of everything.'

It looked revolting, Natasha thought. To her right, Daniel was tucking into his food with his usual enthusiasm. She eyed a forkful of something that glistened almost repulsively. 'Do you know what any of that is?' she asked.

'No, but it doesn't matter as long as it tastes okay.' He gave her a sideways glance. 'You should be more adventurous.'

'I suppose I should be,' she said, shoving her fork into the rice on her plate. Was that how he justified flirting with her friends and lying to her? Being adventurous?

Even without disturbing thoughts rattling around her head, it wasn't a particularly restful meal. There was constant movement as people went up for more food, as waiting staff scurried around, removing used plates and cutlery, refilling drinks, replacing food at the buffet as the platters emptied. A continuous hum filled the air as people chatted and the hotel speakers played anodyne music. Around their table though, conversation was desultory. The odd comment about the food. A moan from Barbara about the heat, followed by a groan from Michele about the chill of the air-conditioning.

'I think my eyes were bigger than my belly,' Barbara said, drawing Natasha's attention.

'It wasn't good?'

'No, it was, very good actually. I've eaten most. I wasn't keen on this...' She tapped what looked like a dark meat. 'It's a bit fishy for my liking.'

'Fishy? Did someone say my favourite word.' Daniel waved his knife in the air as if he was trying to cast a spell. He looked at Barbara's plate, then pushed his closer. 'Slide it over. Can't be too fishy for my liking.'

'My husband, the human dustbin,' Natasha said as Barbara did as requested.

Pulling the plate back, Daniel cut a little off this new addition and tasted it. 'Hmm, it's an unusual texture, almost chewy like calamari, but I agree, it has a strong taste.' He lifted another forkful and held it towards Natasha. 'Would you like to try some?'

She shook her head. 'Doesn't look appealing, I'll stick with what I have, thanks.'

'You don't know what you're missing; it's really good.' He proceeded to prove the point by eating it all, smacking his lips when he was done. He leaned forward to look past Natasha and catch Barbara's eye. 'Thanks, I really enjoyed whatever that was.' He turned to look back at the buffet table. 'I might go and see if they have more of it.'

'Oh for goodness' sake,' Natasha said. 'Finish what's on your plate first.' She smiled to take the sting from her words. 'They have a huge selection of desserts too, and you don't want to be too full to make the most of that, do you?'

He must have seen the sense in this because he didn't get up to look for seconds of Barbara's fishy fish, and instead finished what was on his plate with obvious pleasure. Natasha looked around, her gaze resting on a group at another table. All women, maybe in their early thirties, their faces alight with merriment. Most of the noise in the room was generated at their table. Gusts of laughter, voices rising as one spoke over the other, hands waving in the air, heads thrown back in sheer enjoyment. She and her friends were like that once. She wasn't sure when it had changed. Age, or their various life experiences? If they'd come on this cruise without their husbands, just four old friends, would that have been better?

Dragging her eyes away from the jovial group of women, she looked at Tracy Ann, who was picking at the food on her plate with little enthusiasm. If they'd left their husbands at home, it wouldn't have changed what she'd done, probably wouldn't have stopped her making that ill-advised confession.

Natasha tuned in to the conversation Daniel was having with Blake, who was sitting on his other side. He was talking about the lighthouse, rubbing it in that they'd climbed it while Blake and

Tracy Ann had gone shopping. Boasting. Making himself out to be important.

In that moment, Natasha realised what would have made a difference. If she and her friends had gone on the cruise before she'd met Daniel. He was the catalyst for all the bad changes.

She was still mulling over this when lunch finished and Michele suggested they walk along the beach. Fringed with palm trees and washed with the turquoise waters of the Indian Ocean, it should have been idyllic.

'You look worried,' Barbara said, linking her arm in Natasha's. 'Do you want to talk about it?'

'It's nothing.' There was no point in telling her that she was part of the problem. Anyway, it wasn't true. Not really. Daniel was.

Barbara squeezed her arm. 'Whatever is worrying you, it will all work out. These things always do.'

There was a time when Natasha had believed that too. Work hard, lead a good life, do well, and the world will treat you accordingly.

Now she knew that was all a crock of shit.

34

NATASHA

Many of the passengers had availed themselves of the free-flowing wine at lunch; as a result, the noise level in the coach on the return drive to Kigomasha was ear-splitting. 'Thank goodness it's not a long drive,' Natasha said to Daniel.

'You're becoming a right killjoy,' he said, before turning away to stare out the opposite window.

Maybe it was the noise that was making him unaccustomedly tetchy. The group of women she'd watched at lunch were sitting at the back of the bus. They'd obviously over-indulged and had launched into a singsong that would have been less grating had they been remotely in tune.

The journey wasn't long. They were pulling into the parking space, the coach still moving, when Daniel jumped to his feet to be first off as soon as it came to a halt.

'Daniel!' Natasha would have rushed after him, startled by his quick departure. She left it too late and suddenly there were several in a queue before her waiting to get off. A flustered woman acted like a cork as she tried to locate her many parcels, pulling one from the floor, another from the overhead compartment, at the same time as she maintained a continuous conversation with a man who Natasha assumed to be a husband. He wore a long-suffering look that said it wasn't the first time she'd delayed things.

Natasha bent to peer out the window, trying to see where Daniel had gone. He was nowhere to be seen. She straightened and swallowed the caustic comments that were waiting to be tossed to the woman who was still searching for a missing bag. It took the passenger standing immediately behind to find it jammed under the seat where it had slid during the journey.

Stepping off the coach, Natasha looked around. The shuttle was waiting to ferry them back to the ship. It was already filling, a queue of people building up as the coaches emptied. Tracy Ann and Blake, who'd been sitting to the front of the coach, were already standing in line. 'Did you see where Daniel went?' she asked them, her eyes scanning the area, her brow creased in confusion. 'We got separated getting off the coach.' This wasn't like Daniel. He liked order. He'd have been in the queue. Her brow cleared slightly. Was that it? He'd been annoyed to have been one of the last leaving the ship, had he hurried off to be first in line for the shuttle back? She looked towards where it sat, bobbing gently in the water beside the dock. Maybe he was on board already.

Without her? She had been lost in her thoughts as they made the journey back from the hotel. Had she missed his direction to move as soon as they arrived? Perhaps so, and he'd assumed she was following him when he rushed off. Within seconds, it was too late, then she'd been delayed by that stupid woman.

'He was off the coach as soon as the door opened,' Blake said. He jerked a thumb behind him. 'Last I saw him, he was heading towards the facilities.'

The facilities? Natasha must have looked suitably confused because Tracy Ann leaned closer. 'The toilets, Tasha; perhaps he made too much of a pig of himself at lunch.'

The emphasis on the word pig didn't escape Natasha, who drew a sharp breath before shaking her head and turning to walk away. The facilities, as Blake had so discreetly phrased it, were set in a block on the other side of the large car park. Other passengers were visiting too, a line running ant-like to and fro.

Daniel wasn't among them.

Natasha approached the door to the men's toilet, almost walking head first into Don on his way out. He looked at her in surprise, then pointed to the building next door. 'Wrong one, Natasha,' he said kindly.

'Daniel,' she said, as if that said it all. It obviously didn't as Don looked completely confused.

'Don,' he said, enunciating the name clearly.

As if she was a bloody idiot. 'No, I'm *looking* for Daniel.' The *you bloody idiot* remained unsaid but clear in her tone.

Not a man to take offence, Don held his hands up in apology. 'I think I had too much of that wine over lunch.'

'Can you see if he's in there?' she said, ignoring his excuse. But before he needed to search, Daniel appeared in the doorway. Natasha brushed past Don unceremoniously. 'Where have you been? I was worried!' It was only when he stepped from the shadow of the doorway into the sunlight that she decided to stay worried. You didn't have to be a nurse to know when someone looked unwell, but it was the nurse in her that noted the film of sweat over a face that had taken on a greyish hue, along with his rapid, shallow breathing. 'Daniel! You look dreadful! Have you been sick?'

He managed a shaky smile. 'I think I might have eaten too much.'

'Have you been sick?' she asked again.

'No, I thought I was going to be though. I just feel a bit weak.'

'No diarrhoea?'

He made a face. 'Yuck, no.' He rubbed a hand over his belly. 'It's growling like something wants to get out though.'

'We'd better get back to the ship.' She turned to see how fast the queue was moving. Not fast enough. 'Stand here in the shade,' she said firmly. 'I'll go and have a word, see if I can get us on the next shuttle over.'

'No!' He grabbed her arm. 'What're you going to say? That I'm feeling sick? They might decide not to let me on board at all in case I've caught some bug.'

Natasha frowned. He was right, of course. Although it would take a day or two for symptoms of something like norovirus to manifest itself, the crew were likely to jump to the wrong conclusions. If they got on board, and Daniel remained unwell, the worst that could happen would be that they'd be confined to their cabin. 'Right,' she said, 'then we'd better wait here in the shade until we're ready to board.'

She kept her eye on him as they waited. His colour improved slightly and his breathing slowed. She remembered Tracy Ann's pig comment. Perhaps she'd been right. He had eaten a ridiculous amount of food. 'It'll just be another few minutes,' she said, as the queue moved forward. Nobody had exited the men's toilet for a while; with a glance around, she popped inside, pulled a ream off a roll of toilet paper, and returned to Daniel's side. 'Wipe your face,' she said, handing him the wad. 'That film of sweat looks suspicious.'

He did as she advised with a compliance that made her look at him even more closely.

'Okay,' she said, linking an arm through his. 'Walk slowly, breathe slowly, try not to draw the crew's attention.'

They were in luck. The woman who'd mislaid her bags on the

bus was just ahead of them. She was making such a fuss about her many and varied packages that she drew both crew and other passengers' attention. Natasha guided Daniel to a seat inside the shuttle where he could rest against the bulkhead.

She almost cheered when the same woman made a similar noisy fuss disembarking. In the chaos, Natasha and Daniel slipped by, tapped their crown medallions on the monitor and made their way to the elevators. 'You doing okay?'

'Remind me never to eat so much again,' he said, trying for a lighter note. 'I'll be fine; the cramps have eased.'

'Something didn't agree with you,' she said. 'You'll be fine after a lie-down, but it might be a good idea to skip dinner tonight.'

He checked his watch. 'It's only six; I'll be fine and raring to go by eight.'

She wanted to argue that he'd be better to take it easy, that he should, for a change, listen to her. She didn't, because she realised she simply didn't care.

The elevator was crowded and too full of excited chat about the excursion for anyone to pay attention to Daniel.

Back in their cabin, he kicked off his sandals and dropped heavily onto the sofa. 'I'll have a rest, see how I feel. You don't have to hang around.'

'I'll take a book onto the balcony, let you rest.' She dropped her bag onto the sofa and reached for her Kindle. With a final glance at Daniel, she slid the door open and went outside. She stood for a moment at the rail, surprised to see they were already underway. Sailing towards their next destination: a name she couldn't recall.

With a sigh, she sat on the lounge chair and opened her Kindle. She preferred reading paperbacks but there was no arguing with the convenience of an electronic reader. Especially one that had been preloaded with several books she'd wanted to read for a long time. The one she was reading was addictive enough to keep her swiping pages. It was thirst that eventually stopped her. Standing, she peered through the glass, but the room was empty. Daniel must have gone into the bedroom.

Sliding open the door, she stepped into the air-conditioned coolness and crossed to the fridge for a bottle of water.

She raised the bottle to her mouth and drank as she crossed to their bedroom. When he wasn't there, she approached the bathroom. 'Daniel, is everything okay?'

When there was still no reply, she knocked, then pressed her ear to the door. Then she heard it. A groan.

Startled, she pushed the door open, then yelled out in horror.

Daniel was seated on the toilet, his shorts in a puddle around his feet. He hadn't made it in time. Brown liquid stained his shorts, the floor, and dripped down the outside of the toilet bowl. He shook his head, then groaned again. She could hear the splash as his bowel emptied noisily into the toilet. Sweating, nausea, and now diarrhoea. The diagnosis seemed clear.

She'd liked to have left him there. Turned around, left the cabin, gone to one of the lounges with her Kindle and spent the remainder of the day escaping. But much as she hated him... and how she hated him... she couldn't leave him like this.

The linen shirt he was wearing was plastered to his body in sweat. Reaching down, she undid the buttons and peeled it off. 'You think you'll be able to make it into the bedroom?'

'I'm not sure.'

'Lean on me,' she said, staggering slightly when he did. She grabbed an armful of towels and when they reached the bedroom, hurriedly pulled the covers back and laid them down, two deep. 'Lie on these.' He didn't need to be told twice, collapsing heavily onto the bed.

Stepping back, she looked to the phone. She needed to let the ship's medical staff know.

The number for the medical centre was easily found, and the call was answered immediately by a woman who introduced herself as the nurse-on-duty. 'I think my husband might have norovirus,' Natasha said. 'He's sweaty, nauseous, and has had bad diarrhoea.'

'And this started when?'

'We'd gone on the excursion to Kigomasha. He was fine until we were on our way back. At first, we thought he'd simply eaten too much at the buffet.' When there was no response, she added, 'I'm assuming he isn't the only one on board with norovirus, am I right?'

'No, you aren't. We've been lucky this trip.'

'But it's highly contagious!'

'Yes, it is, which would lead me to believe it isn't what's wrong with your husband.' A heavy sigh came down the line. 'I'll have to contact the doctor, get her to call around to examine him. Stay in your cabin until she arrives.'

Natasha went back to the bedside and stared at the pale, sweating man. Nothing contagious. But maybe, just maybe, she'd be lucky and it'd be something fatal.

35

NATASHA

Daniel's eyes were shut but she didn't think he was asleep. Every now and then, his hands clutched at his belly.

His eyes snapped open. 'I need...' He didn't finish, pushing from the bed and staggering across the floor. The en suite bathroom was closer. It didn't matter. As he moved, a trail of faecal fluid trickled down his legs. He made it to the toilet, sat and exploded, bending over, groaning as it seemed to come again and again in spasms.

The ring of the doorbell offered some hope of relief. With a glance at Daniel, who remained slumped forward, groaning, she hurried to answer it.

'Come in,' she said to the person who stood outside, a woman who wore a disposable gown over her clothes, a disposable hat covering her hair and a high-spec face mask. On her hands she wore blue surgical gloves. 'I'm Natasha Vickery-Orme. It's my husband Daniel who is unwell.' She stepped back to allow the woman to enter.

'I'm Deb Day, the ship's doctor. Please forgive the precautions, but until we know what we're dealing with, it's always better to err on the side of caution.'

'I used to be a nurse, so I know how it works.' Natasha glanced behind her. 'Daniel's in the bathroom. This is the second explosion of diarrhoea since we returned to the ship.'

'I'm told this started on your way back from the excursion, is that correct?'

'Yes, he was fine before that. At first, he thought he'd simply eaten too much. I still think it's norovirus.' Hearing a sound from the bathroom, she shook her head. 'I better go to him.'

'Well, since I'm dressed for the role, I may as well come too.'

'Right, well I'll warn you, he's naked.'

'I think that's the least of my worries.'

Natasha led the way, crying out in alarm when they entered to find Daniel had slid from the toilet and was now on his knees on the floor, his head resting on the wall beside him. 'Hey, come on, let's get you up; the doctor's here to see you.'

It took the combined effort of both Natasha and the doctor to get him to his feet. He hung heavily between them, struggling to put one foot in front of the other as they crossed back to the bed. Dropping onto the towels, he groaned and curled up in the foetal position.

Natasha had seen a lot in her day. More than she'd ever wanted to in the last couple of years, but this deterioration... this was something else.

The doctor took his pulse, blood pressure, and temperature. Above her face mask, her forehead was creased.

'It's norovirus, isn't it? The nurse said you didn't have any on board, but I'm guessing that was a lie.'

'No, it's the truth. We don't have any cases.' Day walked into the bathroom and looked into the unflushed toilet. When she returned to the bedside, a frown had joined the pattern of lines creasing her forehead. 'You're absolutely sure he was fine before he left the ship?'

'Yes, I swear. He was fine until we arrived back in Kigomasha.'

'You went to the hotel in Makangale Beach for lunch?'

'Yes. The food was excellent.' She looked at Daniel and shook her head. 'He likes his grub; he ate a huge meal.' When the doctor made no comment, she asked, 'If it's not norovirus, what do you think it might be?'

'It could be cholera.'

Cholera! Natasha considered the little she knew about the disease and nodded. 'Yes, it would fit.'

'It's prevalent in Africa although we haven't heard of any outbreaks in Zanzibar, but that doesn't rule it out.' Day jerked a blue thumb towards the bathroom. 'I was hoping to see the typical pale diarrhoea that is normal for it, but not seeing it doesn't rule it out.' She stepped back. 'We have rapid dipstick tests for cholera. I'll go and get one. Give me ten minutes. I need to inform the captain too. This is going to bugger up the itinerary either way.'

At the door, she pulled off her protective clothing, rolling them in on each other and dropping them on the floor. 'Until we know otherwise, we're going to have to treat this as an infectious disease. You know the score.' She looked over Natasha's shoulder. 'Try to get some fluids into him. I'll bring some Dioralyte back with me.'

She wanted to ask the doctor to bring a nurse back with her too. Natasha couldn't do this. Couldn't look after a man who'd lied and deceived her. Looking after strangers was easy... someone you loved, difficult... someone you hated, almost impossible.

Once the door swung shut behind the doctor, Natasha returned to the bedroom and looked across the elegant, spacious room, to the bed where her husband lay. She didn't move for a moment, then with a sigh, walked over to his side. He'd stopped clutching his stomach. She hoped that was a good sign. 'Hey,' she said. 'Will you try to drink some water?'

The head bob was barely noticeable but she took it as an affirmative and reached for the bottle she'd left on the bedside table. 'Here you go,' she said, sliding a hand under his head to raise it a little as she held the water to his lips. He took a sip, swallowing almost painfully. The next sip trickled down his chin.

'Okay,' she said, taking the bottle away. It would, in any case, be better to wait till the doctor brought the sachets of Dioralyte to add to the water.

Natasha checked her watch. Ten o'clock. She wondered what her friends were doing and if they'd been surprised at their no-show at dinner. A quick check of her mobile showed that Barbara at least had messaged to ask where she was.

It seemed easier to tell them all together, so Natasha composed a message for their WhatsApp group.

> Daniel's come down with something. Not sure what. Doctor visiting. We're in isolation until we find out what's wrong. Hopefully, I'll have good news tomorrow. Have a drink for us!

She wasn't surprised to have messages from all three of her friends within minutes.

From Barbara:

> Bloody hell! Sending love. Let us know when we can visit, xxx

From Michele:

> God! Is there anything I can do? Anything you
> need? xxx

From Tracy Ann:

> Oh no! Let us know if you need anything, we can
> leave it at the door if we're not allowed in, xxx

Natasha sneered. How many of those kisses were for Daniel?

She put the phone down and returned to his side. He seemed more comfortable. And thank goodness, that awful diarrhoea appeared to have stopped. Or had it? Trying not to disturb him, she lifted the sheet, rearing back at the stink that rose from the puddle of faecal waste under him.

A sharp knock at the door dragged her away to answer it. At least she'd have a fresh sample for the doctor's dipstick test.

Doctor Day was back in protective clothing. She pushed a trolley ahead of her. It was laden with everything they might need for Daniel's care.

'How is he?' she asked, crossing to the bed.

'Seems to be more comfortable, but he's had more diarrhoea. He didn't make it to the bathroom this time; I was just about to clean him up.'

'Is he drinking?'

'Just a sip.'

The doctor nodded. 'Right, well, first things first, let's do the test, see if we can find out what we're dealing with.'

'And if it's cholera?'

'The biggest problem with it is the dehydration, but we can address that, so don't worry.'

She picked up the test kit from the trolley. Natasha held the sheet up to allow access to the generous specimen Daniel had inadvertently provided them. She watched the doctor retrieve a specimen, followed the procedure as it was inserted into a small tube, then waited for a result.

After a moment, Day held it out to show Natasha, who peered at the pink mark, then met the doctor's eyes. 'So that's positive. He has cholera?'

'No,' the doctor shook her head. 'Sorry, that's the control band. If it was cholera, we'd see one or maybe two other markers.' She dropped the test into a rubbish bag attached to the side of the trolley. 'He doesn't have cholera.'

Natasha felt weak. For one hideous moment, she imagined she was coming down with whatever it was Daniel had, but that was impossible. She straightened her shoulders. 'So what now?'

'We treat the symptoms.' The doctor reached for a box on the trolley and handed it to Natasha. 'Dioralyte. We need to get fluids into him. Restore some electrolyte balance.'

Natasha nodded. She opened the box, removed a sachet, and tore it open. The bottle of water was almost full; she tipped the contents of the packet into it and gave it a shake. 'Daniel,' she said, slipping her hand under his head again. 'I need you to drink, okay?'

But although Daniel may have been willing, he didn't seem capable, and the drink trickled from his mouth.

'Right, well, that's no good,' Day said. 'I'll set up an intravenous line. Can you manage to clean him up before I start, or do you need me to help?'

'I can manage.' And she did, switching completely into nurse-mode, working with detached efficiency.

Minutes later, she pulled off the disposable gloves and threw them into the bin. 'All done.'

Dr Day merely nodded before pulling a chair closer to the bed. She set a small tray down beside the pillow and reached under the sheet for Daniel's arm.

'I'm going to let this half-litre run in quickly,' she said, getting to her feet a minute later. 'When it's done, attach the litre bag and let it run in more slowly.' She stretched and yawned behind her mask. 'Right, I'm going to leave him to you. If you've any concerns during the night, you can ring me directly.' She gave Natasha her number. 'I'll come back in the morning, first thing, and we'll go from there.' She looked down on the sleeping man. 'I'm hoping once we've rehydrated him, he'll be feeling a little better.'

And if he isn't? Natasha wanted to ask the question but she was a realist. There was only so much the doctor could do with the facilities on board, no matter how good they were.

'Thank you,' she said.

'Once the litre of fluid goes up, Natasha, you should try to get some sleep.'

And then the doctor was gone, shedding her protective clothing at the door.

Exhaustion swept over Natasha, weighing her down, turning her thoughts into a fuzzy mass that made no sense. She could have gone into the lounge but having draped herself in a nurse's mantle once more, she was strangely reluctant to throw it off. Once the litre of fluid was up, she pulled an armchair through and curled up on it. The gentle sway of the ship should have soothed her. It didn't, and she shuffled to and fro, searching for a place of comfort. Somewhere, she did fall asleep.

It was the stink that woke her after a time she couldn't measure. The room was warmer, exacerbating the smell.

Daniel was asleep. She pulled the chair closer to the bed. It was the nurse rather than the wife who reached for his hand, and for the rest of the night kept it clasped in hers.

She remembered seeing the streak of light as dawn arrived, remembered being amazed by the colour of the sky. The pleasure in it must have done what the sway of the ship hadn't succeeded in doing and relaxed her enough to fall asleep.

When she awoke, she was still holding Daniel's hand. There was a creak in her neck. She stretched, yawned, and blinked gritty eyes so that it was a few seconds before she realised the hand she was holding was cold.

36

TRACY ANN

Tracy Ann was awake early. Without disturbing Blake, she crossed to the balcony door, unlocked it, and slid it open. Stepping out onto their balcony, she was puzzled to see they were still at sea. Perhaps she was mistaken but she was sure the ship was supposed to have docked at six and it was almost seven.

'Morning.' Blake appeared, sleepy faced, rubbing his hands over his bare chest. 'You were up early. Were you worrying about Daniel?'

'Of course,' she said, keeping her face averted. 'Probably worrying more about Natasha if I'm being honest.' If she was being honest, she'd have told Blake the truth about what happened a long time ago, thrown herself on his mercy and let the dice land where it may. Steering the conversation away from either Daniel or Natasha, she nodded seaward. 'We haven't docked. Weren't we supposed to, at six?'

'Must have been delayed,' he said, unconcerned. 'Right, I'm starving. I'm going to have a quick shower.' He sidled up to her, wrapping his arms around her waist. 'We could save time and shower together; what d'you think?'

She turned in his arms and placed her hands flat on his chest. 'The last time we tried that, someone, who shall remain nameless, got ideas and we almost broke our necks!' She tapped his chest. 'You go, but don't take forever.'

'Spoilsport,' he said, kissing her cheek.

When he was gone, she leaned on the rail and stared at the sea. *Worrying about Daniel! Ha!* She hoped that whatever was wrong with him, it was excruciatingly painful and had lasting side-effects. She hated him for blackmailing her, hated him for turning her into a vicious bitch who'd wish pain on someone, who'd be tempted to cause it. Yes – her hands tightened on the rail – she'd like to cause him pain, stick sharp pins in his eyes – no, rusty nails, that was it, rusty nails.

He'd done this to her. Made her as bad as he was.

And Blake didn't have a clue.

Maybe she should leave it at that. She leaned forward and stared into the water. They'd think it was an accident, wouldn't they? They might never find her body. She'd read that it was difficult, that some bodies were never located. When Blake came looking for her, he'd be confused, wondering if she'd decided to skip a shower, get dressed and go to breakfast. The poor man, he'd think he'd offended her in some way. He'd dress and hurry to the restaurant to look for her, and when he didn't find her, he'd still be simply confused. Not worried. That would come later. Maybe an hour after she'd gone over the rail.

Only then would they turn the ship in search of her body.

She looked down at the sea as it lapped against the side of the boat. How long would it take to drown? Would she automatically try to save her own life? Would she swim until she was exhausted, then sink, wondering once again why she'd been so fucking stupid?

Probably the fall would kill her. It was a long way.

She'd be gone and Daniel would simply find some other fool to achieve his aim. She wasn't foolish enough to think he'd feel either regret or guilt.

No, she wasn't going to make it that easy for him. Or for her.

She released her grip on the rail and headed back into the cabin. She'd stop thinking about herself for a change and check in with Natasha, who'd probably had a hideous night.

Picking up her phone, she debated sending another WhatsApp message, then decided to ring. If Natasha had her phone on silent so as not to be disturbed, Tracy Ann would leave a message.

To her surprise, it was answered almost immediately. 'Hi,' she said. 'I hope I'm not disturbing you. I just wanted to check in with you, see how the patient is doing this morning.' She listened to Natasha speak but before she had time to reply, the phone went dead. She was still standing with it in her hand when Blake came out of the bathroom a few minutes later.

She guessed she'd gone pale. She felt weak, numb.

'What's the matter?' he said, putting an arm around her and leading her to the small sofa. 'You look like you've seen a ghost.'

She hadn't, but maybe she would. Maybe the man who'd been haunting her thoughts for weeks would continue to haunt them. 'I rang Natasha.'

'Right,' Blake rubbed his hand up and down her arm. 'Is Daniel worse, is that it?'

'Not worse, no. He's dead.'

37

MICHELE

Michele was staring into the bathroom mirror debating whether to use mascara or not when she heard loud knocking on their cabin door. 'Will you answer that?' When the knocking came again, she tossed the mascara back into her make-up bag and hurried into the cabin. Don was out on the balcony, oblivious to both the knocking and her call.

Whoever was at the door was impatient. The knock came again as she reached it. 'For goodness' sake,' she said, pulling the door open. When she saw Tracy Ann and Blake outside, her first reaction was annoyance but this was swiftly replaced by worry. 'What the hell is going on?'

Tracy Ann didn't wait to be asked inside, brushing past Michele without a word. It was Blake who spoke, and even he didn't make sense. 'It's Daniel.'

Letting the door shut with a clunk, Michele followed them into the cabin. 'We know he's sick.' She frowned. 'I saw the WhatsApp messages.'

'He's dead.' Tracy Ann's words were blunt. Chilling.

And shocking. Michele's hand went to her mouth, her feet

moving backwards until her legs felt the sofa behind, then she dropped onto it, eyes wide. 'Daniel's dead? That's impossible.'

'Natasha told me. She said he died early this morning.'

The balcony door slid open and Don came through, all smiles. 'Hey, are we all going to breakfast together?'

'Daniel's dead.' It was Michele who passed on the news this time.

Don's smile took a while to fade, as if he wasn't sure this wasn't some kind of horrible joke. 'You're serious,' he said. 'Daniel's dead?'

'Natasha told Tracy Ann.'

'Shit! Does Barbara know?'

Since nobody knew the answer, they decided it made sense to go to her cabin. 'It'll be good to be together,' Tracy Ann said. 'We can decide on what to do.'

Michele stared at her. What to do about what? He was dead. And bloody good riddance to him. She wanted to punch the air in glee. Instead, she had to maintain this façade that she gave a fuck that the bastard was dead.

'We need to be there for Tasha,' Tracy Ann said, as if to clarify what she meant.

Be there for their grief-stricken friend, the woman who'd brought that damn viper into their friendship nest. Michele let her anger out in a sigh. It was over, wasn't it? With Daniel dead, there was nobody to prove that Don had known about the insider trading. She hoped it was as simple as that.

They walked together to Barbara and Ralph's cabin. Michele rang the doorbell first, then knocked almost as loudly as Tracy Ann had done on their door a few minutes before.

It was a very confused Ralph who opened it. 'What the hell's going on? Have we to abandon ship or something?'

Blake held a hand up. 'Nothing that dramatic. May we come inside?'

'Who is it?' Barbara's voice drifted towards them.

'Your bloody friends and their idiot husbands,' Ralph said without the slightest trace of amusement.

Michele met Don's gaze and raised an eyebrow.

'Well, let them in!'

Ralph seemed reluctant but eventually, and begrudgingly, stood back to allow the four into the cabin.

Barbara shook her head. 'Ralph was never a morning person,' she explained. 'We all heading for breakfast?' As if that was a rational explanation for them to be hammering on their door. 'I'm hoping we'll find out why we're not in port where we should be. We were looking forward to visiting the medieval village; now it looks as if we won't be doing that.'

'Daniel is dead,' Tracy Ann said. 'It happened early this morning.'

Barbara had been frowning in annoyance at the disruption to their plans. At Tracy Ann's words, she jerked her head around, her mouth an O of disbelief and shock. 'Wha—?' She stumbled towards the bed and sat heavily. 'That can't be!'

Tracy Ann quickly explained her phone call to Natasha. 'She hung up before I could ask any questions, so I don't know more than that.'

'Daniel is dead,' Barbara said, as if testing the words for veracity, the bitter truth of them twisting her mouth. 'Should we go around? Natasha, she'll be devastated.'

'She said they were in isolation yesterday.' Blake reminded them. 'Unless they've discovered what caused his death, she might well still be.'

'We could go, knock on the door, see what the story is. If she can't let us in, at least she'll know we're thinking of her.'

Nobody had a better suggestion so they left Barbara's cabin and walked silently to Natasha's.

Their ring on the doorbell was answered almost immediately by a woman none of them recognised. She didn't introduce herself, merely waited for one of them to speak.

'We're Natasha's friends,' Barbara said. 'We've heard about her husband. Can we see her, or do anything for her?'

'Not at the moment. Later this morning, Mrs Vickery-Orme will be moved into another cabin for the remainder of the voyage. Once she's there, you may be able to see her.'

'It's true then,' Tracy Ann said quietly. 'Daniel is dead.'

'I'm afraid so, but more I cannot say. I'll tell your friend you called. Now, if you'll excuse me.' With a nod, she shut the door, leaving the group in the corridor.

Michele immediately turned to Tracy Ann. 'What was with the question? Did you think Natasha was lying? What is wrong with you?'

'What's wrong with *you*?' Blake put an arm around his wife's shoulder. 'Can't you see she's in shock? We all are. One of our friends is dead. It's going to take a while to process this before we are able to grieve.'

Grieve! Michele turned away before she was tempted to tell him the truth. That she and Don would be celebrating; maybe they'd even open a bottle of champagne later and make a toast to Daniel's passing. For the moment, she'd play the part. 'Yes, of course, you're right, I'm sorry. Come on, let's go to the restaurant; I'm sure we could all do with some coffee, maybe even something to eat.'

Moving past Don to lead the way, she glanced at Tracy Ann, whose head was resting on Blake's shoulder. Michele had no idea what the relationship was between Tracy Ann and Daniel. She'd admitted to kissing him, but Michele had wondered had there been more to it. Expecting to see genuine sorrow, she was taken aback to see the slightest of smiles on Tracy Ann's lips and a definite look of relief in her eyes.

It seemed Michele wasn't the only woman who wouldn't be grieving for Daniel.

38

NATASHA

Natasha wasn't grieving. She was numb. The doctor had answered her panicked call within minutes, and after a brief examination had officially pronounced Daniel dead. As if there was any doubt. His body was cold. He'd died while she'd slept by his side.

When the doctor was finished, Natasha unfolded the clean sheet she'd taken from the trolley and spread it over him. 'I don't understand. He was a fit, healthy man; how can he be dead?' She'd seen death in all its forms over the years, the sad inevitability of dreadful diseases, the shockingly unexpected deaths from catastrophic injuries after accidents, the heart-breaking Covid deaths. But she'd never seen anything like this.

Doctor Day, she noticed, wasn't wearing protective clothing this time. 'You obviously don't think it's something infectious, so what the hell is it?'

The doctor pulled at her shirt. 'I should still be taking precautions, but I wanted to get here as soon as I could. Anyway,' she shrugged, 'I don't believe your husband died from anything contagious. I double checked when I returned to my cabin after leaving last night. There have been no reports of illness of any sort on board. I even checked with the hotel manager at Makangale Beach where you had lunch.' She lifted her hands in the air. 'Nothing.'

'There'll be a post-mortem.' Natasha knew the score.

'Yes. I'll have to speak to the captain. There's a good hospital in Zanzibar City. I'll organise to get it done there.' She put a hand on Natasha's arm and led her into the lounge. When they were both seated on the sofa, she turned to face her. 'Obviously, this will need to be classified as an unexpected death, so I'm afraid I'll also have to inform the security officer.' She raised her hand to stop any argument. 'Much as would happen had his death occurred on land where the police would be informed.'

Natasha wasn't going to argue. It was to be expected.

'I think it would be best,' Day continued, 'if we moved you into another cabin. We don't have a morgue on the ship. What we'll do is crank the air-conditioning way down in here. We should reach Zanzibar City tomorrow.'

Natasha frowned. 'I thought we didn't reach there till Friday.' In three days.

'Dead bodies tend to play havoc with itineraries,' Day said, getting to her feet. 'I need to make a few calls. Sit tight.'

Rather than leaving the cabin, she took herself into the dressing room. Natasha heard the murmur of her voice as it rose and fell, the long pauses where she was listening. They probably had strict routines to follow and it would all click into place. The passengers would miss out two shore excursions on the way to Zanzibar City. They wouldn't be pleased. She wondered what excuse they'd be given. Hardly that a passenger had died from an unknown cause. She imagined the panic that would result and almost smiled.

Daniel would have been pleased to have caused such a fuss.

He had a strange, somewhat nasty sense of humour. What a shame he wasn't there to enjoy it.

She thought of the white-sheeted body of her late husband stretched out on the bed. All his lies had died with him. Now, she wouldn't have to decide whether to stay with him, or to leave and resume the life she was leading before they met.

Charismatic, charming men should have dramatic deaths, not die in their own putrid stink as Daniel had. But perhaps for a lying bastard, it was an appropriate end.

She sat back, resting her head against the wall behind. His death had freed her. She should be grateful. Truth was, she didn't know what she felt. Regret? Possibly. Sorrow? She wasn't sure. Relief. She shut her eyes and felt the sting of tears. How sad that this was what she felt the most. *Relief.*

'Right,' Doctor Day said, returning to the room. 'The captain says we should get to Zanzibar City early tomorrow morning. He'll arrange alternative accommodation for you.' She waved a hand around the cabin. 'I'm afraid it's unlikely to be on this scale though.'

'I don't think that's going to bother me, really.'

'Well, it might; the captain has asked that you remain in your cabin until we reach port. The security officer will see you, of course, but it may be that the authorities will also want to speak to you.'

'The police?' This was unexpected. 'Does the captain think I might have killed Daniel?' A shocking thought crossed her mind. 'Do you? Is that it: *you* think I might have had a hand in it?' She got to her feet and glared at the doctor. 'Seriously!'

The doctor didn't look remotely apologetic. 'I'm merely doing my job, Mrs Vickery-Orme. If we've ruled out any infectious and contagious disease, it does leave one possibility.'

Natasha noticed the doctor had reverted to a more formal address. 'You think I might have poisoned him, is that it?'

'And did you?'

Natasha didn't think that question warranted an answer. If she had poisoned Daniel, she was hardly likely to admit it.

The doctor didn't appear to expect an answer either. 'I'll contact my colleagues at the hospital and get them to expedite a post-mortem. They might be able to give us an indication as to cause of death, although tissue and blood analysis will obviously take time.'

A loud knock on the door startled both women. 'I'll answer it,' the doctor said. 'It might be the security officer.'

Natasha decided she needed some fresh air. Sliding the door onto the balcony open, she stepped outside. Poison. She could see why they'd be suspicious. Poison had long been regarded as a woman's choice of weapon. She had some knowledge of it, of course, but nothing in her repertoire fit with what had happened to Daniel.

They'd do blood tests. Examine the contents of his stomach. Find out what had caused a fit young man to die so suddenly.

The door behind Natasha slid open again and she turned to see the doctor stepping out. 'The odour is getting a bit much in there, isn't it? I've switched the air-con down. You should hear about your new cabin within a couple of minutes.' Day jabbed her thumb over her shoulder. 'That was your friends. They asked me to pass on their condolences. I told them you'd be in a different cabin soon and they could visit you there.'

'Oh, so I'm not under arrest then, am I?'

'Not yet.'

Natasha rested back against the rail. 'I didn't poison Daniel. If I'd wanted to kill my husband, believe me, Doctor Day, I'd have found a neater way to do it.'

39

NATASHA

Doctor Day opened her mouth, but whatever she was going to say died on her lips as the doorbell rang again. As before, it was she who hurried to answer it. When she returned, Emilio, the butler who'd looked after their cabin since they'd boarded, was a step behind.

'He's come to take you to your new cabin,' Day said. 'It appears that you're in luck. Whereas all the penthouse suites are occupied, the Grand Duchess Suite isn't. It's on this deck, so convenient for your friends. You'll be accommodated there for the remainder of the trip.'

She said it as if the greatest honour was being bestowed on Natasha. There was no point in telling the doctor that she'd have been as happy with an inside cabin on one of the worst decks. No point, and it wouldn't have been true anyway; a cabin without some access to outside wouldn't have suited her at all.

'What about my things?' Natasha nodded towards the dressing room. 'I'd really like a change of clothes.' She didn't want to add that she could smell the effluent she'd been dealing with for the last twenty-four hours as if it had become embedded in her pores. The Grand Duchess Suite would have a shower.

'The security officer wants to have a look around the room before you move anything. Afterwards, Emilio can fetch anything you want if you give him a list. Meanwhile, if you want to change out of your clothes, you can avail yourself of the robe in your new cabin.'

Emilio stood quietly, his nose twitching at the unmistakeable odour, his eyes darting nervously in the direction of the bedroom. He'd been pleasantly polite from the beginning but any attempt at friendly banter had been met with a tight smile that said he knew his place and they should know theirs. She guessed he'd take the list of knickers, bras, and assorted items she'd need and collect them all without a blink.

She followed him, leaving the doctor in possession of both the cabin and Daniel's body. Emilio didn't speak as he led the way. Her friends' cabins were in the other direction. She glanced back but the long corridor stayed empty.

They passed several doors before they stopped and Emilio pushed open the door into her new accommodation.

Natasha's first thought was that Daniel would have loved it. Now he'd never know that the penthouse they'd had was left in the shade by this colossal space. A huge living room was furnished with an elegant, three-piece, grey suite that hugged a massive coffee table and faced a giant TV screen. On one end of the room, a table had seating for eight.

'The bedroom is through here, madam.' Emilio held open a door to a room that was possibly twice the size of the bedroom in the penthouse and dominated by a super king-size bed. *With no dead body marring its smooth covers.*

There was an en suite, a separate larger bathroom and a

further single WC. It was the perfect suite for entertaining. Daniel would have been in his element.

'The suite has a guest bedroom too, madam,' Emilio said, pointing towards a door in another corner. 'And a balcony, of course.'

He slid open the door but she shook her head, suddenly weary. 'Thank you. I'll find my way around.'

'If madam would write a list of what she'd like me to bring, I'll fetch them as soon as I'm given permission.'

Realising he expected her to make the list right away, she sighed and crossed to an elegant desk that sat against one wall. In the drawer, as expected, she found writing paper and a pen. Sitting, she tried to think what she'd need, but all that came into her head was knickers. She imagined the rather prim Emilio lifting out handfuls of the lacy lingerie she'd bought for Daniel's delectation. Her snort of laughter had him tilt his head in a question she wasn't planning to answer. Instead, she scribbled a list of things she might need over the following days and handed it to him.

He took the sheet, folded it neatly in half and nodded. 'If there is anything madam needs, my number remains the same.'

And then he was gone and she was alone in a suite built for more than one.

She thought about having a shower to wash the lingering stink from her body. Instead, she crossed to the fridge to check out what alcohol was available. Only the best possibly, but it was the alcohol percentage she was interested in. Neat gin would fit the bill. It might be good to stay drunk till the cruise was over. Or until her stay on it was. If the post-mortem showed up something dodgy, the local police might take a hard line. Take her into custody here in Zanzibar.

If the post-mortem showed up something dodgy.

If...

40

TRACY ANN

'You feeling okay?'

It was the third time Blake had asked Tracy Ann the same question in as many minutes. Once more, one more damn time, and she'd tell him the truth. That she was feeling fucking marvellous. That thanks to Daniel's totally unexpected death, she could breathe for the first time in weeks, that the knots that had tightened since she'd shared a hot tub with him the day before had gone, that the vice that seemed to have been tightening around her head, causing it to ache and her thoughts to become scrambled, had loosened. It hadn't gone, but the pain was easier, her thoughts clearer.

Clear enough to allow her to take a deep breath before answering. 'I'm fine, darling, it's just the shock of it all, you know. Daniel was always so alive, wasn't he?'

'Alive?' Blake tilted his head side to side. 'I'd say larger than life myself.'

Tracy Ann was bent over unlacing her shoes but she looked up when she heard the undertone to Blake's words. Was she imagining it or was there a sharp edge to them? It was so unusual for her normally laid-back husband to be anything other than genial that she was instantly on the alert.

'Yes,' she said, kicking off the shoes and flexing her toes. Wasn't that exactly why she'd been attracted to him in the first place? Everything about Daniel was larger than life – his smile, the glint in his eyes, his obvious charm, charisma, and raw sexuality. And the streak of nastiness that lay just below the surface. Scratch him and it came oozing out to destroy everything in its path.

'There was something about him though.' Blake picked up the remote and flicked on the TV. 'It'll be interesting to see how the captain is planning to explain the decision not to dock in Wete as planned.'

Tracy Ann crossed to the sofa and sat while he searched for the information channel.

'Ha, clever!' He turned to look at her. 'Unconfirmed cholera outbreak. The Nobility Fleet Line unwilling to risk passenger safety, yada yada yada.'

'Maybe that's what killed him. Cholera has been a problem on mainland Africa for a while; maybe it's reached Zanzibar and Daniel came in contact with it while we were on shore.'

Blake switched off the TV and took the seat beside her. 'They'd have done a test for it and obviously it's been ruled out. We've been told we can visit later so whatever killed him, it was nothing contagious.'

She felt his leg press against hers, the heat of it. Daniel was dead but the memory of that night was still with her, still grinding into her soul. She played with the edge of her shorts, pulling her leg away. 'Healthy men don't just die for no reason.'

'Our next stop is Zanzibar City. I'm guessing he'll be taken off.

They'll want a post-mortem done ASAP to prove he didn't die from anything contagious before they'll allow passengers off, I'm guessing. They won't want to take risks.'

'We could be stuck on the ship for days!' The thought appalled her. The ship was suddenly far too small, too crowded. Plus, there'd be no way to avoid her friends and they'd see what Blake couldn't – the sheer relief at the death of their friend's husband. Another thought came to her and she turned to look at her husband. 'What did you mean, "there was something about him"?'

Blake sat back, linking his hands behind his head. 'From the beginning, I felt he was putting on a show for us. The hail-fellow-well-met approach was very calculated, as if he was weighing us up before deciding how to approach each of us. And although his cheerful comments were usually funny, they were often viciously barbed.'

Tracy Ann felt the knots in her belly re-tying themselves. 'I thought you liked him.'

Blake raised his head. He dropped a hand to lay it on her shoulder and gave it a squeeze. 'Like him? No, I never did. But you know that old adage: *keep your friends close and your enemies closer.*' He waited until she nodded before continuing. 'Once he and Natasha married and we were set to be spending more time with him, it seemed safer to keep him closer. Maybe it would have been better all round if I'd let him know the truth.'

'The truth?'

'That I thought he was a devious, lying shit.'

What? A devious, lying shit! Tracy Ann felt Blake's fingers dig deeper into her shoulder, hurting her.

She was so used to thinking of him as a genial, easy-going man who adored her that she was confused, shocked by what was happening. Perhaps she'd taken him for granted. Daniel had worn an ill-fitting mask. Maybe Blake's was better and behind his genial exterior lurked something else.

He had, after all, survived for all these years in the world of politics. He was used to getting things done under difficult circumstances, used to dealing with sleaze. Perhaps, he'd also learned how to get rid of his opponents.

She reached up and laid her hand on his, quietening it, easing the pain he was causing. But it was the pain she'd caused him that was searing through her as she realised that he knew something... *He knew.*

The sleazy world of politics. Blake had once told her that he could acquire whatever he needed to do what had to be done. He had, she assumed, been referencing the day-to-day work he was involved in, but perhaps he'd also meant that he'd learnt how to deal with dodgy politicians.

He couldn't possibly know the truth about what had happened between her and Daniel, but perhaps he believed that they'd been having an affair. The thought made her want to turn and tell him the truth. Confess what she'd done and what she'd been about to do. But she didn't, because she was suddenly very afraid that one confession would lead to another and she wasn't sure she wanted to know what Blake had done.

Daniel was dead. And whatever had killed him wasn't contagious. So what was it? *Poison?*

Her hand tightened on Blake's. What she was thinking was crazy, wasn't it? Did she really think that her gentle husband would kill Daniel because he believed they were having an affair?

She took her hand away and immediately felt his fingers knead her shoulder again. Painfully. This time, she didn't stop him, the pain becoming at one with the ache in her heart, the tense cramps in her belly, and the crippling throb in her head.

She was to blame. She and her stupid desire for a little excitement. And if Blake was to blame for Daniel's death, that too was down to her.

Even dead, the bastard wasn't going to leave her in peace.

41

MICHELE

The relief that flooded Michele and Don was barely contained until they returned to their cabin. There they let it off the leash. Laughter. Hugging one another. Michele dancing a little jig around the room. Don punching the air. She grabbed his arm and they danced together until they stopped and stared at one another with huge smiles and bright eyes. And then they kissed and fell onto the towel swan that sat on the end of their bed, squashing it flat as they rolled together, tearing their clothes off until they were naked and wrapped around one another.

And when they were done, hot, sweaty and satisfied, they lay silently with their limbs entwined.

'Better than make-up sex,' Michele said, her softly spoken words tickling the hair on Don's chest. When he made no comment, she curled fingers around a hair and tugged gently. 'Have I worn you out?'

'No, I'm thinking.'

'Always a dangerous thing to do.' Rolling away from him, she raised herself on an elbow and looked down on his face. He looked unusually serious. 'We're allowed to be relieved that

Daniel is dead,' she said, lifting her hand to lay it against his cheek. 'He was an evil bastard who used people for his own ends. The world is a far better place without him.'

He reached to take her hand and hold it on his chest. She could feel his heart beating. Slowing down after their exertions, but always steady. As he had been for most of their married life. He'd made one mistake – not in getting into debt, not even in getting involved with Daniel. No, his mistake had been in not telling her. In trying to protect her as if she was a Victorian lady in need of being sheltered, and not the life-hardened, resilient woman she was. 'A *much* better place,' she said. 'He'd always want you to do one more thing for him. And if things went tits-up, you can depend on it, he'd have blamed it all on you. You're the qualified accountant, he'd have said, and he'd been misled by you. And he'd say it with that smarmy, fake-sincere expression on his face that made me want to puke.' She was pleased to see this raised a smile. 'Time to get up,' she said, pulling her hand from his, surprised when his fingers tightened on hers to prevent her moving.

'You hoping for another round?' she said with a laugh.

'I love you. I'd love you whatever you did. Stand by you, no matter what.'

She pulled her hand away and shuffled upright. 'No matter what?' She got to her feet, dragging the sheet with her, wrapping it toga-like around her chest as she took a step away. 'What are you talking about?' She raised her chin, her dignified stance spoiled as she tripped on the ends of the sheet trailing along the ground. 'Oh for goodness' sake,' she said, gathering her robes up and crossing to the sofa.

He grabbed his discarded clothes and pulled them on before getting to his feet, his expression unusually sombre. Before he joined her, he opened the fridge and took out a bottle of beer.

Michele watched him, puzzled. There was a time when she could read him like a book. Or so she thought. She let her breath out in a weary sigh. Perhaps she'd been fooling herself and saw what she wanted to. Had that been it? She'd wanted to believe Don was a successful businessman because it would reflect well on her. Behind every successful man, there was a successful woman. Wasn't that it? Was that why she'd been blind to Don's increasing irritability, his pinched expression, the way his eyes darted away if Daniel's name was even mentioned? She hadn't wanted to see.

She refused to be so blind again. 'What is it? You'd better tell me. No more secrets, right?'

He opened the beer, tossed the cap in the bin, and drank deeply from the bottle. Desperate gulps that told her more than words would have done that she wasn't going to like what he said.

The bottle was almost empty when he sat beside her, holding it in his hand, dangling it between his knees. 'I love you. Always did, always will. I'd do anything for you.' He took another swig from the bottle, then put it down and turned to look at her. 'Anything, Michele.'

She laughed, a nervous, high-pitched sound, because she had no idea where this conversation was going, but she was more than ever sure she wasn't going to like it. 'That's good to know,' she said finally.

'You need to tell me how you did it so we can prepare for whatever happens.'

Michele and her girlfriends had often laughed at their partners inability to communicate clearly, or at all. It wasn't funny now. Not in the slightest. 'How I did it? What are you talk—' She stopped abruptly, her eyes widening as realisation dawned. She struggled to stand, swearing softly under her breath when her feet once more became tangled in the sheet. 'Are you fucking serious? You think I killed Daniel?'

'I saw you.' He stood and reached a hand towards her. 'I understand why you did it.' He shook his head. 'If I hadn't been such an idiot, you wouldn't have needed to go to such extremes.'

'Extremes!' This time, Michele's laugh was genuinely amused. 'You think killing Daniel is going to extremes; I'd classify it as going bloody psycho myself!'

'I saw you,' he said again. 'When I lost sight of you in that market in Kigomasha. I thought it was accidental but I'm guessing it was deliberate. You weren't careful enough though; I saw you with that trader, saw you slipping something into your pocket. I'm guessing you bought poison of some sort.'

Her smile was forced. 'It seems I've been caught out.'

42

BARBARA

Ralph was stretched out on the bed. Asleep, or pretending to be. Barbara was on the balcony, standing at the rail, trying to get her thoughts in order. She had to. Ralph would want to go to lunch in a while; she had to have her game face in place before they sat opposite each other in the bright lights of the restaurant. She'd have preferred to have waited till dinner when the more subtle lighting would have given her some chance of hiding the ravages Daniel's demise had wreaked on her face. *Demise.* Even in her head, she found it hard to say dead. She said it now, softly, trying it out for size. 'Dead.' It felt wrong, clumsy, sharp.

Daniel had been so alive. Even now, she could smell the cologne he wore and could feel the heat of his hand through the fabric of her dress. She shut her eyes and sank into the memories, feeling the frisson that every thought or sight of Daniel had sent sizzling through her.

She loved Ralph, had done from almost the first despite their age difference. It hadn't seemed huge back then. Like Daniel, Ralph had been a larger-than-life, charismatic man who had swept her off her feet. She still loved him; she just wasn't sure she liked him much any more.

She wasn't sure what that said about her – that she liked the dynamic journalist but wasn't sure about the retired man slouching around the house, getting under her feet, making her feel old, worn out.

His retirement should have given them an opportunity to travel, to do more things together. It was supposed to be a new beginning, not an end, not a slow spiral towards old age and inca-pacity. Her fingers curled around the rail as she stared out to sea. *Daniel was dead.*

She wasn't sure when she'd seriously considered the idea of having an affair... with anyone. Just to feel alive again. Perhaps around the same time that Ralph's downward spiral seemed unstoppable. Or was it when she realised that she, like her mother before her, looked to be hitting the menopause early, so that at forty, it was all over.

She was good at putting on a front; of being good old reliable Barbara. She'd put on a good front the night they'd gone out for dinner with her friends some months before. Maybe she'd needed an extra glass of wine to keep the smile in place and her voice chirpy. As they often did, they'd arranged to meet their husbands for a drink afterwards. Tired from pretending all was right with her world, she'd have preferred to have gone home; she'd certainly have preferred not to have Ralph joining them. Ralph with the miserable long face he'd been carrying around with him like a dependent child for weeks.

But there was no way out of it so she'd smiled, nodded when necessary, hoped she could get through the night without screaming.

The new wine bar they had decided on was an amazing venue. All moody lighting, lots of glass, mirrors, comfortable seating. It was also crowded. With no seats available, they'd stood with their drinks, separated now and then from each other as the crowd ebbed and flowed, patrons making their way to the bar and back, some leaving, others pushing in. An amazing venue but not one conducive to conversation, which suited Barbara perfectly. It suited her too that Ralph had latched onto Don and was at his side deep in conversation about something or other.

'We'll just stay for one.' Natasha had mouthed the words and grinned when Barbara gave her a thumbs up.

Daniel and Blake had gone to the bar for the drinks, and it was Daniel who brought Barbara's across. 'I got you a large one,' he said, holding the glass of wine out to her. 'You look like you need it.'

A disturbance behind him forced him forward suddenly, the fingers of the hand around the glass pressing against her breast. She felt the warmth of them through the silk of her shirt. It started a roll of heat that swept up her neck and across her cheeks. She could feel a lick of moisture between her breasts, in her armpits. Her eyes flicked to the exit. She needed to get out of there.

Maybe Daniel could read her mind. 'Take a drink, you'll be fine.' He lifted the glass to her lips and held it there while she took a mouthful, gulping the chilled liquid down gratefully.

'Thank you.' He was close enough that she could smell his cologne, something woody and masculine. Close enough that she could see a tiny scar on his cheek and she itched to reach up and touch it, to ask him how he'd acquired it. They were close enough that she was staring straight into his eyes and he was looking into hers. She felt he was seeing right down into her soul and she felt the first stirring of desire for another man.

A harmless flirtation.

That's all it was.

A Band-Aid for a wounded life. A drug to take away the pain, to lift her out of the doldrums, to give her days some meaning. Only when it was too late, only when he'd burrowed under her skin, did she realise she'd become obsessed with him.

Looking back, she could see the truth. It hadn't needed much encouragement for the desperately sad, incredibly stupid, terribly disloyal woman she'd been to fall completely under his spell. Not in love. She understood that now. Despite everything, Ralph was the only man she'd ever loved. But love was one thing, lust something else entirely.

Releasing her grip on the rail, she sat on the lounge chair and swung her feet up. The warm breeze coming off the sea tickled her bare legs and made her smile. A brief twist of her lips. She shut her eyes. It was easy to see now what had happened. Daniel had been an aberration. Under the temporary bandage of her obsession, nothing had healed. Ralph was still in a deep funk; she was still feeling... What? A failure for never having pursued her own goals? Was that it? Did she resent Ralph for the decision she'd made all those years before? Resent him for having suddenly become so old, for dragging her with him?

Daniel – yesterday, she'd hated him with a passion as strong as her obsession had been. Now, she missed him. The way he'd made her feel young and alive. She missed him but she was relieved... No, more, she was glad he was gone.

More especially since she'd seen Ralph look at her oddly when they'd gone to Daniel and Natasha's over-the-top penthouse for the pre-dinner drinks.

In the beginning, she'd been discreet; recently, she hadn't bothered.

Ralph might have been in a bad place but he was a long way from being stupid. She guessed he was suspicious. He might even believe she'd been unfaithful.

In her head, she had. She'd fucked Daniel's brains out.

Only in her head. But Ralph didn't know that.

There'd be a post-mortem. She guessed Zanzibar City would be their next stop and it'd be done there. If they found something suspicious, would all eyes be turned on his friends?

Even dead, was Daniel going to continue to cause them problems?

43

NATASHA

Natasha sent a WhatsApp message to her friends to tell them she was doing okay. If they were surprised she hadn't included her new cabin number, none of them said. Perhaps they understood that she needed time to herself. Time to process Daniel's death.

The fridge held half and full-size bottles of white wine and champagne. It seemed wrong to open the latter, but she did, the pop of the cork ridiculously loud in the silent suite. She took the bottle and a glass onto the balcony. *Process Daniel's death.* As if shock was the overriding factor. It was there, of course; how could she not be shocked by his death? But it wasn't the emotion that was sizzling through her. She poured a glass of champagne and raised it in a toast. 'To being a rich widow.' Because it was still relief she felt mostly. No more worries over that damn prenup, or how she was going to deal with a man she should never have married.

Through the doors, she could hear the distinct sound of a phone ringing. It might be the security officer wanting to speak to her. It was tempting to ignore it, but if she did, they might be concerned and come to see her in person instead.

Taking another sip of the champagne, she topped up the glass before heading inside.

'Hello?'

'It's Captain Alvarez, Mrs Vickery-Orme. I wanted to extend my deepest condolences on the death of your husband and to assure you that we'll do everything in our power to assist you. Is everything in the suite to your satisfaction?'

She wondered if he'd be shocked at her plan to work her way through all the booze the suite offered, and that she was currently drinking champagne. As if she was celebrating. Which she was, wasn't she? Not Daniel's death – or at least not completely – but her freedom. 'Yes, thank you, Captain, it's fine. Your crew have been very helpful.'

'Good, good.' There was silence for a moment before he continued in a more sombre tone of voice. 'We expect to arrive in Zanzibar City very early tomorrow morning. I've contacted the authorities there. We plan to arrange for your husband's removal as soon as possible after we drop anchor. We hope you understand.'

'I understand completely, Captain. I've already said my good-byes. The sooner we find out the cause of death, the better. Anything that would expedite that is fine by me.'

'We appreciate your co-operation, Mrs Vickery-Orme. If there's anything I or my crew can do for you, please let me know. Emilio has been told to take good care of you.'

'I was told the security officer wanted to speak to me.'

'Ah yes. Ms Valentine, our head of security, has decided that it would be best to have that conversation after we get the initial post-mortem results.'

'I see.' And Natasha did. The security officer was waiting to see if she was her husband's murderer, or the wife of a victim of happenstance. It made sense but it was unsettling having to wait.

'We have asked the authorities to have the post-mortem done as a matter of urgency so we expect a preliminary report by mid-morning.' A heavy sigh floated down the line. 'It may not be sufficient to allay their fears but we have to keep hopeful.'

Natasha understood the captain's dilemma. Unless the authorities were satisfied, they would refuse permission for passengers to disembark anywhere in Zanzibar, and the ship's itinerary would be shot to hell.

Proof that Daniel didn't die of any contagious infection would be good news for the captain, but as soon as that was ruled out, as it was bound to be, the authorities would be considering the alternatives. That Daniel had acquired some strange and fast-acting fatal disease, or that he'd been murdered.

Murdered.

It was down to what they could prove.

Natasha wasn't sure what that could be.

44

NATASHA

Natasha swirled the champagne in the glass before she lifted it to her mouth and emptied it in one long gulp. The bubbles made her choke, cough, then snort. Better, she decided, to get the phone calls out of the way before she drank any more.

A message would have been so much easier. One she could cut and paste and send to all. It was tempting but impossible.

It was early afternoon in the UK, a good time to catch her busy mother. She was understandably horrified when Natasha gave her a condensed and sanitised version of Daniel's death. 'My poor darling. What an awful shock. When are you coming home? We can meet you at the airport. I assume your insurance will cover repatriating poor Daniel and flying you home early.'

It was so typical of her mother to jump straight to the practicalities that Natasha had to smile. 'Cruise insurance is particularly high for that very reason. The captain has been very helpful too and of course I have my friends around me.' Her mother didn't need to know that Natasha hadn't seen them that day. Nor did she need to know there was some doubt about the cause of death. She certainly wasn't planning on telling her that the doctor suspected she had something to do with it. 'They have to do the post-mortem here. Some legal requirement.' Her mother was big into dotting every i and crossing every t; she'd appreciate the need to follow protocol.

'So when it's done, you'll get home, yes?'

'Of course.' Actually, Natasha had no idea what she was going to do. She supposed she'd be expected to travel back with Daniel's body, wearing widow's weeds and an expression of intense sorrow. She wasn't royalty; she hadn't packed a black outfit just in case. And she wasn't sure she could do any kind of sorrow.

Daniel had been her escape from a career she'd grown to hate. She'd used him as an easy way out, but how could she have predicted that he'd have had his own agenda?

Because now that he was gone, her thoughts seemed clearer and she decided he had to have done. Something more than the convenience of having an attractive woman on his arm, and available sex. He hadn't had to marry her for either. So why had he? She should have demanded an explanation as soon as she'd heard about the vasectomy. Now she was left with a mystery she'd never be able to solve.

She spoke to her mother for a few minutes more, reassuring her that she was being well-supported and promising to keep her updated.

When she hung up, she slumped back on the sofa. One call down. She needed another glass of champagne before making any more. Maybe the alcohol would loosen her thoughts. It might even allow her to feel something more appropriate than relief. Daniel might have lied, and he hadn't loved her any more than she'd loved him, but they'd had good times.

The alcohol was making her maudlin. Putting the glass down, she picked up her phone and rang a business associate of Daniel's, giving him a much-shortened version of what had happened.

Then there was only the mother and brother. He answered on the first ring. 'Ben Vickery-Orme.'

'Hi, Ben, it's Natasha.' When there was no comment, she added, 'Daniel's wife.' *Late wife, to be exact.* 'I'm afraid I have some bad news. Daniel and I are on a cruise.' Oddly, although she hated euphemisms, when it came to it, she couldn't bring herself to use the blunt *he died.* 'I'm sorry to have to tell you but he passed away yesterday.' She knew the brothers weren't close. Couldn't stand one another, according to Daniel, but she was still taken aback when a gruff laugh rolled down the line.

'His sins caught up with him at last, have they?'

Natasha held a hand to her forehead. 'I'm sorry. I don't understand—'

'Was he murdered by one of the many, many people he pissed off over the years?'

The brothers weren't close, Daniel had said. He hadn't elaborated, hadn't said his brother hated him. But it was there in the savagery of those words. She'd like to have told Ben that his brother had been killed in a terrible accident or had died from cholera or any one of a range of exotic diseases. She didn't think he'd care that his brother had had a dreadful death. From the sound of it, he might even have been glad. 'They're not sure of the cause of death as yet,' she said in answer to his question. 'There'll be a post-mortem tomorrow. Then his body will be sent home where we'll have a funeral—'

'You can stop right there.' The voice was harsh, unapologetic. 'I'll save you the cost of another phone call; I won't be going. It might be tempting to be there, simply to make sure they bury the bastard deeply, or burn him at a high enough temperature, but I'll take your word for it. Believe me, the world is now a better place.'

Natasha wanted to ask what Daniel had done to have caused his brother to hate him so much. She knew him to be a liar, a man of questionable morals. Was there worse to hear about this man she'd married? Perhaps she was better off not knowing. 'I haven't spoken to your mother yet.'

There was a hiss down the phone and when Ben spoke again, his voice was softer, calmer, as if all the anger had leaked away on the ebb of that sound. 'Leave that to me, please. It's not the kind of news a parent should hear over the phone. She only lives a couple of hours away; I'll go and give her news that will sadden her at least. You might think me cruel for not offering my condolences, but to be honest, you sound like a nice person; I think you've had a lucky escape.'

What was she supposed to reply to that? Nothing it seemed. 'Right, well thank you for letting me know. Goodbye now.'

He cut the connection.

She sat in silence until the ring of the doorbell startled her. Dark thoughts had been consuming her. Daniel's sins, hers, those of her friends, all marching through her head in hobnailed boots, making it ache. She looked towards the cabin door as if it was mysteriously going to open and a hoard of police burst through to question her. A silly thought. The captain had been clear: they were waiting for the results of the post-mortem before proceeding.

Seconds later, before she'd decided what to do, the ring was followed by a soft rat-a-tat-tat.

It couldn't be her friends; they didn't yet know her cabin number. Maybe the doctor, returning to apologise for being such a shit. On that hopeful thought, she crossed to answer the summons, surprised to find Emilio standing there. He was holding a tray of something she knew she hadn't ordered in one hand, a small cruise-line logoed holdall hanging from the other.

'Madam must eat,' he said simply, brushing past her. He laid the tray on the dining table and removed the linen cloth that covered an array of food. 'I took the liberty of choosing a selection of canapés and finger food. Small bites, easy to eat.'

Natasha wanted to tell him to take the food and go. That she was happy with the drinks that were so freely available. But he was looking so sympathetically at her, so kindly, and the selection he'd brought looked so appetising, that she smiled and nodded. 'That was very kind. Thank you.'

'I also have those items you requested from your cabin.' He lifted the bag he was holding. 'Would madam like me to unpack for her?'

Having no recollection of what she'd asked for apart from underwear, she hastily shook her head. 'No, thank you, you can drop it in the dressing room and I'll manage from there.'

'As you wish.' He inclined his head and without another word, did exactly as she asked.

Once the cabin door had clicked shut after him, Natasha took the bottle of champagne from the fridge and sat drinking it as she nibbled on the food.

Checking her phone, she saw several messages from her friends, all saying variations of the same thing. *Are you okay?*

Perhaps she should take a selfie of her drinking and eating to send to them to prove she was doing more than okay. To prove she was doing bloody marvellously. And she might have done if she hadn't started to cry big, noisy sobs that seemed to echo around the stupid, over-the-top suite. She wasn't sure why she was crying. Perhaps for the marriage and the future she'd painted in bright, cheery colours. Fake from the beginning. How very stupid she'd been.

Finally, she dried her eyes with the linen napkin and sent a WhatsApp message to alleviate their concerns.

I'm doing okay. Need tonight to get my thoughts in order.

She switched her phone off. Determined not to be interrupted again, she crossed to the door and pressed the button to display *do not disturb* outside. Back on the sofa, she emptied the bottle of champagne into her glass, then relaxed back against the cushions.

Tomorrow... maybe they'd find out what had killed Daniel.

It was a worrying thought. There may be others, like the doctor, who'd point the finger of suspicion straight at her. Natasha would have to pin on her professional mask again and lie her way to safety.

45

NATASHA

Natasha wasn't a big drinker and she was exhausted. Despite worrying about what might happen the following day, she rested her head on the back of the comfortable sofa and fell into a heavy sleep. When she awoke, the room was in partial darkness, nightlights glowing from the base of the long console opposite. They were enough to light her way from the room, insufficient to do much else. She sat for a moment, relaxing into the slight sway of the ship, wondering if she should simply stay there till the morning. It was a deeper rocking movement that drove her to stand and investigate.

Out on the balcony, the air was fresh without being cold. The sea was definitely rougher, the white horses, visible from the light of the ship, bigger than before. Maybe a storm was coming. Daniel had wished for one, she remembered suddenly. He wasn't expecting to have caused one.

A sudden chill made her shiver. With a last glance over the railing, she headed back inside. It made more sense to go to the bedroom, try to get back to sleep.

After a quick visit to the bathroom where she stripped off her clothes and threw them into the corner, she pushed open the door to the bedroom. Normally, someone would have turned down the covers and switched on the light, but not that night thanks to her request to be left alone. She felt along the wall hoping to find a light switch, muttering in frustration when there was nothing.

In seconds, her eyes had adjusted to the darkness, finding shades of grey in the blank space ahead. Making out the shape of the bed, she walked carefully towards it, hands extended uselessly. When a light came on without warning, she squealed in surprise and twisted around, but there was nobody there. What had she expected? The ghost of Daniel, dripping in shit, searching for whomever had ended his charmed life so soon? When the light went out, throwing her once again into darkness, fear scurried through her. Maybe he wasn't the only one who was to die on that cruise. A step backwards and the light came on again. By the time the deafening sound of her heart thumping had faded, she'd realised what was happening. Her movement was triggering sensor lights built into the base of the bedside table.

Before she was plunged into darkness, she found the main light switches and flicked them on. The bed was dressed with cushions and a throw, all of which she gathered and dropped on a chair in the corner. Then, naked, she slid between the sheets and prayed for sleep to come.

It did, eventually, but instead of the blank escape she'd experienced lying on the sofa, her slumber was coloured with hideous visions of Daniel in the last hours of his life, but in her dreams, instead of faecal matter, it was writhing snakes that were slithering from every orifice. No amount of twisting and turning helped to escape the image and she finally gave up. Grabbing a robe from the bathroom, she went back to the lounge, switched on the TV, and channel surfed until dawn, filling her head with anything she could find rather than dwell on the past or consider what the next few hours might bring.

At first light, she stepped out onto the balcony and watched as signs of life appeared: small fishing boats, container ships, motor boats. The distant shoreline gradually took a more solid form as they neared Zanzibar City. Natasha knew from reading the ship's itinerary that they could dock in the city itself but it seemed the authorities weren't taking any risks. Only minutes after dropping anchor, a motor boat approached, growing larger before vanishing to the port side of the ship.

Should she go on deck to wave Daniel's body off? Maybe take one of the white pillowcases with her and wave it as the launch pulled away? Get stuck into the role of grieving widow she'd need to display later? Not so much for her friends who wouldn't be so easily fooled, but for the security officer and any other official who might think it necessary to speak to her.

A glance in a mirror told her she wouldn't have to act too much. The sleepless night and the strain of the last couple of days were writ large on her face, making her look haggard and wretched. Too damn wretched to stand on deck waving a white flag of surrender.

Back in the cabin, she reached for her phone and wrote a message to her friends.

> Would love if you could all come to see me this morning. Maybe after breakfast. Same deck, further towards the bow, cabin number 1261.

There was no point in telling them it was the Grand Duchess suite; they'd find that out for themselves when they arrived.

It was only six. Her friends were early risers – apart from Michele perhaps – but they were unlikely to arrive before nine. She had hours to make herself somewhat presentable.

In the dressing room, she opened the case Emilio had packed for her. The list she'd given him had been vague and random. Apart from underwear, she'd asked for dark clothes. He'd taken her literally. Unfortunately, her dark clothes were mostly cocktail dresses, and dressier blouses and trousers. The dresses were of the tight-fitting, low-cut variety that Daniel had preferred. It was almost tempting to pull one on. She smiled when she imagined the security officer's face if she opened the door in such a revealing outfit. More merry widow than grieving one. Until she knew what the post-mortem revealed, it was unwise to look as if she was revelling in Daniel's departure.

Luckily, Emilio hadn't stinted on what he'd brought, so she was able to cobble together a decent outfit, layering a semi-transparent chiffon black shirt over a black T-shirt, and teaming them with matching trousers. With her skin so unnaturally pale, she looked like Morticia Addams. The thought put the Addams Family theme tune into her head. She was humming it and even clicking her fingers as she went to the main door to disable the *do not disturb* notice.

Too restless to read, or to concentrate on TV, she made herself a cup of tea and took it out onto the balcony. But when she sat, her eyes drifting over the view, it was a motor boat on the way to the harbour that caught her attention. Was Daniel's body inside? The thought made her stand so abruptly that tea sloshed from the cup. Brushing the spillage from her leg with a hand, she returned to the cabin. The next hour was spent with the same inability to settle and she gasped in relief when she heard the doorbell. Relief, then worry. She checked her watch. Only eight. Too early for her friends, too soon for the security officer.

Emilio, she guessed, opening the door. And she was right.

'Good morning, madam,' he said. 'I've come to clear away, and to fetch you whatever you would like for breakfast.' He didn't seem to be a man who needed to wait for a reply. Or an invitation. He stepped forward, assuming, rightly as it happened, that Natasha would move aside to allow him to enter. She could have shut the door in his face but he'd been helpful and kind, in his rather reserved, distant way. Anyway, the remains of the food he'd brought the previous evening was an unappetising mess on the table. It wouldn't bother her friends, but she wanted to give the security officer a good impression from the start. To show that Natasha was a woman who liked a certain standard of living, a woman for whom chaos was an abomination.

Not a woman who would kill her husband.

46

NATASHA

With a difficult day stretching ahead of her, it seemed sensible to eat something. Natasha asked Emilio to bring her some toast. 'A couple of slices, with marmalade and butter. Nothing else.' She laid heavy emphasis on the last two words.

'As you wish.'

There was a coffee machine, of course. An all-singing, all-dancing one that took her a few minutes to figure out. It was spluttering out deliciously aromatic coffee by the time Emilio returned.

'Perfect, thank you,' she said as he put a toast rack on the table along with a small dish of marmalade and another of butter. Before she could stop him, he'd turned to pour her coffee into the waiting cup. It seemed rude to tell him she was capable of doing it herself, so she sat and waited till he brought it across, waiting a moment longer as he opened the fridge and took out the jug of milk.

He peered into it suspiciously. For a moment, she wondered if he was going to lift it to his nose to sniff. He didn't, merely saying, 'I'll bring a fresh jug of milk when I come again.'

'Thank you. If you'd bring a large one please, I have friends coming later.' *Now please go away.*

Perhaps he read her mind, because he gave one of his jerky little bows before turning and walking away. He didn't leave though; he went into the bedroom. She heard him moving about. No doubt picking up the abandoned cushions and pillows and returning them to their proper place.

It was a few minutes before she heard the distinct sound of the main door being opened and the gentle click as it shut. Only then did she relax. The coffee was good, the toast slathered in butter and marmalade probably was too, but she couldn't bring herself to eat more than a couple of mouthfuls before giving up.

She made another coffee and took it out onto the balcony. Even with a light sea breeze blowing, it was warm. She pulled a chair into the shade and sat with the cup clasped between her hands, sipping occasionally as she stared through the rail to the shore. At that moment, somewhere over in the city, someone was cutting into Daniel's body. Looking for his secrets.

They'd find some. No doubt about it.

Secrets. If she'd never discovered his, if Barbara hadn't seen fit to spill the beans, would she feel differently now, would she be sincerely grieving? She really wasn't sure. The woman she'd once been would never have been happily married to a man for whom truth was an optional extra. She'd known his business dealings were shady; she'd stupidly assumed his dealings with her weren't. His money had offered a lifebelt of safety that had dragged her from the world she knew, one that had become frightening and uncertain. It was why she'd married him, but once more she considered the conundrum – why had he married her? She'd never asked, and now she'd never know.

Daniel had died with his secrets intact. Now it was up to Natasha to ensure the secrets of his death were kept too.

47

THE WIVES

Michele woke with a groan. They'd drunk a bottle of champagne in their cabin before heading down to the very swish French restaurant for dinner, choosing it because it was the one restaurant her friends had said they weren't interested in trying. They had an excellent meal, accompanied by a very nice bottle of red wine and followed by a brandy. Or was it two? She laid a hand across her forehead. Actually, it might have been three. No wonder her head was thumping.

Don was snoring gently. She turned to look at him, smiling when she saw that the lines of stress were already beginning to fade. Never again. She'd take a more active part in his business, do their accounts herself. If there was any fallout from Daniel's shady dealings, she'd absorb it, confess she'd taken on more than she was capable of, play the fool, accept whatever was handed out.

She reached for her mobile, squinted to read the message from Natasha then dropped her phone onto the bed with another groan. They had to go, of course, had to be there for their friend. But, bloody hell, it was going to be tough to maintain a sad demeanour for any length of time. Barbara, she guessed, would be sorrowful enough for all of them. Tracy Ann? There was a puzzle. There was no mistaking the look of relief on her face the previous day. Maybe Michele would try to get her in a quiet corner later, see if she could probe that rather self-contained shell of hers and prise out some information.

She raised herself up on an elbow to stare down at her sleeping husband. Perhaps it would be better to set Don on her; he'd proven that he was more observant than she'd given him credit for.

Observant, but he'd not seen everything.

* * *

Tracy Ann stood naked in front of the bathroom mirror and brushed a finger over the bruise on her shoulder. It was tender to touch, almost painful when she lifted her arm. In all their years together, the ones before they were married, the ones after, Blake had never once hurt her. Not even accidentally. She'd have described him as a gentle, sensitive man. Yet, there was no denying that his fingers had dug into her flesh. Deliberately. Painfully.

Her head drooped as her eyes filled. The marks both Blake and Daniel had left on her body were one thing, the heavy weight on her heart another. What to do for the best? She didn't know. That Blake was suspicious was blindingly obvious. Would it be better if he knew the truth? She squeezed her eyes shut, pushing a tear out to career down her cheek when she thought of the video Daniel had made. How ugly and sordid it had been. How utterly depraved she'd appeared to be.

And now, what would happen to it? Daniel had said he'd uploaded it to his laptop. Would Natasha find it? If only Tracy Ann had been brave enough to confess the whole episode to her

instead of leaving it at that stupid kiss, the almost innocent beginning to that lewd chapter in her life. She could have told her then;
she couldn't now. Couldn't speak ill of the dead. So even in death,
Daniel wins.

If Natasha found the video, would she be angry enough to
send it to Blake? Tracy Ann didn't know. At one time, she'd have
thought not, but her friend had changed over the last couple of
years. She'd become harder, more brittle, and then she'd married
that scheming, manipulative little shit.

And now he was dead. And Tracy Ann was scared that Blake
might... just might... have had something to do with it.

* * *

Barbara refused to go down to any of the restaurants for dinner.
'You go if you want,' she told Ralph. 'Give Don a shout, see if you
can tag along with them. I saw you chatting with him the other
night.' *Making more of an effort than he ever did with his wife these
days.*

'We need to get something to eat.'

*To keep their strength up for all the fun and games. For the dancing.
For the vigorous sex life they had.* She wanted to spit it all out, to
offload all the venom she had stored up for months. If she started,
it would ooze out in a cankerous mass of spite and resentment.
And she wasn't sure it would ever stop. She ran a hand over her
face, wiping the anger away. When she looked up, there was only
defeat in her eyes. 'I'm not hungry.'

Ralph looked at her for a moment, then shrugged. 'I'll pop
down to the buffet. If you like, I could bring you back something.'

He was being kind. In the rather distracted way he'd been
since he'd retired. As if it was all too much of an effort. As if his
wife didn't warrant more than the bare minimum.

'I don't want anything.' Her voice now sharp, cutting, almost vicious. She didn't look to see if he was upset by her tone, afraid she'd feel guilty if he did, or feel even more miserable if he didn't.

She waited until she heard the click of the cabin door shutting behind him before getting to her feet. On the balcony, the setting sun was casting a glow on the coastline. Barbara leaned on the rail and watched as the light faded, focusing on the changing colours, refusing to give space to any of the thoughts that were demanding attention.

As darkness descended, beads of light began to appear along the coast and randomly out at sea. That's when Daniel forced himself back into her head. It was apt. He'd been a light in her dark days. He was gone. She'd try to get help when they returned home. For her, and for Ralph. And maybe their relationship was salvageable. Maybe. But that light, that magic that Daniel had brought into her life, it was gone, and she desperately missed it.

She hadn't lied to Ralph; she wasn't hungry, but she was weary. Back in the cabin, she switched on the *do not disturb* sign and did the minimum ablutions before pulling on a cotton nightdress and crawling into bed. She was asleep before Ralph returned.

A solid night's sleep gave her little solace. Nor did the early-morning message on her phone from Natasha. Almost a summons. Barbara's first thought was to ignore it, her second to castigate herself for being such a cow. This was her best friend. She'd lost her husband. The role of grieving wife was hers. Barbara would paste on her old-reliable face and go to offer her support.

She'd commiserate with the friend who was married to Daniel, ignore Tracy Ann, the woman he'd been having an affair with, the one he'd chosen over her, and try to remember the light he'd brought into her life.

She'd try to forget how much, at the end, she'd hated him.

48

NATASHA

Natasha was still restless. A minute sitting on the sofa was as much as she could bear, then she was up, pacing the floor. She stood a few minutes out on the balcony watching the coastline, eyes straining for any sign of a motorboat heading their direction, one that might bring news to change everything.

Wishing she'd told her friends to come immediately, she picked up and dropped her mobile in a regular cycle of indecision. The arrival of Emilio to clear away the breakfast offered limited diversion. He'd already proven not to be a great conversationalist but whereas before she'd have commented on the weather or on whatever excursion they'd planned for the day, now there was nothing she could say. Unless she was to comment that she hoped they were using sharp knives when they cut through Daniel's skin, fat, and muscle.

Emilio had brought fresh milk and clean cups. He put everything away and tidied up without a word. He unnerved her and she was glad when he'd finished.

'Is there anything else I can do for you before I leave, madam?'

She wondered if, like the doctor, he suspected she had something to do with her husband's death. Or if he'd resented having to clean up the mess she'd left behind. The one Daniel had created with his death. 'No, there's nothing, thank you.'

When he'd gone, she picked up her mobile again. Almost nine. Her friends would be here soon. They'd be here for her. Despite everything. Despite Tracy Ann's inappropriate kiss, Barbara's silly crush, and whatever was going on with Michele. They would be there for her now that she needed them so badly.

When the doorbell rang, she almost cried out with relief and hurried to answer it. And there they were, her friends and their husbands, huddled together in the narrow corridor that was filled with their cries of disbelief, of sympathy, hands and arms, hugs and kisses, until Natasha was laughing in relief, and crying in sorrow. 'Come in, come in,' she said, pulling away and waving them inside. 'As you can see, they've been good to me.'

It was Michele who vocalised what Natasha guessed the rest were thinking, her loudly voiced, 'Bloody hell!' making everyone smile and breaking the uncomfortable silence.

Natasha led them towards the lounge area. 'Wouldn't Daniel have loved this? He'd have been cock of the walk.' She turned, forcing herself to smile. 'Would anyone like coffee, or tea?' Just as if this was a social event and she was lady of the manor. She caught the strange looks her friends were exchanging, and laughed. A brittle, sad sound. 'Nothing prepares you for how to behave when a partner dies. It looks like I'm falling back on the coping strategy I used as a nurse. Be professional, but slightly distant.'

'You don't need to do that now,' Michele said, putting an arm around her and leading her to a seat. 'We're here for you. Sit down, talk to us.'

Natasha allowed herself to be pushed down onto the sofa. She felt all their eyes on her, searching, probing. Should she cry?

Howl? If she wanted, she could put on a good act. After all, she'd seen the reality of devastated sorrow often enough. It wouldn't be too hard to give a reasonable facsimile of grief. She would have done, if there was even a small part of her that felt Daniel deserved it. There wasn't. Not a tiny bit. Not an atom.

Ever since the phone call to his brother, things had been slotting into place. Michele's dagger looks every time she looked at Daniel, Tracy Ann's confession, Barbara's obsession. Her friends were decent people. Natasha had known them a long time. Only one thing could have made them behave as they had done. Daniel. In the last few hours, it had dawned on her. She'd brought a viper into their friendship group.

'They're doing the post-mortem this morning,' she said. 'Hopefully, we'll soon have a cause of death. Then the ship can return to its itinerary.'

'It's nothing contagious obviously.'

Natasha looked at Tracy Ann. The woman who'd admitted to kissing Daniel. Who'd looked very cosy beside him in the hot tub. Her face was set in lines of regret. Were they as fake as Natasha's, or did she genuinely miss him? Had he been an escape from her abusive marriage, or the cause of it? 'Obviously,' she said, looking her directly in the eye. 'Or you'd have caught whatever it was.' She regretted her words when she saw the quick look of shock slide across Tracy Ann's face, her eyes flitting to Blake and away as quickly. Damage control, Natasha was good at that. She waved a hand around the room. 'You'd all have caught it. We were together nearly every day. We were in the bus together on the way back from that damn lunch.' She shook her head. 'It'll be something he ate. You know the way he liked to try just about anything.'

Nods all around in agreement. Silence settled over them. A heavy weight of it that none appeared to either want or know how to break. Natasha had no idea how soon the security officer would arrive. It seemed suddenly important that she spoke to her friends before she did. Wrapping her arms around herself, she rocked once, then got to her feet. 'Listen, I don't mean to be rude, but do you think I could have some time alone with my girlfriends?'

It was almost amusing to see how quickly the three men agreed to leave, Ralph not even trying to hide his relief, the other two making a fairly poor stab at it.

Natasha waited till they'd left before retaking her seat with a grunt. 'Well now, with them out of the way, let's get down to it, eh?' She leaned back in the seat so she could look at her friends, one after the other, her eyes drifting over each, head to toe and back. 'Right, tell me then, which of you bitches killed Daniel?'

49

MICHELE

Michele heard both Barbara and Tracy Ann gasp from shock. Her own reaction might have been similar if she hadn't noticed that Natasha's grief was sorely lacking. If Don had died, Michele would be a devastated mess. She wouldn't be offering tea and coffee, dressed to kill in an outfit that might have been black but was screaming its sexy credentials all the same.

Interesting that Natasha was assuming it was one of them who'd killed Daniel. Not one of the men. Was she working under the assumption that poison was a woman's tool? A silly one given that she, of all people, must be only too aware of the infamous doctor, Harold Shipman, who'd poisoned so many of his patients.

'Don thought it was me,' she said, drawing three pairs of startled eyes towards her. She held her hands up in surrender. 'It wasn't, honest.'

'Then why did he think it was?'

Michele dropped her hands to the sofa, fingers caressing the soft plush of the fabric. 'We got separated at the market in Kigomasha. When he found me, I was putting something into my bag.

He said I looked,' she curled her forefingers in the air, '"furtive".
So when Daniel died, he assumed I'd bought something dodgy.'

'But you hadn't?' Barbara said.

Michele turned to glare at her. 'Of course I hadn't! What I had
bought was a fake Rolex. I was going to give it to him for our
anniversary next month.'

'But why did he think *you'd* have wanted to kill Daniel?' Tracy
Ann asked.

Michele heard the emphasis on the *you'd* and mentally patted
herself on the back. She'd been right. Whatever had been
between Tracy Ann and Daniel hadn't ended well.

'Yes, I'd like to know the answer to that too.' Natasha leaned
forward, resting her elbows on her knees, her gaze intent. 'Just
why would Don leap to such a conclusion?'

'I don't like to speak ill of the dead—'

'But you're going to?' Natasha sniffed loudly and sat back,
folding her arms across her chest.

'You want to know why Don would leap to such a conclusion?'
Michele waited till Natasha gave a jerky nod before continuing.
'Right, I'll tell you. Because your precious Daniel was a manipula-
tive, conniving little shit. That's why!' It felt good to get the words
out. Her one regret was, she hadn't said them to him. Hadn't faced
the bastard. She looked at the expressions on her friends' faces.
Only Barbara looked horrified. Both Natasha and Tracy Ann
looked as if what she'd said was nothing new. 'Three months ago,
Don mentioned to Daniel that his business wasn't going too well.
In fact, as I learned afterwards, Don was up to his eyeballs in debt.
A few days later, Daniel mentioned an investment opportunity. It
was a sure thing, he said. You know the way he is... was... so damn
convincing. If Don had mentioned it to me, I'd have been suspicious. I had already come to the conclusion that Daniel was a man
for whom charity began and ended in his colossal ego. But Don

wanted to sort everything out without worrying me so he borrowed money and went for it.' Michele huffed a sigh. 'And it was good. He made a killing.'

'Sounds like Daniel did a good thing,' Barbara said.

'A good thing.' Michele wagged her head side to side. 'No, I was right. Daniel had a hidden agenda. A few weeks later when they met up again, and Don thanked him for the advice, Daniel pretended to look shocked. He insisted he'd only mentioned it as part of a conversation and hadn't expected Don to use the knowledge. He said he was appalled to have been taken advantage of and stormed off.' Michele smiled. 'Honestly, you have to hand it to Daniel, he had it down to a fine art. The following morning, he rang Don, apologised for leaving so abruptly, then let the great, big, snarling cat out of the bag. That the information Don had used wasn't public knowledge. Daniel insisted he'd told him, but of course he hadn't.'

'Insider trading,' Tracy Ann said. 'That's illegal, isn't it?'

Michele glared at her. 'Of course it's bloody illegal. A criminal offence. Don could go to prison. His accountancy body would cut him off. He'd be ruined.'

Barbara frowned as she tried to follow the story. 'But didn't Don look into it before investing?'

'That's exactly what I said when I heard,' Michele said, 'but it seems that Daniel had stressed the need for speed to capitalise on it, so as soon as Don got the money, he bought the shares.'

'Okay,' Barbara said, 'but couldn't he have sold them again when he found out?'

'It was too late. Daniel was right about one thing. Speed was essential. The following week, the share price jumped after the company announced a major breakthrough. Don thought he'd been lucky, sold the shares and paid off our debts.'

'But Daniel told him the truth,' Natasha guessed.

'Yes. He insisted he'd told Don that the company was expected to make an announcement the following week, but he hadn't.' Michele looked around the room. 'You all know my husband. He's as straight as they come and would never have got involved in anything illegal. He was horrified. And then, when he was still trying to take it all in and decide what to do, Daniel stuck the knife in. He asked Don to find him a way to hide a large amount of money from the tax man. Of course, Don said he couldn't do that. He told him that tax evasion, which is what Daniel was looking for, was a criminal offence and they could face charges if they were caught. That was when the lovely Daniel showed his true colours. He said if Don didn't help him with the tax evasion, that he'd have no choice but to report him for insider trading.'

'I don't understand,' Natasha said. 'Wouldn't Daniel have gone to prison for it too?'

Michele's laugh was high-pitched and slightly maniacal. It startled her as much as her friends. 'Sorry,' she said running a shaking hand through her hair. 'I've been holding it together for so long. It's funny to be falling apart when it seems like it might be over.' Natasha was waiting for an answer. It was time, it appeared, to spell it out for her. 'No, Daniel wouldn't have gone to prison because your devious, cunning, bastard late husband hadn't invested, had he?' Her laugh this time was a sad, weary sound. 'Poor Don, he's such a fool really; he'd no chance against an expert like Daniel.'

'So Don agreed to do what Daniel wanted?' Barbara and Tracy Ann asked at the same time. Neither laughed, each sitting forward as if enthralled by what they were hearing.

'When Don finally told me what was going on, we looked at the options, but there didn't seem to be any that didn't involve the authorities.' She smiled at Natasha. 'So perhaps now you can understand why Don thought I might have had something to do with Daniel's death.' The smile faded and an ugly expression crossed her face. 'To be honest, I'd have killed him in a heartbeat if I thought I could get away with it.'

She would have done. She'd intended to. Don's suspicions were correct. He'd just chosen the wrong small package. Not the one she'd bought in the market. The one hidden in the lining of her toilet bag. Her initial plan was to crush a few of her sleeping tablets, add the mixture to some food, then wait until Daniel became drowsy and push him overboard. But she guessed it sounded easier than it would be in reality. So instead, using money she'd got from the sale of every decent piece of jewellery she owned, she bought a capsule of cyanide on the dark web.

She'd thought it through, had planned to give it to him the last morning they were on the ship. A final goodbye drink that would be more final than he'd anticipate. In the chaos of disembarking, she hoped it would be more difficult to get help when he collapsed. And far too late for any antidote to be given, even if the ship's doctor could have guessed the cause of Daniel's illness. By the time a post-mortem could be arranged, she was assured that any traces of cyanide would be gone. Not that it mattered. Who'd have suspected her? Now of course, it didn't matter.

She met Natasha's gaze calmly. 'So, I didn't kill him, but I'm sure as hell not sorry he's gone.' Michele tilted her head. 'I don't think I'm the only one either, am I?'

But it wasn't Natasha who answered.

'No, you aren't,' Tracy Ann said. 'I'm delighted the bastard has met with a sticky end. And I'm glad it was a shitty, horrible death too. It was exactly what he deserved!'

50

NATASHA

It was so unexpected that for a moment, there was silence. Then everyone spoke together, high-pitched, strident words that mingled together and made no sense.

It was the doorbell that silenced them, heads turning, mouths open, eyes wide.

Natasha stood shakily. There wasn't time to take in all she'd heard. Wasn't time to hear if Tracy Ann was going to add more drama to the mix. 'That might be the security officer. If it is, leave as quickly as you can, and for goodness' sake, say nothing.' She looked from one of her friends to the other. 'I mean it, say absolutely nothing. If she should ask, we're best friends and our husbands got on well. Everything was rosy in our garden. Okay?' She wanted some acknowledgement, almost snarling, 'Okay?'

Barbara looked shaken. Whether it was by what Michele had told them, or by Tracy Ann's gleefully vicious statement, wasn't clear, but looking at her, Natasha knew she was the weakest link. As the doorbell chimed again, she crossed and put a hand on her shoulder. 'It'll be fine, just relax, remember what I said. We were all happy with each other. Okay?'

'Yes, yes, okay.'

'Okay?' Natasha waited until Michele and Tracy Ann gave jerky nods of agreement before going to answer the door. 'It might only be Emilio wanting to get me lunch or something.' She hoped it would be. It would be better to finish this conversation before talking to the security officer. She took a deep breath to steady herself before pasting a neutral expression on her face and pulling the door open.

The first thing that struck her when she saw the figure framed by the doorway was that she'd been wrong. The white uniforms worn by the crew weren't in the slightest bit sexy. Close up, the startling polyester sheen and the sharp creases struck her as being cold, unfriendly, unnatural. It suited the rigidly unsmiling face of the woman who wore it.

'Mrs Vickery-Orme?'

'Yes. You must be the Ship Security Officer.'

'Yes, Allison Valentine. May I come in?'

Natasha guessed it wasn't really a question. 'Please,' she said, and stood back. Expecting the officer to wait in the small hallway, Natasha was taken aback when instead she walked straight into the lounge. She found herself almost trotting behind to keep up with the officer's long strides, then almost walking into her when she stopped abruptly.

The arrival of the grim-faced security officer caused the three seated women to jump to their feet. There was such a collective look of guilt on their faces that Natasha raised her eyes to the ceiling. It was almost as if *guilty* had been carved on each of their foreheads. 'My friends came to offer their condolences,' she said. 'They were just leaving.'

Valentine's eyes were steady and searching. 'You were travelling together?'

'Yes,' Natasha said. 'We've been friends for years. And our

husbands are too. Friendly, I mean. We're all friendly together.' *Shut up. Stop babbling. Take a breath. Get your brain in gear.*

'I'll need to speak to each of you,' Valentine said, looking deliberately from one to the other. 'And your husbands.'

Natasha saw the look of panic on her friends' faces. No matter how innocent they might be, Valentine's whole demeanour was intimidating. If she spoke to each of the women on their own, goodness knows what they'd say. Making a quick decision, she turned to the officer with a smile. 'Would it be easier if they stayed? You could speak to us all together.' She turned back to her friends and, hidden from Valentine, gave them a wink. 'You wouldn't mind staying, would you?'

'It would make initial fact gathering easier,' Valentine said as one after the other, the women shook their heads.

'Right,' Natasha said. 'That's settled then.' As if they'd all agreed to a damn party. She waved her friends back into their seats. 'I think we could all do with some coffee.' Actually, she could do with a drink, and from the expression on her friends' faces, they could too.

'Coffee would be good,' Valentine said, taking a seat on the empty sofa. 'While we're waiting for it, perhaps I could ask you for your names?' She tapped the screen of the iPad she was carrying, looked at it intently for a moment, then nodded. 'If you wouldn't mind?' Her eyes fixed on Tracy Ann.

'No, yes, of course.' Tracy Ann stumbled and smiled. 'I'm Tracy Ann Robinson. My husband is Blake.'

Valentine tapped her screen, then looked at Michele.

'Michele Turner. My husband is Don Turner.'

'Thank you. And finally...' Valentine looked to Barbara.

'Barbara Gittens. My husband's name is Ralph.'

'Thank you.' Valentine tapped the screen a few more times. 'Right, so that's the full cast identified.'

Natasha, in the process of crossing with a full cup of coffee in each hand, stopped and tottered a little when she heard these words. It was as if they were all actors in some ghastly play. Coffee had lapped over the edge of one of the cups and puddled in the saucer. 'Still don't have my sea legs,' she excused herself. Handing the unspilt coffee to Valentine, she returned to the drinks station. How much longer could she put off hearing what the security officer had to say? She was earlier than Natasha had expected. She guessed strings had been pulled to have the post-mortem done as quickly as possible.

Minutes later, sitting with her untouched coffee on the table in front of her, she sat back, her hands resting on her knees. There was something about the security officer's expression which said she'd need to hold it together. The waiting wasn't helping, but she could bring that to a quick end. 'I assume the post-mortem has been done.'

If the security officer was surprised at the blunt question, she didn't show it. 'Yes, it has. I had a call from the doctor in charge of the private clinic where it was performed.' She hesitated, looking from Natasha to her friends. 'Toxicology reports haven't come back as yet, however the clinic has reached a conclusion based on their extensive knowledge of the subject.'

The subject? Natasha frowned. 'Do you mean my husband? How do they know anything about him?'

It had been Daniel's idea to come to Zanzibar. What had Michele said... that Daniel didn't do anything without an ulterior motive.

What else had he not told her?

51

NATASHA

Valentine looked puzzled. 'Your husband?' Then her frown cleared. 'No, sorry, you've misunderstood.' She held a hand up. 'Wrong choice of word, forgive me; perhaps condition would make more sense. I was referring to your husband's cause of death.'

Natasha held a hand to her forehead for a second, then reached for the coffee and took a few sips. Maybe caffeine would clear her head, get the grey cells working, because she was finding it hard to make sense of anything. 'It was cholera after all, was it?'

Valentine shook her head. 'That's what they were expecting to find, but it wasn't.' She sipped the coffee, then put the cup back on the saucer. 'What they did find were haemorrhages in the liver, oesophagus, stomach, and conjunctiva. They also discovered cerebral cortical oedema.'

'What?' Barbara looked at Natasha as if she would be able to translate.

She could. 'Putting it simply, they're saying that Daniel died from internal bleeding, and swelling on the brain.'

'But it wasn't anything contagious, was it?' Tracy Ann asked. 'We're not in any danger, are we?'

'Not everything is about you,' Michele said sharply.

Tracy Ann glared at her. 'And you're not worried?'

Michele turned away from her and looked across the table to where the security officer was sitting quietly, observing them. 'You said the clinic had extensive knowledge of whatever he died from, which I take to mean they know exactly what it was, so why don't you tell us?'

The security officer glanced at Natasha as if asking for permission to disclose the information. 'I think we would all like to know,' she said.

'Based on their extensive knowledge,' Valentine said slowly, 'the clinic has put the cause of death down to chelonitoxism.'

Natasha felt her friends' eyes on her, waiting for her to clarify. 'I've no idea what that is, I'm afraid.'

'It's a type of food poisoning. Rare in most parts of the world but unfortunately, although not common, has been seen several times in this region. Sea turtle meat.' She said this last as if it explained everything.

Natasha wasn't any wiser and shook her head. 'I'm sorry, I don't understand; you're saying Daniel ate sea turtle meat and it killed him?'

'Contaminated sea turtle meat to be exact. There have been a number of cases over the years. A woman and her children died from ingesting it only a year ago. The locals are urged not to eat it, but it's considered a delicacy and it's hard to stop old customs.'

'Daniel would try just about anything,' Natasha said with a sad smile. 'Always the first in line for something new.'

'How ironic that it's what killed him,' Tracy Ann said.

'Those octopus dishes he ate,' Barbara said with a shiver. 'Honestly, I half expected them to slither from his plate.'

'And those sea snails,' Michele added. 'They had to have been the worst.'

'So he would have tried something new?' Valentine asked. When they all nodded emphatically, she tilted her head to one side. 'But where did he get it? It's not served on board. I checked with the kitchen. Nor was it served at lunch when you all went to Makangale Beach. There have been no other cases reported anywhere in Zanzibar. I had a long conversation with the authorities on Pemba Island. They say they're strictly enforcing a ban on catching sea turtles to avoid just this situation.'

'But as you said, it's hard to stop old customs,' Natasha said. She got to her feet and walked to the balcony door. She imagined Daniel's body, torn apart and stitched together again, lying in a refrigerated drawer somewhere in the just visible city. *Torn apart and stitched together.* She wondered if she could do the same with her life. 'He must have got it from one of those stalls in the market,' she said, turning back to face the security officer.

It was Michele who shook her head. 'But you didn't go to the market. You went to the lighthouse and didn't have time to visit it before we had to leave on the coaches for lunch.'

'The lighthouse,' Natasha nodded. 'That's right. The last few days have been such a blur, I'd almost forgotten.' She returned to her seat and angled her body to face the security officer. 'I remember now, there were a couple of food stalls on the way back; Daniel insisted on stopping to have a look.' She held a hand to her mouth, eyes widening in realisation. 'That was it. Oh my God, that was it. He insisted on trying some of the food they were selling. I begged him not to be so foolish, that their hygiene could be dodgy, but he wouldn't listen.'

'Street stalls between the lighthouse and Kigomasha?'

'Yes, there were just a couple. I was conscious of the time, you know, for the coaches. We didn't want to miss them, so I was walking on, but he insisted on investigating what they were selling. He was chewing on something when he caught up with me.'

Valentine tapped on her iPad. 'That sounds like it might have been the source. I'll contact the authorities on Pemba.' She put the iPad down and sat back with a sigh. 'To be honest, it's unlikely they'll be able to find the vendors. Locals come out to make money when cruise ships arrive and vanish when they're gone. If they were separate to the official market, it's likely they had no licence to be selling anything.'

'So nobody will be held responsible?'

'The authorities will do their best.' But it was obvious from Valentine's tone of voice that she thought it unlikely anyone would be held accountable. 'Meanwhile, and I'm sorry to have to talk about logistics during such a difficult time, but I'm afraid it's necessary. You'll want your husband's body to be repatriated to the UK, of course. I can ask the clinic to arrange that for you if you like. I just need your permission to act on your behalf.' She glanced around the room. 'The captain has indicated that you're welcome to keep this cabin if you should choose to continue the journey until we arrive back at Dar es Salaam in a couple of days. The alternative is to disembark now and catch a flight, but it's likely to be a few days before all the essential paperwork is in place to release your husband's body.' She got to her feet. 'Now that the authorities are satisfied that there's no contagion, we have permission to disembark here, but there are two other cruise ships in port so the captain has decided to return to Wete. He is anxious to get underway as soon as possible, which unfortunately means you need to make a decision quickly.'

Natasha stood and extended her hand. 'You've been very helpful, thank you. I think it's best that I remain on board, with my friends. If you could make the necessary arrangements, and let the captain know, I'd appreciate it.'

Valentine held on to Natasha's hand. 'I think you've made the right decision. We're all sincerely sorry for your loss. Please contact me if you have any questions or worries. I have no doubt the captain will visit you himself later too.'

'You're all very kind,' Natasha said, wondering if it would seem strange to pull her hand away from the security officer's strong, clammy grip, grateful to be spared the decision when her hand was dropped, and the officer, with a final nod to the other three women, turned and left the cabin.

52

TRACY ANN

When Tracy Ann discovered that Daniel's death was due to his own stupidity in eating from a roadside stall, she felt her tense shoulders relax. *Blake hadn't been involved.* She wanted to punch the air in relief before she remembered the ugly words she'd spat out before the security officer had arrived. She'd meant every word she'd said, but she wished she could take them back. She'd seen the shocked expression on her friends' faces and she'd wanted to say the words hadn't come from her, not from the person they'd known for so long, they were coming from the woman Daniel had forced her to be. That deceitful, disgusting, treacherous slut he'd made of her. Even as the security officer spoke, the words she'd blurted out hovered just out of sight, waiting to be explained away.

She could lie. Say she'd simply been supporting Michele. Tracy Ann glanced at her friend. If she'd known what Daniel had done to her and Don, she might have been able to share what had happened to her. It would have been good to have talked about it with someone, instead of letting it eat away inside her. But Daniel had cleverly isolated each of them in their misery.

She should forget about it now. Put it behind her. It would be easier if she could be certain that damn video would vanish. Would Natasha find it while going through his computer or his phone? She seemed very composed. Probably in shock. The truth would hit her soon. Perhaps then she'd look at his phone messages to search for something of his to cling to in the empty days ahead. And she'd find that awful, awful video.

Tracy Ann had only seen it once. It had been enough to have seared the memory into her soul. No, she couldn't let Natasha find it accidentally. It was past time she told the truth. She'd tell her friends, use it as a trial run for the story she'd tell Blake. She knew now that she had to. Whatever he had guessed, it wasn't the truth. He deserved to know. And maybe, if he knew everything, he might forgive her.

She tuned back in to what the security officer was saying.

'...he is anxious to get underway as soon as possible, which unfortunately means you need to make a decision quickly.'

Natasha wanted to remain on board. Tracy Ann took it as a sign. It was time to spill the effluent that had clogged her mind for weeks.

There was an uneasy silence after the security officer had left. As if nobody was quite sure how to proceed. It was the perfect opportunity, yet she sat silently, wondering if she was doing the right thing. Weren't some secrets better kept? Was she using the threat of that video to force herself to speak? Hoping for forgiveness. From Natasha, from Blake. From herself.

'I need to tell you all something,' she said, so quietly the words barely rippled the air. She cleared her throat, sat up straighter and tried again. 'I need to tell you all something.' The words too loud this time, eyes snapping around to stare at her in surprise.

Natasha held up a hand. 'Not if it's more horrible criticism of my late husband, please.'

Tracy Ann locked her gaze on Natasha's. For the first time, she realised that there was no real sorrow in the blue eyes. Her friend looked tired, worn out, but not as devastated as she'd have expected. Maybe it wasn't only she and Michele who had secrets.

'It's a story,' Tracy Ann said. 'I'll tell it, you can decide yourself whether it's criticism or not.' Instead of beginning, she got to her feet, crossed to the under-counter fridge, and took out a bottle of wine. 'I hope you don't mind me helping myself, but tea or coffee isn't going to oil the wheels of this tale.'

She didn't wait for an answer, pouring wine into four glasses and taking them two at a time to the table before retaking her seat and drinking half a glass in two greedy, noisy gulps. 'Right, well, I'll start in the traditional way, shall I?' She put the glass down and sat back, her hands grasping her knees. 'Once upon a time, there was this middle-aged woman who had it all. A lovely home, great kids, a husband who adored her. And then her single friend met and married a man. One not as handsome as her own husband, but who had an air of excitement, of danger, of...' she searched for the words, '...sexual magnetism.' She nodded as if that was it, as if that was exactly what had made her behave as she'd done. 'I love Blake, but he's so...'

'Boring?' Natasha said when once again, Tracy Ann seemed lost for words.

'No, not boring, safe. Blake is safe.'

'Safe?' Natasha sneered. 'Come on, we've seen the bruises!'

Tracy Ann looked puzzled for a second, then she sighed. 'You knew I'd lied about tripping coming out of the hot tub?' She didn't wait for an answer. 'I had to lie to explain the bruises away to Blake, you see. Daniel caused them. The ones on my hand, and the one on my thigh. He wasn't happy that I hadn't got him the information he'd asked for.' She'd like to have added that Blake had never hurt her, but sadly that wasn't true any longer. 'I've never doubted Blake, not for a second. I know he loves me, and I love him. I just...' She sighed and gave a wavering smile. 'I'm almost forty. I've only ever slept with and loved one man. Suddenly, I felt like I'd missed out on something, because when you and Daniel walked into a room, the air seemed to crackle around you—'

'Crackle!' Natasha laughed.

'No, she's right,' Barbara said. 'You always looked as if you'd just come from bed. Like there was some kind of static charge coming off you.'

'A static charge,' Tracy Ann said. 'Yes, that was it. And I suppose I wanted to see what it was like.'

'So, what?' Natasha reached for her wine and took a sip. 'You decided it would be a good idea to seduce my husband?'

'It wasn't like that. He fascinated me, I suppose, and maybe I made it obvious. Looking his way a little too often. Laughing at his stupid jokes a little too heartily.' She finished the wine, reached for the bottle, and refilled the glass. 'Remember that party you gave in your swanky apartment a couple of months ago?'

Natasha shrugged. 'We gave a lot of parties, but yes, I remember.'

'I'd gone to use the bathroom, but there was someone in it. I turned to go back into the living room but Daniel was there, standing in my way. He grinned at me. "I'll take you to the en suite in the spare bedroom," he said, and took me by the hand, pulling me along. His grip was tight; I'm not sure I could have got away, even if I'd wanted to.'

Even if she'd wanted to. Tracy Ann shut her eyes on the memory of her hand in his, the energy that seemed to sizzle from him. She'd felt the first flicker of lust as she was led along that hallway. And another when he'd pushed open the door to that bedroom and pulled her inside. It was dark apart from the ribbon of light at the bottom of the door he'd quickly shut behind them. There must have been a light switch, but he didn't reach for it. Instead, he'd pulled the hand he held until her breasts were pressed against his chest. He let her go then and ran his two hands over the curve of her bottom, his thumbs catching the edge of her knickers through the soft fabric of her dress.

'Kiss me,' he said.

She was a slave to the wave of emotions that were washing over her. Disbelief, desire, basic lust. 'It was as if it wasn't real,' she told her friends. 'As if I'd suddenly taken a starring role in *Fifty Shades*. So, I did what he said. I kissed him.'

'Yes, you confessed this already,' Natasha said, as if suddenly bored by the whole thing.

'But not all of it.' Tracy Ann's words were laced with shame.

Natasha got to her feet. 'I'm sorry, please spare me the details of how you fucked my husband!' She sat down again, heavily, and reached for the glass. She held it, stared into the wine, but didn't drink.

'I didn't,' Tracy Ann said. 'We didn't. After we'd kissed for a while, he led me to the bed. I thought we were going to make love; I wanted to. Right in that moment, I would have done anything he'd asked. I didn't care about Blake, not about you, not about myself.' She felt the tears come then and brushed them away angrily. Tears of self-pity, of humiliation. It still hurt, still stung. It probably always would. 'He pushed me down onto the bed, then moved away for a minute. I thought maybe he was taking off his clothes, but he'd gone to switch on the en suite light. He shut the door over so the room was still in semi-darkness. But he still had all his clothes on. He stood there, looking down at me and told me to lift up my dress and take off my underwear. And I did exactly what he told me to do.' Even when she'd caught sight of his expression in the dim light and was surprised to see, not lust, but a twisted kind of anger. Perhaps even then there'd been time to escape. But she was already lost.

She met Natasha's eyes, then looked at her two friends. 'You all know me. Mrs Respectable. I can't explain why I did what I did. It was all so fantastic, you know. As if I'd wandered into the script of a bad, no, a very bad, erotic thriller.'

'What happened?' Barbara's voice was hushed.

'He told me to beg,' Tracy Ann said, through the tears that had overflowed and were clogging up her voice. 'He said if I wanted him to fuck me, I was to beg for it. And, God forgive me, I did. I spread my legs, begged him, and kept begging.'

'And he did.' Natasha's voice was low, brittle.

'No.' Tracy Ann whispered the one sad, pathetic word.

Michele sat forward, eyes wide in horrified disbelief. 'What?'

'No, he didn't. He turned, switched on the main lights, and looked at me as if I'd crawled out of a sewer.'

Natasha snorted. 'Are you telling me that after all that palaver, nothing actually happened?'

'Nothing happened?' Tracy Ann's laugh was a shrill, slightly manic sound. 'Oh, something happened all right.'

'You just said—'

'I said he didn't fuck me, and he didn't, but what he did do, what that charming, charismatic, dangerously exciting shit did, was to video it all.'

53

NATASHA

Natasha's mouth was suddenly dry. Her hand shook as she reached for the wine glass to take a gulp, then another. She shouldn't drink, she'd hardly eaten anything, but it suddenly seemed necessary. A quick glance at her friends told her they were as dumbfounded as she was. 'I don't understand,' she said finally.

Tracy Ann pressed her lips together and swallowed loudly before managing to answer. 'He videoed me begging him to fuck me. Have you any idea what that looks like? I'll tell you, shall I? It looks exactly what it sounds like. Hideous. Degrading. Humiliating. I know because he sent it to me. Later that night. I watched it, then had to explain to Blake why I threw up.'

'Why?' It was Barbara who asked, in a voice devoid of any emotion. 'This is Daniel we're talking about. He wouldn't do such a hideous thing.'

'Would you listen to yourself!' Michele said. 'Did you not hear a word I said? He was an evil bastard.'

Barbara looked at her with tear-sodden eyes. 'But why? Why would he do such a thing?'

'Blackmail,' Tracy Ann said. 'He told me if I didn't get him the information he wanted that he'd send the video to Blake.'

'The information?' Natasha resorted to parroting while her brain tried desperately to catch up. 'What information?' But she didn't need to ask really; she knew exactly what Daniel would be looking for. Any kind of inside knowledge that Tracy Ann could obtain from her unsuspecting husband.

'Don't you get it, Natasha?' Tracy Ann said, looking at her almost pityingly. 'Don't you understand? He wasn't standing over me with a phone, videoing me. It was all set up before. All premeditated. He knew exactly what he was doing.'

'No.' Natasha gave a harsh burst of laughter. 'You're trying to tell me that he'd set up some kind of video system in our spare bedroom and deliberately lured you in, in order to compromise you?'

'I'm trying to tell you that Daniel had it all planned out for a long time.' She reached a hand towards her. 'Do you remember before we met him, that you said it wasn't serious, just a fling. Remember?'

'I suppose.' But yes, she did remember, clearly. He'd been a bit of fun when she'd desperately needed it, but she didn't think the relationship was going to go anywhere.

'And then you brought him to that party in Michele's house and introduced him to all of us, and we all thought he was lovely—'

'I didn't,' Michele interrupted. 'I thought he was a bit dodgy from the get-go.'

Tracy Ann ignored the interruption. 'And then suddenly, you were moving in with him. And before we knew it, you were talking wedding bells.'

'You're trying to tell me that he married me to gain access to Blake?'

'And Don,' Michele said. 'Yes, that all makes perfect sense. Don, Blake, and Ralph used to meet up, but they never invited any of your various boyfriends to join them. It was only when you married him that Daniel was invited along.'

'Come on!' Natasha stood and crossed to the door, staring over the rail to the distant coast. Strangely, it all made sense now. All of it. His curiosity about her friends. The prenup. The marriage was only ever meant to be a short-lived event. Just long enough to get him what he wanted. By the sounds of it, he was well on his way. She had wondered why he'd married her. Now she knew. How much longer would he have continued the charade?

How much longer would she?

That thought hopping into her head startled her. She pulled open the sliding door to the balcony and stepped outside. There was a soft breeze blowing. She could smell the sea, a faint, nose-crinkling smell of something mechanical, an even fainter waft of perfume drifting over the barrier from whomever was sitting on the balcony on the far side. Behind her, through the door that had slid shut behind her, she could hear the faint murmur of her friends' voices. They'd be in there, exchanging experiences. Michele and Tracy Ann anyway. Or did Barbara have an equally awful tale to tell?

How stupid she'd been. Natasha's hair blew around her face, catching in the tears that had started to fall. She remembered the night she and Daniel had met. The drinks had been flowing freely and she'd taken advantage, knocking them back as she tried to forget whatever she'd had to deal with that day. Because nothing was coming easily to her any more. Then there he'd been. Handsome, smiling, charming. And he'd listened to her.

She thought he was being kind. And perhaps he was. But he'd also have seen how vulnerable she'd been. How broken. She'd tried to bury herself in the great sex but it hadn't worked. And then that party in Michele's house. Tracy Ann had been correct. Things had changed after that. Daniel had started to talk about their future. The invitation to move in with him had come as a surprise. One she'd grasped with both hands as her work life imploded around her.

She heard the door behind slide open, then felt an arm loop around her shoulders.

'You okay?' Barbara said, pulling Natasha closer.

'I thought marriage and motherhood were going to save me from falling apart. What an idiot I was, eh?'

Barbara waved a hand towards the cabin. 'Michele and Tracy Ann are talking about going to lunch. I know you have a lot of thinking to do, but you need to eat something so why don't you come along?'

Sit around, in her newly single state, while her friends and their husbands made polite small talk. While they tried not to appear too cheerful, tried not to celebrate that her beastly monster of a husband was no more.

No, it was too much to ask of her. Anyway, they weren't done here. 'You seemed as shocked as I was when Michele and Tracy Ann told their sorry tales.'

'Yes, of course I was.' Barbara moved away to stand at the rail, her hands loosely grasping the curved, wooden bar that edged it.

'Had you no sad story of your own to add?'

'No, it seems I was lucky. I only ever saw the charming side to Daniel.'

'Really?' Natasha waited, watching as her friend's hand tightened on the rail, knuckles whitening as the pressure increased. Such tension. Natasha knew what that was like. Every part of her seemed to have blanched in the last couple of years. But this wasn't about her. Not this time. 'The charming side, eh? If that's true, then why did you kill him?'

54

BARBARA

Natasha was startled into taking a step backwards as Barbara turned abruptly. 'You're crazy,' she said, then brushed past, slid open the door and slipped inside. 'Fuck's sake!'

The loud and unexpected swearing silenced Michele and Tracy Ann who were sitting on the sofa, heads together, holding hands. 'You never swear,' Michele said, in a tone of voice that said her whole world seemed to be in a freefall.

'Well, I'm fucking well swearing now,' Barbara said. Reaching for the wine bottle, she shook it, swearing again to find it empty. 'Bugger, shit, bugger.'

'There's a whole fridge full.' Natasha had come in behind her; she took the empty bottle from her, dropped it into a bin where it rattled loudly, and opened the fridge. 'We could even have champagne, if you feel like celebrating.'

Tracy Ann got to her feet. 'What the hell is going on!?'

Barbara jabbed a finger towards Natasha. 'Ask her! Now she's accusing me of having killed Daniel!'

'What?' Michele held a hand to her forehead. 'Would one of you explain what the hell happened out there?'

'I told you,' Barbara said, sitting heavily onto the sofa. 'Natasha's looking for someone to blame, and she's chosen me.'

'It's guilt,' Tracy Ann said. She crossed to where Natasha was still standing with the fridge door open. 'It's understandable. You're feeling guilty for not stopping Daniel eating that contaminated meat, so you're trying to find someone to blame. Barbara is an easy candidate. We all know how much she fancied him.' She reached for Natasha's hand and drew her towards the other sofa. 'Sit down, I'll make us some tea.'

Natasha started to laugh. 'Tea, that's your bloody answer, is it?'

'I think it's better than champagne.'

'And you call me the reasonable one of us,' Barbara got to her feet, crossed to the fridge, and took out a bottle of wine. She unscrewed the cap and poured into the nearest glass. 'Anyone else feel the need? No?' She put the bottle down without replacing the lid.

Tracy Ann busied herself making tea. She didn't ask, making one for each of them and placing them on the table. 'We should get some food too,' she said, looking hopefully towards Natasha. 'Maybe you could ask that nice Emilio to bring some.'

'Yes, let's make it a fucking party,' Natasha said. 'We could ask him to get paper hats and poppers. A party to celebrate the death of the monster.'

'Stop it.' Barbara's voice crackled. 'Just stop it.'

'You were really taken in by Daniel's surface charm, weren't you?' Michele said, casting her a pitying glance. 'I'm surprised at you. You're normally so—'

'What? So sensible? I've been bloody-well sensible all of my life, I just wanted—' She broke off and pressed her lips together, fat tears squeezing from her eyes to run an erratic path down her cheeks.

'You wanted a bit of excitement,' Tracy Ann said. 'Just like I did. He played us.'

Barbara picked up her glass and took a noisy gulp of wine, then wiped the tears away with the back of her hand. 'If you hadn't been so scared that Blake would find out, you could have told us and spared us the extra heartache.' She wouldn't have fallen so hard for Daniel had she known what a scheming prick he was. Had she known, everything would be different. She turned to look at Michele. 'And you! If Don wasn't so bloody scared of you, he'd have told you what was going on and you could have stopped Daniel sooner.' She jabbed a finger at Michele and Tracy Ann, her voice harsher, louder. 'You two wives and your stupid husbands, Natasha and her monstrous one—'

'And what kind of wife are you?' Michele jumped to her feet and glared down at Barbara. 'You should be encouraging Ralph to tell the truth, not perpetuating that pathetic lie!'

'What?' Barbara frowned. 'It's not a pathetic lie. Ralph is finding retirement more difficult than he'd expected.'

Michele opened her mouth to speak, then shut it again. As realisation hit her, anger faded from her eyes. 'You don't know.'

'It seems I don't.' Barbara looked at her glass and wondered about drinking the rest, filling it up, drinking that. Perhaps she should simply hold the bottle to her mouth and drain it. Alcoholic oblivion seemed a good option for whatever it was that Michele was going to say. She didn't need to be a mind reader to know, from the suddenly sympathetic, almost pitying expression on her face, that it was going to be bad. 'Spit it out, Michele, before it chokes you.'

'Ralph told Don in confidence.'

Barbara snorted. 'Well, since he obviously broke that by telling you, you might as well tell me.'

'Have it your own way.' Michele didn't meet her friend's eyes. 'Ralph didn't retire. He was made redundant.'

Natasha was almost amused. Her friends were so wrapped up in themselves that nobody had yet addressed her accusation. 'Is anyone listening to me?' She waved to attract their attention. 'Remember me? The widow?'

'At least you have the honesty not to say *grieving* widow.' Barbara put down the wine glass she'd been holding and picked up the tea. 'Tracy Ann was right; we should get some food.'

'Stop it!' Natasha shouted at her, her face screwed up in frustrated anger. 'Stop trying to wriggle out of it. You killed Daniel.'

Tracy Ann offered herself up as peacemaker. Approaching Natasha, she laid a hand on her arm. 'You need to stop. Stop feeling guilty for what happened. We all knew what Daniel was like; he did what he wanted, with no regard for what anyone thought.'

Natasha brushed her hand off. 'I lied, okay!' She crossed to the sofa and sat, straightening the crease in her black trousers, fiddling with the cuff of her shirt.

Michele took the seat beside her. 'Hang on a minute. Are you saying you lied to the security officer about Daniel eating from that roadside stall?'

'Give the girl a medal.' Natasha's voice was scathing. 'That's exactly what I'm saying.'

'But...' Tracy Ann started, then stopped and shook her head.

Michele glanced over her shoulder to where Barbara was sitting, seemingly unconcerned. 'You can't be serious with your accusation.'

As if this was something Natasha was going to make up! 'Think back to the lunch in that hotel on Makangale Beach. A buffet lunch, where we all went up to help ourselves.'

'Right,' Michele and Tracy Ann answered in unison.

'Daniel came back to the table with a plate of the most weird and wonderful, remember?' She waited until both women nodded before continuing. 'We were almost finished when Barbara pointed to something on her plate with the tip of her knife and said she didn't like it.'

Tracy Ann shook her head. 'I don't remem—'

'I don't care if you remember or not,' Natasha cut her off with a snarl. 'I'm telling you what happened. Barbara was so clever. She didn't make the mistake of offering it to Daniel – oh no, that would have been too obvious – but she spoke loud enough to get his attention, saying that it was too fishy for her liking.' Natasha looked at Barbara, who was sitting, staring straight ahead, barely blinking. 'I remember, he said, "did someone say my favourite word" and he held his plate out for you to give it to him. He ate the lot, told you that you were wrong, that it was delicious.'

'But if it was from the buffet, it's not Barbara's fault,' Tracy Ann said. 'Sounds like she was lucky she didn't eat it.' She turned her head to smile at her friend. 'We could have lost you as well.'

Michele caught her hand. 'No, I don't think that's what Natasha means.'

Confused, Tracy Ann looked back at Natasha. 'For goodness' sake, what the hell's going on?'

'Whatever it was, it didn't come from the buffet. I know because I saw Barbara slipping it from her bag to her hand, then sliding it onto her plate. She was discreet and it was just luck that made me glance her direction. At first, I thought she'd slipped food in from her breakfast that morning. To be honest, I wasn't even suspicious when she handed it over to Daniel.' She met Barbara's eyes across the room. 'I remember I watched your expression change, a certain satisfaction crossing your face. I didn't understand, of course. How could I?'

'But...' Tracy Ann said, then stopped again.

'Oh for fuck's sake, would you say something more than *but!*'

Tracy Ann wrapped her arms around her chest as if to defend herself; it made Natasha want to go over and punch her. She really was a tiresome woman.

'Get on with it, would you?'

'Why did you lie to the security officer? Why didn't you tell them about the lunch?'

'Tell them that my oldest friend deliberately killed my husband, you mean?'

Tracy Ann unwrapped her arms and lifted her chin, almost defiantly. 'If that's what you're saying.'

Natasha got to her feet, anger making her body rigid, her steps jerky as she walked across the room, needing distance from her friends. *Her friends, ha!* She turned to glare at Tracy Ann. 'You don't believe me? You think I'd make something like this up?'

'You made up the story about Daniel eating from the roadside stall, didn't you?'

Michele, obviously deciding to take Tracy Ann's side, nodded. 'Yes, you did. So you've already proven yourself to be a convincing liar.'

'I think we've all proven to be that, don't you think?' Natasha said caustically.

'Stop it, all of you!' Barbara got to her feet and stood with her hands on her hips, facing them. 'Yes, I did it, okay. I killed the bastard. And I'd do it again.' She looked from one to the other of them, her gaze lingering on each of their faces. 'And I don't believe there's one of you who wouldn't have done the same if you'd been given the chance. So just be grateful I did the job for you.'

Tracy Ann grabbed hold of Michele's arm and clung to it as she stared at Barbara as if unable to believe what she was hearing. 'You killed him!'

'And you wouldn't have? To have stopped him?'

'I would.' It was Michele who answered, her voice hard and firm.

'He lied to me, was using me. So yes,' Natasha said. 'I'd have done the same.' She looked at Tracy Ann. 'Wouldn't you, to have stopped him sending that video to Blake?'

Tracy Ann looked horrified, but Natasha could see the truth in her eyes. If she thought she'd get away with it, if she'd had the guts, she'd have done the same. 'There is something that's puzzling me though,' Natasha said, taking a seat, crossing her legs, and relaxing back to look up to where Barbara still stood. 'We three have a good reason, but you, you drooled over him. You always looked as if you'd eat Daniel without salt, so what reason did you have for killing him?'

56

BARBARA

Why had she killed Daniel? Barbara wasn't sure she could explain. She had virtually drooled over him. He was the embodiment of sex. Sparkling with charisma. Oozing charm. She'd been feeling so old, so worn out and past it; he'd been a jolt of joy, of excitement. And the deeper Ralph had fallen into that trough of despair the more enticing Daniel had become. *Ralph, why hadn't he told her he'd been made redundant? What kind of wife was she that he'd felt the need to lie? What kind of woman?*

Months of brain fog, of feeling lost, and then Daniel came into her life. Being nice. Paying her attention. Tempting her. Turning her into the kind of woman she'd never been. A woman who lusted after a married man – her best friend's husband, for pity's sake. A woman who'd throw away years of fidelity for a quick fumble.

Daniel with his sly glances, his fingers brushing against her when he passed by. His breath on her skin when he stood behind her – just that little bit too close. *But not close enough.*

She shut her eyes as she was overcome with myriad feelings of lust, of longing, of absolute hatred. Despite all she'd learned that day about him, despite trying to convince herself that she hated him, she still couldn't stop the wanting. It was only then that she realised who she hated the most – herself.

She sat and looked up at the faces of the three women who stood waiting for her to speak. 'Daniel had an uncanny ability to find someone's weakness. Don's, Tracy Ann's, mine, even yours, Natasha. He found it, then used it. For financial reward, to get what he wanted, or as in my case,' her face twisted in bitter lines, 'just because he could. Because it was fun for him to make a pathetic, sad woman lust after him.' She patted the seat beside her. 'Sit down; you're all giving me a crick in my neck.'

She half-expected Natasha to object with one of her increasingly caustic remarks, but she sat without a word.

Barbara waited till they'd stopped shuffling about before she continued her story. 'That day in Kigomasha, after Ralph and I had explored the mangroves, we returned to the town. We still had time to spare before the coach came, so we wandered over to the market. I left Ralph admiring some wood carvings and strolled along aimlessly until I got to the edge of it where some food stalls had been set up. I think they were mostly for the benefit of the locals rather than tourists, and I was about to retrace my steps when I remembered something I'd read the previous year in a copy of the *Metro* I'd picked up on the bus. A small article about a woman and some children who'd died after eating contaminated turtle meat. So, I bought some.'

Natasha stared at her and shook her head. 'You say that as if it was the most natural thing to do!'

Barbara shrugged. 'One of the hawkers had a bit of English. He explained that I needed to cook it very well to prevent any illness. Then he wrapped it up and handed it to me.'

'And you gave it to Daniel, knowing it would kill him.'

'Not all turtle meat is contaminated.' Barbara had hoped it

was. As she'd passed the small slab of meat onto Daniel's plate, she hoped it would kill the bastard. Now, having heard what an absolute monster he was, she was more than certain she'd done the right thing. 'You could say he was simply unlucky.'

'I don't believe I'm hearing this,' Tracy Ann said. 'You gave him that meat, knowing it would probably kill him. I know we all said we wanted him dead, but...' She took a deep breath. 'It was all just talk. You murdered him!'

'What are we going to do?' Michele looked from Natasha to Barbara and back.

'Nothing.' Natasha's voice was quiet but firm. 'As far as the authorities are aware, he ate something from one of those stalls. They'll look, but they won't find anything, or anyone. As long as we stick to the story, everything will be okay.'

'But...' Tracy Ann swallowed, then shook her head. 'No, you're right. You're both right. Yes, oh my God, yes, if I'd had the opportunity, if I'd been brave enough, I'd have killed the bastard myself.'

'The world is a safer place without him,' Michele said.

Barbara felt her shoulders relax. She hadn't been certain her friends would take it this way. She should have been; they'd been friends a long time, and Daniel, after all, was an evil bastard.

'We never speak of this again,' Natasha said. 'Ever. And you don't tell your husbands.' She looked pointedly at Michele. 'Understand? Not a word to Don.'

'Not a word.' Michele held a hand to her forehead. 'Unsurprisingly, thanks to all these revelations, my head is thumping.' She got to her feet. 'I'm going to my cabin for some paracetamol. Much as I'd like to stay away though, I will be back.'

'Take my medallion to let yourself in.' Natasha pointed to where it sat on the top of a console.

Michele wasn't gone long, letting herself in and dropping the medallion back where she'd found it. 'Did I miss anything?'

'Nothing.' It was Barbara who replied.

'Good. I'm going to make some more tea.' Only when she'd put a cup in front of everyone and retaken her seat, did the conversation resume, almost exactly where it had left off.

'I'm not sure anyone would believe us, even if we did talk about it,' Tracy Ann said. 'Who'd imagine Daniel would marry Tasha just to get access to Blake and Don? It's all so unbelievable.'

'Ah,' Michele said, putting her cup down with a smile. 'It might make more sense if I tell you that the sum of money Daniel wanted help to hide was ten million pounds.'

57

NATASHA

Natasha blinked. It was the only movement she was capable of making. That, and breathing, and her heart was beating. She could hear it in the silence of the room. A loud thumpty thumpty thump. What she was finding hard to do was to compute what Michele had just said. *Ten million.* Was it possible? She'd known Daniel owned the apartment – all three point five million pounds worth of prime London real estate – and she'd guessed there'd be some money too. But not this much.

'Looks like you're going to be a very wealthy, grieving widow,' Barbara said. 'Considering the prenup you signed, it looks like I've done you a favour.'

Natasha heard the strain in her voice. Did Barbara really think she was strong enough to handle the guilt? Natasha didn't believe she was. Perhaps it would be better to speak to the security officer again. She could tell Valentine that in the stress of the moment, in her shocked confusion, she'd mixed things up. Now that her head was clearer, she remembered that although Daniel had been tempted, he hadn't actually eaten at the street stall. Maybe she could drop something into the conversation about Barbara having asked him to taste something from her plate at that lunch. Just a hint would be enough to arouse the security officer's suspicion. Turtle meat hadn't been on the hotel's menu. It had to have been bought elsewhere. Natasha imagined her sending their photographs to the police on Pemba Island. They'd hurry to that market in Kigomasha and ask if anyone remembered a foreigner buying turtle meat. Of course they'd remember. Barbara had said the seller had been emphatic about cooking it properly. He'd easily be able to pick out her round, weary face from a lineup of photographs.

Yes, it would be better to speak to Valentine before Barbara's secret corroded her resolve and it leaked out, because if it did, they'd all be destroyed for having agreed to keep it. Now that Natasha was going to be seriously wealthy, she needed to be free to enjoy it.

If there was a twinge of guilt for what she intended to do, it was brushed away. Their friendship, strong and long as it had been, had been damaged by their various revelations and was unlikely to recover. Her decision was made: as soon as her friends had left, she'd ring the security officer.

When the doorbell sounded, Natasha pushed the thought to the back of her head and got to her feet. 'Maybe your wish has come true and it's Emilio with some food.'

But it wasn't Emilio. It was Blake and Don. Blake looked a little embarrassed as he asked, 'We were wondering if you wanted to go to lunch.'

Grateful that he hadn't added the asinine *you need to eat*, she waved them inside. 'I don't, but I'm sure your wives would like to.'

'If you need them to stay, that's okay,' Blake, ever the gentleman, added. 'We just thought we'd check. Or perhaps we could order food here. Eat together.'

Natasha patted his arm. 'Thank you, but to be honest, I think I could do with a rest. As I'm sure you understand, I haven't been sleeping too well.'

'Of course,' he said, looking even more embarrassed.

'Are you sure you'll be okay?' Michele asked.

'We're happy to stay, you know,' Tracy Ann said. 'Or we could take it in turns to keep you company.'

As if Natasha really was the sad, grieving widow. 'Thank you, but honestly, I'll be fine. I'm going to try and get an hour's sleep.' *Go away, get out and leave me alone.*

They were still reluctant to leave and it needed Natasha to almost herd them along before she managed to get them to the door. She pulled it open. 'Thank you all. I really do appreciate your support.' Lots of hugs, kisses and promises, then they were gone.

Natasha shut the door and leaned heavily against it, the weight of everything that had happened over the last few days pressing into her. Who was she kidding? The last few days had been the cherry on the top of a hideous couple of years where she'd seen the worst the world could do. She'd allowed the horror of it all to taint and change her. Probably irredeemably. She had some of what she'd wanted. Enough money to never have to return to nursing. She didn't have the husband, or the children that she'd thought might make her life better – more like that of her friends – what a silly idea that had been. Close up and personal as she'd been with the three women the last few days, she didn't want to be like them. Stepford wives with their secrets.

Pushing away from the door, she crossed the spacious suite. She really should eat. The thought made her smile but instead of lifting the phone to ring for Emilio, she slid open the door to the balcony and stepped outside. It was a glorious day. The air felt thick with the heat of the mid-afternoon sun. *Ten million pounds.* She'd never need to spend a miserable, cold winter in the UK again. Resting her forearms on the rail, she stared as Zanzibar City seemed to disappear into the sea. No doubt the captain was desperately trying to cobble together the itinerary that Daniel's death had so rudely interrupted. If Natasha joined in, if she went on excursions, would other passengers look at her askance? Probably, and she wouldn't blame them. There was a time when she'd have been equally as condemning.

But she had more important things to think about. She needed to ring the security officer, but first, she needed to get Michele and Tracy Ann on their own, tell them she'd been playing it cautiously, that she'd never really intended to let Barbara get away with murder.

The security officer hadn't struck her as a stupid woman. Natasha would have to act her ass off. The way she had earlier when Barbara had confessed that she'd given Daniel that contaminated turtle meat – because as Natasha had watched her take it from her bag and slip it onto her plate, she hadn't known what it was, but she'd known there was something wrong with it, and she could have stopped it there and then. Barbara had said it tasted awful. Natasha could have warned Daniel that the awful taste might be due to contamination of some sort. He was adventurous, but he wasn't an idiot. But she didn't open her mouth. Instead, as he ate, she watched Barbara. Saw her expression change from apprehensive to supremely satisfied and she knew she'd been right.

Even then, Natasha could have saved him, but by then, she knew she didn't want to.

She stared into the white horses that galloped alongside the ship as it cut through the waves, and thought that justice had been served along with that turtle meat.

'You enjoying the sun?'

Natasha almost tripped over her feet in her haste to turn

around. 'Bloody hell, you scared the wits out of me! What are you doing, creeping up on me like that?' She frowned and stared into the room behind. 'How did you get in, anyway? I know I shut the door after you all left.'

'Easy. I took your crown medallion.'

58

NATASHA

Natasha stared as Michele swung the crown medallion to and fro. 'Why would you do such a thing?' She peered through the glass doors behind, wondering if everybody had returned. There didn't appear to be anyone there and she brought her gaze back to Michele, who had a strange smile curling her lips. 'I thought you were all going for lunch. What happened?'

'What happened?' Michele sighed as she continued to swing the lanyard. 'Your big mouth happened. If you'd just let it lie. Nobody had to know it was Barbara who'd given Daniel the contaminated meat. We were all in agreement that the world was a better place without him.' She swung the lanyard again, harder, higher, then she let it go and it sailed over the rail into the sea below.

'What the hell!' Natasha turned and leaned over the rail, then jerked around, her expression confused. Nothing was making any sense. The tiredness she'd felt earlier swept over her, making her feel weak. 'Why did you do that? What is wrong with you?'

'You made us all promise to keep what happened a secret but I could tell by your face, even by the words you used, that you were never going to keep quiet about what Barbara did.'

Sometimes, it was a bad idea to have friends who knew you too well. 'Listen, Michele, I wasn't kidding when I said I was going to go for a lie-down, so if you wouldn't mind leaving.'

'Feeling tired, are you? A little weak? Legs a bit wobbly?'

It was exactly how Natasha was feeling. Confused too. 'Barbara isn't strong enough to keep it a secret. It's better if it comes out now. She could plead temporary insanity, or something.'

'Or something.' Michele sneered. 'The press would have a field day. They'd dig into her background and into ours. They'd pull Daniel apart in the search for the truth. Everything would come out.'

Natasha hung heavily on the rail. Strangely, although her body felt weaker, her mind was suddenly clear. 'Everything would come out? You did get into some shady financial dealings with Daniel, am I right?'

Instead of answering, Michele asked, 'Do you know how much debt we were in before I discovered what was happening? Don had remortgaged our home, taken out loans, maxed out several credit cards. We were drowning in debt. A million pounds might just about have cleared it all.'

'Then that tip Daniel gave you paid off.'

'I might have exaggerated that a little,' Michele said.

Natasha saw the truth in her friend's face. 'You did help Daniel evade tax, didn't you?'

'When I took charge and saw how much debt we were in, I knew we had no choice. So, yes, we did. And got well paid for it. But then, being the greedy bastard he was, Daniel wanted more and more increasingly shady work done. It was only a matter of time before it all came tumbling down. Then this cruise came along, like an answer to our prayers.'

'And Barbara did you the favour of killing Daniel.'

'My dear friend, Daniel was never going to leave the ship alive. I had a plan, but thanks to Barbara, it never needed to be implemented. It was all going so well, but then you went and opened your stupid mouth, and I knew it wasn't over.'

Piercing clarity came when it was too late to be of any help. Natasha remembered Michele making tea for her earlier. 'You put something in my drink, didn't you?'

'A couple of pills, just to make it all a little easier.' She closed the distance between them and laid a hand gently on Natasha's arm. 'I am sorry, but you know how it is; Don will always come first for me. Anyway,' she took her hand away and stepped back, 'your life is a mess. I'll speak to the newspapers afterwards, tell them how losing Daniel destroyed your life.'

Afterwards. It looked as if Natasha wasn't going to get to enjoy any of that ten million after all. Her brain was still strong enough to attempt to fight. 'You don't have to do this. We can work things out.'

'Don't be silly. That line is too far in the past now to ever go back.'

'The crown medallion.' A note of triumph filled the words. 'They'll be able to see it was taken from the room. See it in your cabin. They'll know there was something wrong.'

Michele stepped closer again and gently patted Natasha's cheek. 'Ah, but you see, I'm not that stupid. I dropped yours outside when we left. It was a risk. One of the staff might have found it, or another passenger. But it was still there when I returned. And, of course, I'm not carrying mine.'

'We're friends.' And they were, but hadn't it always been Natasha and the wives. Even when she'd married Daniel, she'd never really made the club. She guessed they knew her heart wasn't really in it.

'Once you're gone, things will be okay.'

Well, that's all right then. Happy to die, in that case, but she was damn well going to hang on to her sense of the ridiculous.

'Tracy Ann and Barbara will be devastated and will cling to one another for support.' Michele smiled. 'I'll make sure they do, and by focusing on you, Daniel will quickly become an unpleasant memory. It's unlikely they'll find your body but we'll hold a memorial service for you. Talk about what a good friend you were, yada yada yada.' Michele's smile was wicked. 'I'll make sure I have a drink for you.'

After all Natasha had been through. All she'd survived. Was it really going to end like this? 'You'll never know if I'm really dead, and I promise you, I will haunt your days. You'll see a woman who looks a little like me, and you'll wonder, did I make it somehow? Was I perhaps rescued by a passing fishing boat, and brought to shore, vowing revenge?'

Michele shrugged. 'It's a risk I'll take.'

'It's not too late to change your mind,' she pleaded. When she felt Michele press a kiss to her cheek, she thought she'd got through to her until she saw her set, determined expression. 'A Judas kiss,' she whispered.

'Just a last goodbye.' Michele almost gently released the fingers that were desperately clinging onto the handrail, then slipped her arms around her waist.

Natasha would have liked to have asked what medication she'd been given. Had a long conversation about it, maybe over a glass of wine. She'd miss that. She'd miss life. Once, it had been good. It could have been again. All too late now.

It was frighteningly easy to be shoved up and over the rail. And then... well then she was floating on the warm air, the chiffon sleeves of her now even-more-suitable blouse billowing in the breeze. Like a bird in flight.

There was enough time in the few seconds it took to fall almost one hundred feet to worry about the pain of drowning. She needn't have worried – the rapid deceleration when she hit the water killed her first.

EPILOGUE
MICHELE

One Month Later

Natasha's body was never found. It was late the following morning before her friends became worried by her silence, and another hour before the man overboard cameras were checked.

'They're not continuously monitored,' the captain explained to them as they crowded into his office, their faces pale and strained. 'But we've been able to ascertain that a person went overboard yesterday afternoon. I've ordered the ship to return to the co-ordinates and have also requested that coastguard send vessels to assist in the search.' He wiped a hand over his face. 'We hope to be able to locate your friend's body but I have to inform you, the chances are slim. It has been considerable hours.'

'We should never have left her alone,' Barbara said, her voice thick with tears.

'She was so emphatic that she was okay; we should have guessed there was something wrong. That she'd planned this.' Michele shook her head. 'I didn't realise Daniel's death had hit her so hard.' She met her friends' eyes. There wasn't the slightest hint of suspicion in any of them. Nor was there in the captain's. It had all gone swimmingly. The thought almost made her laugh and she hurriedly held both hands over her face.

Natasha's body wasn't found despite the best efforts of the several small boats that searched the area. It was the end of the cruise for the friends. They disembarked and were taken immediately to Dar es Salaam where they caught a flight home.

Michele refused to feel any regret for what she'd done. If she could have trusted Natasha to keep her silly mouth shut, it wouldn't have been necessary. Truth was, she'd have done anything to protect Don, and the life they had together.

She still would.

In the weeks since, she'd met up with Barbara and Tracy Ann several times and they were meeting again that night. Michele was first to arrive at the new bar they had taken to frequenting which held no memories of nights with Natasha.

Although they spoke often of her, nobody mentioned Daniel. It was as if he'd never existed. Which was just what Michele had hoped.

'Hi.' Barbara flopped onto the seat beside her, dropping her handbag on the table and unwrapping a long, woolly scarf. 'A miserable night.'

'I'll get you a drink. The usual?'

'Please.'

Michele ordered a large G&T for Barbara and another wine for herself, carrying both glasses back to the table. 'Tracy Ann sent a message to say she'd be a bit late.'

'Good,' Barbara said, lifting her glass and taking a mouthful. 'I wanted to talk to you.'

'That sounds ominous.' Michele felt something twist in her gut as she took in her friend's weary, pale face. It was all going so well. *Don't spoil it now, you silly cow.* 'Go on then, what is it?'

'I'm not sure I can live with the guilt,' Barbara said, wrapping her fingers around the glass. When Michele made no comment, she looked up from it and added, 'You know. For what I did.'

'You rid the world of a monster.'

'Yes, and I really did think Natasha would cope, you know. I never thought she'd do what she did. It's all my fault; if Daniel hadn't died, she'd still be with us.'

It was hard to argue the point. 'You just need to let it go. There's no reason to keep beating yourself up about it.'

'I don't think I can.' Barbara took another mouthful of her drink. 'I'm thinking about going to the police, telling them what I did.'

The police! It would result in just the kind of interest Michele wanted to avoid. 'Natasha wouldn't want you to do that. Remember, it's what she said.' Only Michele had seen the lie in her eyes, setting her on that final path. Or what she hoped would be final. She'd worried that Tracy Ann might be the weak link, but there hadn't been a peep from her. It looked as if Barbara was going to be the one to worry about.

'Listen,' Michele said, pressing Barbara's arm. 'I was thinking we should go on another cruise, just us three women this time. We could throw some flowers into the sea, have some kind of farewell ceremony for Natasha. What d'you think?'

Barbara nodded. 'I think it would be a lovely idea.'

'I'm sure Tracy Ann will be game too.' Michele squeezed the arm she held again. 'I'll find one that goes soon, okay? Meanwhile, don't worry. If, when we get back, you're still thinking about going to the police, I'll go with you.'

'You will?' Barbara smiled and laid her hand over Michele's. 'That would mean a lot to me, thank you. Okay, I'll wait till then, but I think it will be the right thing to do.'

'It's important to do the right thing.' And Michele would.

She'd tossed the vial of cyanide overboard before they'd left the ship, but the crushed sleeping tablets had worked a treat on Natasha. The same trick would work as well on Barbara. Murder would be easier the second time around.

Michele was already practising the words in her head.

Poor Barbara, she never really recovered from the death of her friend.

ACKNOWLEDGEMENTS

The Wives is my twenty-eighth published book, and my tenth for Boldwood Books. What an amazing journey it has been, and how many wonderful people I have met along the way, some of whom have become good friends. The writing community – those who write, read, publish or shout about books – is an amazingly generous one that I'm privileged and delighted to be part of.

There are many people to whom I owe a great big thank you:

All of the wonderful Boldwood team, especially my editor, Emily Ruston, copy editor, Emily Reader, proofreader, Shirley Khan, and marketing executive, Niamh Wallace.

Thanks also to the Valerie Keogh Supporters' group, some of whose names I have used in *The Wives*.

I'm grateful to everyone who reads my books, to those who blog about them, to those who review and shout about them.

I've enjoyed a number of cruises, the last with the Princess Cruise line on the *Royal Princess* around New Zealand. I'd been thinking about basing a story on a cruise ship so took the opportunity to have a word with the Ship Security Officer, Andy Carroll, who kindly volunteered his valuable time to answer some of my questions. Thanks, Andy, I hope I haven't let you down.

The Wives are cruising on the *Duchess Mary* – it isn't a real ship but an amalgamation of the few cruise ships I've been on, plus the one in my imagination.

As usual, I've had the support and encouragement of writing friends, and my family. Thanks to every one of you.

I love to hear from readers. You can contact me here:

Facebook: https://www.facebook.com/valeriekeoghnovels

Twitter: https://twitter.com/ValerieKeogh1

Instagram: https://www.instagram.com/valeriekeogh2

BookBub: https://www.bookbub.com/authors/valerie-keogh

Author Central: https://www.amazon.co.uk/Valerie-Keogh/e/B00LK0NMB8

ABOUT THE AUTHOR

Valerie Keogh is the internationally bestselling author of several psychological thrillers and crime series. She originally comes from Dublin but now lives in Wiltshire and worked as a nurse for many years.

Sign up to Valerie Keogh's mailing list here for news, competitions and updates on future books.

Follow Valerie on social media here:

facebook.com/valeriekeoghnovels
x.com/ValerieKeogh1
instagram.com/valeriekeogh2
bookbub.com/authors/valerie-keogh

ALSO BY VALERIE KEOGH

The Lodger

The Widow

The Trophy Wife

The Librarian

The Nurse

The Lawyer

The House Keeper

The Mistress

The Mother

The Wives

THE

Murder

LIST

**THE MURDER LIST IS A NEWSLETTER
DEDICATED TO SPINE-CHILLING FICTION
AND GRIPPING PAGE-TURNERS!**

**SIGN UP TO MAKE SURE YOU'RE ON OUR
HIT LIST FOR EXCLUSIVE DEALS, AUTHOR
CONTENT, AND COMPETITIONS.**

SIGN UP TO OUR
NEWSLETTER

BIT.LY/THEMURDERLISTNEWS

Boldwood

Boldwood Books is an award-winning fiction publishing company seeking out the best stories from around the world.

Find out more at www.boldwoodbooks.com

Join our reader community for brilliant books, competitions and offers!

Follow us
@BoldwoodBooks
@TheBoldBookClub

Sign up to our weekly
deals newsletter

https://bit.ly/BoldwoodBNewsletter

Made in the USA
Las Vegas, NV
02 November 2024

10807733R10164